ALSO BY
AKEMI DAWN BOWMAN

Starfish
Summer Bird Blue
Harley in the Sky
The Infinity Courts series

GENERATION MISFITS

AKEMI DAWN BOWMAN

FARRAR STRAUS GIROUX
NEW YORK

Farrar Straus Giroux Books for Young Readers
An imprint of Macmillan Publishing Group, LLC
120 Broadway, New York, NY 10271

mackids.com

Our books may be purchased in bulk for promotional, educational, or business use.
Please contact your local bookseller or the Macmillan Corporate and Premium Sales
Department at (800) 221-7945 ext. 5442 or by email at
MacmillanSpecialMarkets@macmillan.com.

Library of Congress Control Number: 2020919566

ISBN 978-0-374-31374-6
10 9 8 7 6 5 4 3 2 1

Printed in the United States of America by LSC Communications, Harrisonburg, Virginia
First edition, 2021
Book design by Cassie Gonzales

To Danielle—for Oreo milkshakes,
too many tacos, and midnight adventures

CHAPTER ONE

When the mustard-yellow bus appeared at the top of the hill, eleven-year-old Millie Nakakura felt her heart triple—no, *quadruple*—in beats per minute. It was like watching the sun rise on the horizon, signaling a new day.

And today, *everything* seemed new.

She had a new haircut—bangs and a bob, which had only sort of turned out like the photo Millie had shown her mom. She had a new pair of red Converse, and a new backpack decorated in smiling pieces of sushi and rice balls. She had a new binder covered in all her favorite Pokémon, which she was certain would be a great conversation starter. (How could anyone not think Alolan Vulpix was the absolute cutest?) She even had a new pad guard for her flute, which some might argue was exciting to absolutely nobody, but those people had never met Millie's dad.

And most important of all, Millie was starting sixth grade at a new school. Her *first* school, really, because being homeschooled always felt more like "home" than "school."

Millie looked toward her parents at the front of the car. Her mom checked her hair in the mirror, again and again. Her dad drummed his fingers against the steering wheel almost exactly in time to Millie's racing heart.

Maybe nerves were similar to sneezes, and you could pass them off to other people.

Not that her parents had any reason to be nervous. None of this was new to them. They'd already experienced classes and teachers and best friends.

A smile grew in the corner of Millie's mouth.

Friends.

It sounded like all the hope in the world bottled up in one tiny word.

Millie could feel her face giving away everything she was thinking. She was worse than an open book—there might as well be a flashing neon sign above her head, because anybody in the world could take one look at her and know exactly what she was feeling.

She hadn't been this excited since Generation Love released their second album last year. The fact that a new school could compete with the world's greatest J-Pop group was *kind of a big deal.*

Millie clutched her flute case in her lap. The silver YAMAHA logo caught her eye, reminding her of all the arguments it had taken to finally convince her parents to let her attend a real school. She'd threatened to quit flute, though she wasn't sure the choice to quit was really hers at all. But it made her parents discuss their options. Or rather, the *only* option: Brightside

Academy, a K-to-twelve magnet school for performing and visual arts.

It was a compromise—Millie had to keep doing the one thing she hated in order to have the one thing she wanted more than anything. But maybe flute wouldn't be so bad at Brightside Academy. Band seemed like as good a place as any to make friends.

And the chance to go to school and make friends was all she'd ever wanted.

Most wishes were fleeting and forgotten, like shooting stars and fountain pennies. But some wishes stuck. *Permanently.*

And every now and then—when the planets aligned, and there was a full moon, and some otherworldly presence was feeling generous—some wishes could come true.

Even the big ones.

The school bus slowed to a stop next to the curb, and a flickering red stop sign appeared.

Millie took a breath and reached for the door handle, freezing in terror when her parents did the same.

"You don't have to go with me," she said hurriedly, eyes scanning the herd of students on the nearby pavement. Emphasis on *students*—not parents.

Her mom, Jane, turned around, confusion swarming her hazel eyes. "We just want to say hello to the bus driver. I think it's important to know who's driving our eleven-year-old daughter to school every morning."

"But parents don't do that," Millie blurted out. She could see the way her mom was moving closer to the door, like she had already made up her mind.

Millie begged every star, penny, and four-leaf clover in the world not to let her parents get out of the car. Because this was her new beginning—she wanted it to be perfect.

Perfect did *not* involve her parents walking her to the school bus like she was a toddler who couldn't go anywhere without having her hand held. They'd already insisted on driving her to the bus stop so she didn't have to walk nearly a mile on her own. Wasn't that enough?

Millie's mom frowned. "How do you know parents don't do that?"

Millie was prepared. She had to be when it came to her parents. "I googled it." It wasn't a lie. Millie googled *everything*. Not knowing things made her anxious, and if there was ever a sliver of hope she could win an argument against her parents, she needed to be a walking Wikipedia page.

Her dad, Scott, turned to the side and shrugged matter-of-factly. "Well, if she says she *googled* it . . ."

Jane looked back at him with a raised brow. They were having a silent debate.

Millie's desperation grew as the crowd outside the window began to shrink. "Please? I don't want to be late."

Finally, a sigh. Her mother's fingers drifted away from the handle.

"Okay, fine," Jane said. "But call us if there are any problems at all."

Scott looked over his shoulder. "No cell phones in class."

Jane eyed him testily. "Unless there's an emergency."

"If there's an emergency, the school will call us. Besides, you said *problems*—she's starting school, not a job on an oil rig." He turned around. "Don't call us unless you have to, and do not answer your mother if she texts you during school hours."

Unless it's an emergency, Jane mouthed with a small smile.

Millie nodded too many times. "Bye, Mom. Bye, Dad." She threw herself from the car and bolted for the dwindling line at the parked school bus.

She tried to pretend that her parents weren't watching her every move, even though she knew they would be, somewhere in the background.

But at least they were finally in the *background*, and not front and center, for once. It would take her a while to get used to such a concept.

Millie's heart thumped harder with every step she took up the stairs, down the aisle, and into one of the navy blue seats. And it raced the hardest when her eyes landed on all the new faces around her.

Classmates. Peers. Friends.

At that moment, the possibilities felt infinite.

Maybe tomorrow one of them would even be sitting next to her. They could talk about teachers, and homework, and how hard it was to remember their locker combinations.

Millie bit down on her lip and tried not to think about

throwing up. Because even though she was excited, she was nervous, too.

Because what if nobody liked her?

She clasped her hands, shoved them in her lap, and forced her eyes out the window, hoping the view of the familiar Oregon suburbs would calm her down.

What did she really have to worry about? She was going to school as a band major. By default, she already had a million things in common with everyone. Mozart, Rachmaninoff, Handel . . . And okay, maybe Millie didn't particularly like any of those things—classical music had nothing on J-Pop—but there were bound to be kids she had things in common with.

Right?

Thirty minutes later, the bus pulled up alongside the collection of buildings that formed Brightside Academy. Millie had visited the campus for orientation, but with an army of yellow buses outside and students socializing in the courtyard, everything felt different. More colorful, somehow.

Which made sense, because Brightside Academy encouraged its students to express themselves. It was uncommon to have a school with such a relaxed dress code—especially when that dress code also involved a uniform. But at Brightside, students took their fashion choices very seriously.

Millie adjusted her tie and sweater-vest self-consciously. Her mom had been certain the red Converse would be too loud, but it turned out there were things even Jane Nakakura didn't know.

Because individual footwear was just the beginning of a very long crescendo.

Students had hair in nearly every shade of the color wheel. They wore jewelry, and patterned socks, and had backpacks decorated with fuzzy key chains. They carried paint canvases, instrument cases, and big duffel bags with the names of dance schools and theater companies printed along the sides.

They looked like they *belonged* at Brightside Academy. Which made sense, because most of them had been going there since kindergarten.

It wasn't just that the school felt different.

It felt *alive*.

Millie grinned, the buzzing in her heart shooting through every vein in her body. She was alive, too, and it felt electric.

They *had* to accept her. Because she wanted to feel like she belonged there, too.

And for one brief moment, she was too hopeful to be afraid.

Crossing her fingers on both hands, she closed her eyes, took a breath, and joined the crowd.

CHAPTER TWO

"You're not supposed to be here."

Millie's embarrassment coiled through her. Her eyes drifted toward the rest of the students scattered around the room—the ones who *weren't* in the wrong homeroom. Maybe they weren't listening. Maybe they weren't paying attention to Millie's big mistake at all.

Two boys with nearly matching floppy hair exchanged glances and grinned.

It was enough to make Millie certain *everyone* was silently laughing at her.

The homeroom teacher held the yellow slip of paper toward Millie and pointed to the whiteboard. "The homerooms are alphabetical. This one is for names starting with *M*."

Millie fumbled for words, her grip on her flute case tightening. "My name is Millie." Was that even her voice? It sounded a million miles away.

The teacher let out a noise of understanding. "Ah. Yes, but

it's alphabetical by *last* name. Na—Nako—" She squinted hard at the paper. "Nay-ko-kara?"

Millie wasn't sure if it was rude to correct a teacher—it was pronounced Nah-kah-koo-rah—so she stayed quiet.

"You're looking for the *N to O* room, with Mr. Holland. Do you know where the Science labs are?" the teacher asked before rattling off a few quick directions.

Some of the students giggled. Millie felt like every spotlight in the world was pointed right at her. All she wanted to do was flee.

The teacher handed her the yellow schedule, and Millie stepped quickly into the empty hallway and headed for the Science labs. It was eerily quiet, like a shopping mall first thing in the morning. All the doors had little windows above the handles, so each time she walked past and looked inside she could see a classroom full of students.

She was very aware of being on the outside looking in.

Millie tried to fight the tremble in her shoulders. She wanted to be in a classroom with everyone else, meeting new people like everyone else. But instead she was the only person in the entire school who had turned up to the wrong homeroom.

Did everyone know that "alphabetical" meant "alphabetical by last name"? Would Millie have known, too, if she hadn't missed the first six years of public school? And if so, what *else* was she bound to get wrong?

It was a silly mistake. A small one, even. But to Millie, it felt like she'd face-planted in front of the entire school.

By the time she found her homeroom—she got lost, *twice*—Mr. Holland was wrapping up.

"Well, hello," he said when he saw Millie in the doorway. "A straggler."

Millie felt her ears burn when everyone in the classroom turned to look at her.

Mr. Holland didn't seem to notice. He held out his hand. "Schedule?" he asked, taking the piece of paper from her. "I see we have Earth Science together for first period. So unless you get terribly lost finding your seat, you won't have to worry about being late for your first class of the day." He chuckled, and a few of the other students joined in.

Millie blinked, not sure if she was supposed to be in on the joke, or if she *was* the joke.

Mr. Holland gave her a packet of information and some forms her parents would need to sign. She took a seat in the back of the classroom and tried to tell herself things would get better as soon as she calmed down.

But things didn't get better.

Even though she wasn't late for first period, Millie got lost on her way to Math and walked in during roll call. She was relieved to be on time to third period—until she realized she'd left her flute in the Math room. Too embarrassed to tell the teacher, she waited until the bell rang to run back to get it, so she was late for fourth period, too.

By the time her lunch hour rolled along, she was convinced

everything was going wrong. And the worst part was, not one student had said a word to her all day.

Generation Love had a song about taking charge of your own destiny. Millie had listened to it so many times she'd memorized every word—despite the lyrics being in Japanese. It had a good beat, and the choreography in the music video was amazing, but it was the meaning behind the words that tugged at Millie's heart the most. They taught her to be brave. To take charge.

It was the same song that gave Millie the courage to tell her parents she wanted to go to a real school.

And maybe a little bit of courage was still lingering around, waiting for Millie to reach for it. She couldn't change the fact that the morning had gone horribly, but maybe she could start over. Maybe lunch could be like a fresh start—a second chance to meet new people and enjoy school and not mess anything up.

Millie took a breath and lifted her head. Maybe all she had to do was be brave, just like Generation Love said.

Millie stepped into the cafeteria and felt immediately overwhelmed. It was chaos. Everyone was filling the empty chairs so quickly Millie started to worry there was a seating chart she didn't know about. And if there wasn't, what was she supposed to do? What were the rules? Did she just put her things down at a table and say hello to the people sitting there?

Something told Millie it was a lot more complicated than that.

She adjusted the straps on her backpack and decided she'd worry about where to eat once she got her food. With nervous steps, she made her way to the lunch line and copied everything the person in front of her was doing—she grabbed a red tray, picked up a carton of strawberry milk (even though she preferred chocolate), ordered a chicken burger, fries, and coleslaw, and then paid the man at the register. It seemed logical that as long as she was doing whatever the person in front of her was doing, she wouldn't mess anything up.

When the student she'd been copying sat down at a nearby table, Millie tried to quell her nerves. All she had to do was find an empty table. Once she was seated, she could gather her thoughts and try to forget the entire morning.

She could *reset.*

Millie only managed two steps before she tripped over her own feet and stumbled forward, crashing into a girl with dark curly hair.

Fries flew everywhere. The chicken burger split into three sections and landed at the girl's feet. And the coleslaw splattered all over the girl's sweater-vest—a sad, gloopy mixture of cabbage, carrots, and mayonnaise.

"Oh my God!" the girl shrieked.

Millie opened her mouth to apologize. She was pretty sure she managed the words, but she also couldn't feel her mouth move, or hear her voice, or focus on anything other than the girl's flailing hands in front of her.

Some of the kids turned to see what had happened. A few looked concerned.

But most of them had erupted in laughter.

"I didn't mean to—" Millie stopped. Was that her voice? It sounded like a squeak.

The girl held up her hands, suddenly aware there were people laughing. "It's fine." She looked over her shoulder at her two friends who were watching Millie with curious, peering eyes. They looked angry on their friend's behalf, even though the girl covered in coleslaw looked more embarrassed than anything.

Millie knelt to the floor and began plucking stray fries from the linoleum.

The girl hesitated for a moment, conflicted. Millie got the feeling she wanted to help.

"Come on, we'll help you clean up in the bathroom," one of her friends announced, the metal legs of her chair screeching as she stood up. The other girl followed.

The curly-haired stranger glanced briefly at Millie before turning toward her friends.

As they started walking away, Millie heard one of them say, "So gross. Who actually asks for the coleslaw? Everyone knows cafeteria coleslaw is the *worst*."

Millie's cheeks turned beet red. Nobody had told her about the coleslaw. Nobody had told her *anything*.

She cleaned up as quickly as she could, set her tray on the lunch cart, and shakily walked back through the cafeteria, unsure of what to do next.

Every table looked full, which only amplified the fact that there was no room for her.

All she wanted was a friend. Just one. One person to make

her feel like coming to Brightside wasn't the worst decision she'd ever made.

Was that so much to ask?

Millie looked up at the last table—the one closest to the doors. A student with short brown hair and plenty of freckles sat alone. Millie recognized them from Math class. Their name was Ashley Seo, which was easy for Millie to remember because of Asuna Seo—a J-Pop singer who was half Japanese and half Korean and sang the theme song on one of Millie's favorite anime shows.

Maybe it was a sign?

Millie reached for an empty chair. "Is it okay if I sit—" she started.

But Ashley didn't let her finish. "No."

Millie froze, startled. She wanted to mention their shared class, and to point out how Ashley's name reminded her of one of her favorite singers. But she couldn't get the words out. Something garbled and hurried came out instead. "I—in—the Math."

Oh no, Millie wanted to cry. *Now I'm even* speaking *wrong.*

Ashley didn't look up. "I'm not interested in making friends." When Millie's hand wilted, Ashley continued, "And even if I was, you'd be wasting your time. At Brightside, people stick to their own major. No one stays friends with someone outside of their little groups." Ashley motioned toward the other tables to show Millie what they meant.

Clusters of students were pebbled around the room. Some groups had sketchbooks; others had instruments. The curly-haired girl and her friends still hadn't returned, but the dance bags they had left behind were still slumped on their chairs.

Millie's heart sank. How was she ever going to make friends when there were so many guidelines she didn't know about?

She looked back at Ashley, who stood up abruptly and swung their bag over their shoulder.

"You can have the table. It's too crowded in here for me anyway," they said, and walked out of the cafeteria doors with all the calmness Millie didn't have.

Maybe Ashley hadn't meant to be rude. Maybe they had even meant to be *helpful*.

But all Millie could think about was what a disaster the day had been and how totally and completely unprepared she was for school.

When she returned to the bus at the end of the day, she forced her gaze out the window. She didn't want to risk anyone seeing the tears well up in her eyes or the way her lip had started to quiver.

More important, she had to figure out a way to stop crying before she stepped off the bus and saw her parents.

She'd made enough mistakes for one day.

Letting her parents see how right they were about school just couldn't be one of them.

★

CHAPTER THREE

The days rolled along like tumbleweeds in slow motion. Millie couldn't believe it was still the first week of school. It felt like she'd been there for a hundred years.

And the worst part?

Despite her best efforts, things didn't improve. They got *worse.*

On Tuesday, she found out the girl she'd spilled food all over was Luna Acevedo—a sixth-grade dance major, and one of the most popular girls at Brightside Academy.

In other words, Millie wasn't surprised people weren't lining up to be friends with her. Most of the students had known each other since kindergarten—there were bound to be unwritten rules about social etiquette. And assaulting Luna Acevedo with coleslaw and a chicken burger was probably breaking *at least* five of them.

But Millie wasn't ready to admit defeat. There was still band, after all, and Ashley *had* said most friend groups revolved around people's majors. Maybe she just needed more time to meet people. Preferably people who hadn't heard about the cafeteria incident.

But on Thursday, Millie found out that the band director was moving her into Wind Ensemble II. It was the top band at the junior high level, made up of mostly eighth graders. And something told Millie the odds of making friends when almost everyone was two years older were not great. Even if band majors *were* supposed to stick together.

And then it was Friday. Most of the students had hurried to the band room after lunch, so by the time Millie arrived, there was a crowd spilling out into the hallway. Everyone was trying to get a better view of the piece of paper taped to the door.

Chair Placements.

Millie swallowed the lump in her throat. Even though she hated how suffocating playing the flute had become, there was still a small part of her that remembered when it used to be fun. When she *enjoyed* playing classical music.

That small part of her was excited to see the results. She'd practiced really hard for her audition, and she only messed up once when she forgot to breathe in the right place. A side effect of being constantly nervous.

But the other part of her—the *bigger* part of her—was terrified to look at the results. What if she was last chair?

To everyone else, it was just a chair placement. And she'd already been moved to top band; most people would *expect* a sixth grader to get last chair. But to Millie, it was the difference between her parents being proud of her and letting their disappointment crush her like a tsunami.

She hated letting them down. She hated how it made her feel small and guilty and unable to breathe. And most of all, she hated feeling so responsible for her parents' happiness to begin with.

When the crowd dwindled, Millie made her way to the door, her eyes finding the section that read *Flutes.*

And there was her name, second from the top: *Millie Nakakura—second chair.*

Her stomach somersaulted and backflipped and cartwheeled all at once.

She wanted to smile with relief, but when she turned around, any ounce of excitement evaporated.

Kelly and Dia, two eighth graders, were scowling from the flute section. Millie knew from overhearing other students that they were best friends *and* the top flutists in Wind Ensemble II since last year.

Millie looked back up at the result sheet. Kelly was first chair; Dia was third.

They weren't expecting to be separated at all, let alone by a sixth grader.

Mr. Thomas, the band director, appeared at the podium and waved at the students still in the doorway. "Everyone, please sit down, and try not to worry about the results. There will be plenty of time for chair challenges once we've gotten into the swing of things."

Millie found her chair, feeling the heat of Kelly's and Dia's stares when she opened her case and put her flute together. It became more and more obvious how upset they were the longer the class went on. Every glance they exchanged had to pass right over Millie. She felt like an awkwardly placed window, forcing them apart.

She considered offering Dia her chair, but she worried that would only make things worse. Plus, her parents would be furious.

And she'd rather deal with Kelly and Dia than her parents' disappointment.

When the bell finally rang, she hurried to her next class, taking comfort in the fact that the sixth-grade classrooms were on a completely different side of the school from the eighth-grade ones.

She could feel defeat bubbling up from the pit of her stomach, but she tried to force it back down. Hope was the only thing protecting her heart.

And just when Millie didn't think her week could get any more horrible, it did.

It was unmistakable, written in bright red marker: *20%*.

She stared at the piece of paper in her hands and tried to make sense of it. Of how this could've *happened*.

She'd failed her first test.

Ms. Woods, her Geography teacher, paused beside Millie's desk. "You didn't include a proper heading, and you put your name in the wrong corner. That's worth twenty points on its own. Did you not read the board?" Her brow was lifted slightly, like she hadn't fully decided whether to be concerned or disappointed.

Millie scanned the whiteboard with confusion. She had no idea there were rules on how to write your name. Her words tangled up on the edge of her tongue. "I, um, didn't know about the board."

"And what about the additional reading?" Ms. Woods pressed. "Did you forget to go over the pages, or are you just having a hard time with the material?"

Millie felt her shoulders wobble and shake, like she'd become one of those comical dancing skeletons. Like there was barely anything holding her together. She couldn't find the words to explain how she hadn't even known there *was* additional reading.

All she could do was shake her head.

Ms. Woods sighed, giving Millie a look that said, *I know you can do better*, before moving down the row of desks.

Except Millie *had* done her best, and she was still getting everything wrong.

When the final bell rang, Millie made her way onto the bus and pushed herself into a window seat. She could still feel the Geography test nearby, bursting out of her notebook, crushed against the fabric of her backpack. It was a monster that grew and grew, and by the time she spotted her parents' car outside the window, she felt like the monster would swallow her whole.

Millie stepped onto the sidewalk with heavy shoulders and looked up to see her mom waving from next to the car.

Jane wrapped her arms around Millie for a quick hug before sliding back into the driver's seat. "So?" she asked once they were both inside. "What's the news?"

Millie grimaced. Her parents had been talking about chair placements all week. She knew they'd be excited, but this was even worse. Her mom was jubilant.

"I got second chair," Millie mumbled. She clicked her seat belt into place and stared hard at her flute. It suddenly seemed to weigh a thousand pounds. Between the pressure of band and the monster in her backpack, Millie felt like there was barely room for her in the car.

"That's wonderful!" Jane exclaimed, oblivious to Millie's furrowed brow. "Your dad will be so proud. Second chair in top band. What a way to start the school year, huh?"

As the car pulled away from the parking lot, Millie thought about telling her mom what had happened with her Geography test. She knew it was the right thing to do, but she also had no idea what to say. It wasn't like she hadn't studied; she'd just been studying the wrong material.

Besides, her mom was so happy about band . . .

Millie bit down on her lip and stared out the window.

Her dad was waiting by the front door when they got home. He held his hands open like he wanted the news.

"Second chair!" Jane exclaimed from behind Millie.

"That's fantastic," Scott said with a smile. His ink-black hair was combed neatly to one side. "I knew you could do it."

"Thanks," Millie said, and her test must've developed a pulse because she could feel it beating through her like a jackhammer. She wanted to shove her backpack in a corner and never open it again, but there was Math homework and reading assignments and notes to go over . . .

It was more overwhelming than Millie wanted to admit.

"I'll make you a snack," Jane said, hanging her purse on a nearby hook and disappearing into the kitchen.

"You know, if you practice a little harder, I bet you'll be first chair in no time," Scott said, and Millie's heart sank. Her dad continued, "You've got the technique, you just have to work on your tone. Remember what Anna told you about practicing your vibrato, even when you don't have your flute?"

Millie squeezed the handle of her flute case. How could she ever admit she was having a hard time at school when even *second chair* in *top band* wasn't good enough?

"I have to use the bathroom," she said abruptly, struggling to keep her lip from wobbling.

"Okay." Scott nodded. "Don't forget, you've got a flute lesson in an hour and a half." The corners of his eyes wrinkled when he smiled. "You can tell Anna about your chair. I'm sure she'll be thrilled for you."

He turned and headed for the kitchen.

Millie held it together for all the steps it took to get to her bedroom. The moment her door closed, she let her backpack fall to the floor, her face crumpling like a fistful of tissue paper.

She might not have wanted to tell them about her test, but her parents hadn't even *asked* about school. She'd waited all week for them to be interested in whether she'd made any friends or if she liked her teachers. Anything to make Millie feel like there was an opening in the conversation to bring up her feelings.

Because she wanted to talk to her parents. She wanted their advice. She wanted them to tell her how to make everything better.

But all her mom and dad seemed to care about was band.

Sometimes it felt like there wasn't room for them to care about anything else.

Millie wiped her tears with the back of her hand and hurried to her dresser, where her limited edition Generation Love headphones were sitting in the same place she always kept them. They were dependable. Constant.

She took out her phone, scrolled through her playlists, and found the mix of her favorite Generation Love songs. The sound poured through the headphones, making Millie think of sugary-pink cupcakes and bubble gum. She sank into her bed and closed her eyes.

Generation Love was the closest thing to a friend she had. It didn't matter that the five-person band lived in Japan and were too busy singing in stadiums and making music videos to have any idea who Millie was.

Because when she listened to their perfect harmonies and happy choruses, she felt a little less lonely than she had before.

And in her heart, that was what Millie wanted more than anything in the world.

CHAPTER FOUR

On Saturday evening, Millie clicked the latest post on Generation Love's biggest fan page, and an explosion of silver and pink pixels took over most of the screen. In the center was a live countdown.

In another twenty-three minutes, their new music video would be unveiled.

Millie was giddy with excitement. She'd been waiting weeks for this—months, if you counted the time before she knew the video was going to be official. And even though she loved checking the fan forums for rumors and leaked images of Generation Love on set, enough was enough. She wanted the real thing.

Swaying in her chair to the sound of their latest single in the background, Millie scrolled down the page until she reached the comments section, where fans from all over the world were busy sharing their pure, unfiltered love for the ultimate pop group. Most of the comments were written in Japanese, but there were still plenty in English that Millie could read without using auto-translate.

GennerLove13: OMGGGG IT'S ALMOST HERE

KiyokoHeartsGL: *refreshes the page a billion times even though it's not noon in Japan yet*

JpopIsL1f3: ASDKJFKDFHE I CAN'T BREATHE

ChiyoFanForeverrr: literally having a GL video unveiling party right now, there are fourteen of us camped around the computer eating chicken wings and we CANNOT WAIT

Millie felt a tinge of jealousy pulse through her. She couldn't help it. There were people out there throwing actual parties with actual friends—something Millie had never had in her life.

But at least she had the internet, where she could live vicariously through strangers on Generation Love forums.

"There you are," Jane said, peeking through the office doorway. "It's getting pretty late, Millie. I think you should head up to bed."

Millie's brows lifted in alarm. "But the new Generation Love music video is coming out soon!"

Jane frowned and stepped into the room. "Can't you watch it in the morning?"

"It won't be the same. All the biggest fans watch it as soon as it releases so they can talk about it. It's like"—Millie paused, desperate—"a community thing, I guess."

"Hmm." Her mom stepped around the desk to look at the computer and placed a gentle hand on Millie's shoulder.

Millie tensed, hoping her mom wouldn't read too many of the comments. She was worried she wouldn't get it.

And her parents had a habit of putting a stop to things they didn't understand.

"I'm not comfortable with you being in chat rooms, Millie," Jane said sternly. She was wearing a plaid sweater that looked more like a shawl, and every time she moved the threads brushed against Millie's arm.

"It's not a chat room." Millie pulled away, her voice clipped and fragile. "It's a fan page."

Jane stepped back and crossed her arms. "If you're talking to strangers online, it's the same thing to me."

"I don't even post anything! I just like to read what other people are saying." When Jane's forehead crumpled, Millie added quickly, "The forums are a big part of what makes the videos so special. Everyone likes to write about what they think. It's kind of like going to a concert and being around people who all love the same music as you do." Not that Millie had ever been to a concert that wasn't a wind symphony or a flute choir. Besides, Generation Love rarely performed in the States, and when they did it was only ever in major cities, and tickets cost a *fortune*.

Jane sighed.

Millie bit the edge of her lip.

"Fine." Jane leaned forward and kissed Millie's temple. "You can stay up for the video and a few extra minutes to read the comments. But after that it's bedtime." She paused near the door. "Didn't any of your teachers give out homework for the weekend?"

Millie twisted her fingers together nervously. "No. I mean, not that I know of."

"That doesn't sound like you're very sure." Jane frowned, eyes processing Millie like a computer. Though for all the times Millie's parents tried to read her, they rarely seemed to get it right. "Are you having a hard time adjusting at school?"

Millie stiffened. She hadn't expected that.

It was the perfect opportunity to tell the truth. If she confessed everything she was feeling, maybe her parents could even help her understand the rules about homework and teachers and socializing.

But before Millie could open her mouth, Jane said the words that made Millie's heart shrink. "Because if this is too much for you, we can go back to homeschooling."

Alarm bells went off in Millie's head, making her ears ring. It had only been a week, and her parents were already talking about pulling her out of school. There was no *way* Millie could admit she was struggling. Her time at Brightside Academy would be over before it ever really started.

Millie pressed her lips together and shook her head. "School is fine. And I did all my homework yesterday." The homework she *knew* about, anyway. She couldn't be completely sure she hadn't missed something, but now wasn't the time to explain that to her mom.

Maybe there'd never be a good time. Not when Brightside was at risk.

Jane's gaze softened. "I'm glad to hear it." She pointed a finger at Millie and scrunched her nose. "Just a few more minutes, okay?"

Millie hummed in agreement, and her mom disappeared back through the doorway.

Almost instantly, Millie's shoulders began to relax, like she'd been holding all the tension in without even realizing it. And then her eyes drifted to the framed photograph sitting beside the computer monitor. Even though their faces were slightly blurred and brimming with youth, the teenagers in the photo were unmistakably younger versions of Scott and Jane.

Scott was holding a flute; Jane was holding an oboe. And even in their arguably dorky and outdated marching-band uniforms, they still smiled like their faces were drinking up the sun.

It had always been like that—Scott and Jane, the unbreakable duo. They'd been together since they were teenagers, and for most of their lives, it was them against the world. It was no wonder they didn't understand the importance of making friends. They had been each other's *best* friend since practically the beginning of time.

Millie refreshed the forums again and again, trying to sink back into the excitement rather than the bubbling frustration behind her rib cage. It was hard, but she managed.

When the countdown hit zero and the newest Generation Love music video appeared, Millie lost herself in the music, and the colors, and the joy from strangers all over the world.

And for the next ten minutes, she felt like she was a part of something beautiful.

CHAPTER FIVE

The cafeteria smelled like overcooked cheese and slightly burned pizza crust. Millie took a small bite of her slice, trying her best to pretend she wasn't the only person in the cafeteria with an entire table to herself.

She rummaged through her notebooks and found a pair of bright green earbuds. After putting them in, she scrolled through her most recent Generation Love playlist. There was something comforting about listening to music in a crowded room. She was still alone, but she didn't *feel* as alone, and maybe that was the magic of a good personal soundtrack.

She was about to play her favorite ballad—"Lost Star," from Generation Love's most recent album—when the laughter coming from a nearby table caught her attention. She looked up and saw Luna Acevedo tuck a dark curl behind her ear and lean toward her best friends, Ruby and Annabelle, the three of them looking over their shoulders at the same time before bursting into a wave of giggles.

Millie followed their gaze across the cafeteria and saw Rainbow Chan, her oversize red glasses and argyle socks making her stand out in the crowd. She was a sixth-grade theater major, which Millie found peculiar. Rainbow seemed like the kind of person who would rather take part in a disappearing act than a stage performance.

Millie knew her from English class—*before* her schedule had been switched to accommodate Wind Ensemble II. Rainbow was the first person Millie thought she might get along with, mostly because Rainbow was always so flighty and nervous. Millie thought at the very least they'd have that in common.

But the moment they made eye contact in class, Rainbow's face had turned a startlingly deep shade of red, and she never looked Millie's way again.

Rainbow shuffled through the aisle, her arms cradled around herself awkwardly and her eyes darting about like she was lost.

And maybe she was. Because if there was one thing Millie had learned pretty quickly about school, it was that lunchtime was the one hour of the day when everyone was completely predictable. People sat at the same tables, with the same friends, eating more or less the same food. They were creatures of habit.

But Millie had never seen Rainbow in the cafeteria before. She wasn't even sure this was Rainbow's lunch hour.

"Rainbow!" Ruby shouted from a few yards away.

The sound made Rainbow stiffen. When she looked toward the voice, her entire body recoiled. She didn't just look lost—she looked like an animal caught in danger.

Even though the exchange had nothing to do with Millie, curiosity got the better of her. She couldn't look away.

Ruby's smile stretched across her face. "I didn't know you still went to this school."

Annabelle looked smug beside her. Luna busied herself with a slice of pizza.

Rainbow tugged at her sweater-vest, her eyes tracing the space surrounding the girls. It was obvious she didn't want to talk to them.

But Ruby didn't seem to care what Rainbow wanted. "What brings you to the cafeteria? Did you finally get sick of living off tofu and rice crackers?" She smirked at Annabelle, whose laugh practically bubbled with venom.

Rainbow shifted her weight, fingers tapping against her leg. When she spoke, her voice was barely audible above the lunch-room chatter. "I forgot my lunch at home."

"I'd use that excuse, too." Annabelle snorted.

Luna adjusted the built-in straw on her water bottle, seemingly too preoccupied to notice what was happening beside her.

Rainbow tugged the straps of her backpack and pushed forward toward the lunch line, but Ruby's voice stopped her.

"You're going to eat outside, right?" Ruby asked innocently.

Rainbow looked over her shoulder, confusion swirling through her glazed eyes.

"It's just that you smell like patchouli oil or bug spray or whatever it is your parents wash your clothes with. It's going to make everyone sick, and I mean, we're trying to *eat*."

Rainbow's cheeks flushed with color, and she didn't waste a moment before lowering her head and hurrying back out of the cafeteria doors as Ruby and Annabelle laughed cruelly beside Luna.

"Did you see her socks?"

"She is *so weird*."

Millie wanted to turn the music up, to drown out the noise of their meanness. But she couldn't. She couldn't unsee what had happened, and no amount of J-Pop was going to morph the room into something other than what it was.

The cafeteria was terrifying. How was Millie ever going to fit in? Rainbow Chan had been at Brightside Academy for years and never bothered anyone, and she was being picked on for something as minor as her *lunch*.

Millie shoved her earbuds back into her bag, dumped the rest of her uneaten lunch into the trash can, and headed for her next class. She'd get there too early and would have to wait in the hall, but anything was better than having to listen to the horrible things Ruby and Annabelle were saying at Rainbow's expense.

But when she reached the doors, a flyer on the nearby bulletin board caught her eye. It was bright blue, like cotton candy at a carnival, with big, bold lettering.

Do you love Japanese pop music? Want to make new friends?
Then come and join J-Club! We meet in Room F-206 every Thursday at 3:15 p.m.

Millie had to read the flyer three times because she was convinced her eyes were playing tricks on her.

A club. For *J-Pop.*

She felt her soul explode from her body until it was flying ten thousand feet in the air. Because this was the answer. This was going to change *everything.*

All she had to do was get her parents on board.

Jane took a bite of potato salad. Scott reached across the table for a second helping of green beans.

Millie stared at the chicken leg she'd mostly left untouched. She'd loved them when she was younger, but now she hated the grease and the mess. Except her parents didn't seem to notice her face fall every time they carved a roast chicken and put the leg on her plate.

They hadn't noticed how much she'd changed over the years. How much she was still changing.

And it was more than just her distaste for chicken legs.

Millie shuffled anxiously in her chair, catching her parents' attention.

"You okay, sweetie?" her mom asked with round, happy eyes.

"You've been acting strange since you got home from school." Her dad paused. Creases appeared between his eyebrows. "Did something happen in band?"

"No," Millie said irritably, though she tried to hide it. It might help her cause more if her parents *didn't* know how frustrated she was with them. "I—I just have something I want to ask you."

"Oh yeah?" Her mom's face settled into a smile and she took a drink of water.

Her dad chewed a mouthful of green beans, his eyes watching Millie curiously. "What is it?"

Millie sat up straighter. "Well, you see, there's this after-school club—"

"A club?" her mom repeated.

Millie flinched at the interruption, but kept her voice steady. "Yeah. And I'd really like to join. It would be perfect for me. And there's a late bus so you wouldn't have to pick me up from the school or anything."

Jane looked at Scott, who lifted his shoulders like the decision was up to her.

"I mean, we would definitely support any extracurricular activity that would help with your studies. Or band—is this a band club?" Jane asked.

Millie felt a tremor in her stomach. It felt like the world was a few seconds from splitting apart. "Not exactly . . ."

Jane barely seemed to hear her. "Or a flute club! Do they have that already? If they don't, I bet you could try to start something like that yourself."

Scott nodded encouragingly. "You kids could probably even try out for solo ensemble as a group. Along with your own solo, of course. A flute ensemble—imagine that!"

Millie swallowed. She could imagine it, all right. The added pressure. The extra time spent practicing. And all the hours she'd have to spend with Kelly and Dia, who would probably never in a billion years agree to a flute ensemble in the first place.

And worst of all, it felt like the complete *opposite* of J-Club.

Millie bit her lip and tried to steady her breathing. "Why does everything always have to be about flute?" She could feel the weight of her dad's disappointment already starting when he lowered his chin. Like not wanting to play the flute was hurting him somehow. Her voice cracked, but she fought to get the words out. "I just thought—if I joined a club where it wasn't about work or a competition—maybe it would be easier to make friends."

Jane set her fork down and folded her hands together. "Honey, we aren't sending you to school to make friends."

"Socializing is a huge part of school," Millie tried. "And I just want to fit in."

"You'll fit in by being yourself," Jane said. Her voice was full of love, but it didn't reach Millie through the walls of frustration and annoyance she'd been building for months.

Millie made a face. "You don't go to Brightside. You don't know what it's like."

Scott narrowed his dark brown eyes. "Hey. Watch your tone."

Millie sank into her chair. They weren't even *pretending* to listen to her.

Jane sighed and ran a finger over the silver chain around her neck. "We just don't want you to get distracted. You're at school to learn, not to worry about making friends. It will happen naturally; maybe even in band. Just give it time."

Millie opened her mouth again to argue, but she couldn't find her words. They were probably hiding out with her bravery, which she could never seem to find when she needed it most.

Her parents went back to their meal as if nothing had happened. Millie didn't even get the chance to bring up J-Club, because what would be the point? They'd never let her join. It wasn't academic enough, and it would do nothing to help with chair placements, honor band, all-state, and whatever other expectations her parents had of her.

Millie felt her stomach knot over and over again. It wasn't fair. She wished they cared more. She wished they could at least *try* to understand her.

But neither of them could see why this was so important to her. Why making friends felt like *everything*.

They believed so deeply they were doing the right thing.

How was Millie ever going to compete with that?

★

CHAPTER SIX

"Everyone, please pass your homework to the front of the class," Mrs. Devon said, marking the whiteboard with swooping blue letters.

Millie looked nervously to the side, hoping her classmates would look as confused as she felt. They were rummaging through their backpacks and binders, pulling out stapled pages at almost exactly the same time. Like everything else at Brightside, they were moving too fast for her to keep up.

A girl with copper hair tied back in a ponytail sat to Millie's right. She seemed friendly, or at the very least approachable. It was enough to make Millie think it was safe to ask her a question.

Leaning to the side, Millie kept her voice as low as possible. "What homework did we have?"

The friendliness in the girl's face disappeared instantly. "Vocab," she replied, and busied her eyes in her notebook.

Frowning, Millie pressed on. "What vocab? I don't remember Mrs. Devon saying anything about an assignment yesterday."

"It's on the whiteboard," the girl answered curtly. And then she sighed, a twinge of pity in her eyes. "No offense, but we have vocab every day. It's not that hard to remember."

Millie's entire face began to boil. She could feel her classmates turning to stare. They all thought she was lazy, or forgetful, or a bad student.

But that wasn't it. Millie was just *confused.* She felt like an alien from outer space who had accidentally ended up in an earthling school. She felt like someone who didn't understand how anything worked.

The girl with copper hair looked away, uninterested. Because nobody wanted to be friends with the person who never did their homework.

The whiteboard wasn't much help either. The middle section was covered in Mrs. Devon's neat cursive. There were some page numbers to the left—maybe something to do with today's lesson. And on the right was a section that read *Planner*, with a list of more page numbers.

Nothing said *Homework* or *Vocab* or *THIS IS DUE TOMORROW*. Shouldn't something as big as a homework assignment be *clearer*?

Millie's muddled thoughts were forced aside when the boy behind her waved a stack of lined paper near her shoulder.

"Here," he said impatiently.

"Sorry," Millie mumbled, taking the pages and avoiding eye contact with the teacher when she stopped in front of her.

"Millie, where's your homework?" Mrs. Devon asked, her

eyes peering over the top of her glasses. They felt like lasers, making Millie shrink into her chair.

"I don't have it," Millie said quietly.

Mrs. Devon shook her head and lowered her chin. "That's the second assignment you've missed this week."

Millie opened her mouth to tell Mrs. Devon she was confused, but she couldn't conjure up the words. Not in front of the whole classroom.

She was too embarrassed to draw any more attention to herself.

So Millie stared at her clasped hands in shame and waited for Mrs. Devon to walk away.

In band, Millie could hardly focus on the notes. She kept seeing Mrs. Devon's disapproving face in her mind, and all the students turning to stare. She was attracting bad attention, and she didn't know how to stop.

She'd rather be invisible than noticed for all the wrong reasons, like poor Rainbow Chan and her argyle socks.

"*It's not that hard to remember,*" the copper-haired girl had said. But she was wrong. Everything about school was hard for Millie to remember.

Mr. Thomas tapped his baton against his podium stand. "Flutes, you aren't quite getting this section right. Can I hear each of you play the line—starting at measure twenty-three?" He motioned toward the first chair.

Kelly lifted her flute and played the line perfectly.

Millie's heart was caught in a storm, pounding angrily

against her chest. It didn't matter that she'd been playing the flute since she was six years old. Playing in front of people didn't just make Millie nervous—it did something to her entire nervous system.

Mr. Thomas nodded toward her. "Millie?"

She placed the mouthpiece below her lip and played the line. First her fingers wouldn't cooperate and she hit a wrong note. And then her breath quivered, causing the notes to sound weak and airy.

She sounded like someone who could barely play the flute at all.

"Hmm," Mr. Thomas said when Millie finished. "Make sure you're holding the G for the full two beats. Let's practice that line at home, okay?"

Millie's cheeks burned. Beside her, Kelly and Dia snickered.

Mr. Thomas continued down the line, and each flute player hit all the right notes in the right tempo.

Millie wished a sinkhole would open up right below her and swallow her into the earth so she could disappear forever.

She spent the rest of band moving her fingers over all the keys, hoping the rest of the flute section would hide the fact that she wasn't playing a single note. It wasn't because she didn't know them—she could play the entire song without even looking at the sheet music. But she was distracted.

For weeks, everything had been going horribly wrong.

Millie was embarrassing herself practically on a daily basis.

She had just proven to the entire band that she was the weak link. Most of her teachers thought she was a bad student. Nobody wanted to be her friend. And J-Club was meeting tomorrow, and Millie didn't have permission to go.

She felt like every door in the world was slamming in her face at once.

And maybe she couldn't change what people already thought about her, but J-Club? It was an opportunity for a fresh start with people who would understand her. Maybe they could even *help* her.

But her parents would never let her join a club for fun. They didn't see the benefit of making friends. They didn't understand how lonely Millie felt and how desperately important it was for her to feel like she belonged at Brightside Academy.

Like she belonged *somewhere*. The truth was, more often than not, Millie felt like she and her parents came from different worlds.

J-Pop was about as foreign to her parents as playing the flute had become to Millie. And if Millie couldn't be convinced to be excited about honor band, there wasn't a chance in the world she could convince her parents to be excited about J-Club.

It wasn't practical enough. *Educational* enough.

And then, sometime between the xylophone solo and the trumpet section butchering their entrance, Millie remembered something she'd heard in a Generation Love interview.

Chiyo Aoki, the lead singer of Generation Love, once talked

about her audition for the group during an appearance on a Japanese talk show. She admitted to being so nervous that she didn't even tell anyone she was auditioning. Instead, she told her parents she was attending a study session after school and then took a train across the city to try out for the new pop group.

Maybe Millie needed to be more like Chiyo. Maybe she needed to take control of her destiny. And even though her plan would involve lying to her parents, Millie told herself it was the only way.

Chiyo had chased after her dreams, and look where it got her. She was the lead singer of the biggest pop group in Japan. Millie had to at least *try*. The future of her social life—and happiness—depended on it.

So she spent the rest of the day thinking of the perfect lie, and by the time she got home, it hardly felt like a lie at all.

"I have to stay late tomorrow after school," Millie said, her pen hovering over her Math homework.

Jane looked up from across the table. She was going through the mail, a mess of envelopes sprawled in front of her. "Why? Did something happen?"

"No," Millie said, trying to sound casual. "But some of the teachers suggested I join Advanced Studies. It's a teacher-run after-school study session to help students with test-taking and essay-writing. It's good for someone like me, who is behind on that kind of thing." She couldn't believe she got all the words out without tripping over her tongue.

"I hardly think you're *behind*," Jane said, her voice sounding almost defensive.

"I am," Millie replied stiffly. When her mom raised a brow, Millie softened her expression. "It's not your fault. It's just that things move a lot faster at school. I want to make sure I'm on the same level as everyone else."

Jane seemed to chew on her thoughts, her fingers tap-tap-tapping against the nearest envelope. "Well, I don't know. I'd have to talk to your dad about it when he gets home."

Millie shrugged. Inside, her heart was about to explode. She had to pretend she didn't want this. That it was more the school's idea than her own.

After all, her parents had a history of disapproving of the things Millie wanted most.

"It's not a big deal if you don't want me to go. It was Mrs. Devon's idea." The lies left a bitter aftertaste in Millie's mouth. She tried to remind herself it was for a good cause.

"I mean, if your teacher thinks it would be helpful . . ." Jane's voice trailed off. "And it's teacher-run?"

"Every Thursday."

"And there's a late bus?"

"Yes."

Her mom smiled. "Okay. Well, I don't think that should be a problem. I guess it's never too early to start practicing for the SATs."

Millie couldn't even bring herself to be annoyed at the comment. Because her mom had said *yes*.

She bit down on the inside of her cheek and went back to her Math homework, too terrified to let her mom see how she was glowing from the inside out.

Because tomorrow, when her parents thought she was in Advanced Studies practicing essay-writing, Millie would be in J-Club meeting people who shared her passion.

It didn't matter that she had lied to her parents and felt a horrible sense of guilt deep in her belly. Because on the surface, Millie felt like a firework, fizzing and popping and ready to burst.

Tomorrow, she would finally make *friends.* And that was worth ten thousand lies.

Besides, Millie's lies weren't hurting anyone. Maybe that meant they weren't really so bad.

She repeated the thought to herself, again and again, and by the time she was in bed, ready to sleep, she realized she had finally started to believe it.

CHAPTER SEVEN

The campus felt transformed after the final yellow bus pulled away from the curb. Millie never knew school could be so *still*.

She pulled at the straps of her backpack self-consciously. Even though she wasn't doing anything wrong, it still felt like at any moment a teacher would appear to scold her for missing the bus or for wandering through the school without a hall pass.

Her eyes darted around the empty courtyard. She was hoping to spot somebody else who might be headed to J-Club, but she couldn't seem to find any clues. Key chains, stickers, pins — the usual markers of a J-Pop fan — were nowhere in sight.

If anyone nearby was as obsessed with Japanese pop music as Millie was, they were being incognito about it.

Millie made her way past the PE locker rooms and the track field before she had to cross the road that separated the music, dance, and theater buildings from the rest of the campus. The flyer, which Millie kept tucked away in her binder, said to meet in Room F-206, which was the orchestra room.

Maybe it meant some of the people in J-Club were music

majors, which was a good start. The more things they had in common, the better.

She passed the band room, feeling her chest tighten at the sound of the jazz band rehearsing late. It reminded her how excited her parents were at the idea of a flute choir.

They'd be upset if they ever found out Millie was lying. Furious, even. But Millie needed this more than her parents could possibly understand.

Pushing the sound of saxophone riffs and cymbal crashes from her mind, Millie turned the corner and made her way toward the orchestra room.

She stared at the big blue door for a while, wondering if it would be weird to knock or weirder to walk right in. What were the rules? Why was socializing always so complicated?

With a timid breath and shaky hands, Millie pushed the door open and stepped inside.

The first thing she noticed were all the chairs. Most of them were folded and stacked at the back of the room, but a handful were still standing near the podium.

The second thing she noticed was how empty the room was, apart from one girl who stood out against her beige surroundings like a carnival at the edge of the sea.

She had bubblegum-pink streaks in her black hair and eyes that rounded into saucers when she spotted Millie near the doorway. Her bow tie was loose around her neck, and her sleeves were pushed up past her elbows, revealing at least ten rows of rainbow-hued bracelets.

Millie couldn't remember if she'd seen her around school before, which probably meant she hadn't. It would be impossible to see someone so colorful and *not* remember them.

Maybe that was a downside to going to a K-to-twelve school. Sometimes people got lost in the crowd.

"Are you here for the J-Club meeting?" the girl asked, head tilting to the side.

Millie barely had a chance to nod before the girl leaped out of her chair and clapped her hands excitedly, bouncing on her toes like she'd just heard the greatest news.

"Oh my gosh, yay!" She hurried toward Millie and threw her arm forward. When Millie didn't move, she grabbed hold of her hand anyway and began shaking furiously. And then words exploded out of her like she was an actual volcano. "Hi, I'm Zuki! It's so nice to meet you. Did you see the flyer? Is that why you're here? I knew they would work. Charlie Franklin from Science said nobody would ever join J-Club when there was already Anime Club and Manga Club, but I knew he was wrong. I can't wait to tell him tomorrow what an old expired jug of milk he is. Do you know Charlie? He's the worst—don't talk to him, if you can help it. All he does is make fun of *ev-er-y-thing*. Are you in sixth grade, too? I've never seen you around. You must not be an orchestra major, or I'd definitely remember you. I play the violin. Ms. Jimenez lets me use this room for J-Club meetings, but we have to put all the chairs away when we're done. Which isn't too much work, but it will be even less work now that there are two of us!"

She was still shaking Millie's hand, her eyes too busy bursting with excitement to notice.

"Um. I'm a band major," Millie said timidly, and Zuki seemed to settle long enough to release her hand.

"Oh, cool! We're practically neighbors then. Do you want a Starburst?" Zuki skipped toward her fiery-orange backpack and pulled out a disheveled, half-eaten pack of candy. "I ate all the pink ones already—they're my favorite." She held it up to Millie with a toothy smile.

Millie hesitated before taking one of the yellow pieces.

Zuki didn't stop grinning. "Good choice." She turned quickly, her movements sharp and impatient, and picked up a binder from one of the chairs. It had the name *Tina Suzuki* written on the front, with a collage of stickers plastered all over. Zuki caught Millie's gaze and tapped her finger against the writing. "It's just in case I lose it somewhere. Only my parents call me Tina. And teachers. And people I don't know very well." She paused for a second before tumbling into a laugh. "So I guess *everyone* calls me Tina, but I don't really like it. It doesn't say anything about me, and names should say something, you know?" Her eyes tripled in size again, fingers gripping the binder in front of her. "Oh my gosh, I forgot to ask *your* name!"

Millie couldn't help but break into a smile, and when she did, she felt her nerves start to settle. Zuki's unapologetic enthusiasm was infectious. "I'm Millie. Millie Nakakura."

Zuki wagged a finger energetically. "You're Japanese, too! I knew it. You look a little like Miyuki from Generation Love. Do you listen to them?"

Millie's heart felt like a helicopter, knocking everything in the wrong direction. "Yes!" she practically shouted. "They're my absolute favorite."

"Me too!" Zuki squealed, thrusting the binder forward again. "Chiyo is my favorite member, of course." She motioned toward her pink streaks, pointing to the stickers of Generation Love and Chiyo's identical pink hair color. "But I love all of them. Do you have their new album? I've been listening to it nonstop for weeks."

"So have I," Millie nodded a thousand times. "Chiyo is my idol, too. But I also like Hana, because she's so funny."

"*So* funny," Zuki agreed, turning several pages in her binder before presenting it to Millie. "I was working on this playlist. It's what I think are their top ten hits, but I'm struggling to narrow it down. Their album *Sugar Pop* was just so good, but now with *E-Volve* out, it's just too many good ones to choose from." She sighed dreamily, like not knowing how to pick her favorite songs was the most perfect problem in the world to have.

Millie had never related to someone more in her life.

She scanned the list, recognizing every song title as easily as if she were looking through a favorite box of crayons. And it felt good to finally feel like she was speaking the same language as another human being.

Her smile was so wide her cheeks started to hurt.

They sat down to compare their favorite songs, taking turns playing each example from their phones like they needed to be reminded how much they loved them. And with each song, their excitement grew bigger and wider until it filled the entire room. They barely took a breath to stop talking, and by the time the late bell rang, Millie couldn't believe a whole hour had passed already.

Zuki stuffed her binder into her backpack. "You're coming back next Thursday, right?"

"Definitely," Millie said, her entire body feeling like it was buzzing.

Zuki looked relieved. "Good. Because you're vice president now. I'm so glad to finally have someone to plan things with!"

"I can't believe we're the only two members," Millie said in genuine disbelief. "We can't possibly be the only people in this school who like J-Pop."

Zuki laughed, walking side by side with Millie toward the door. "I've been trying to recruit people for *forever*, but nobody ever turns up. Well, except for the time when these two art majors stopped by and realized this wasn't Anime Club." She rolled her eyes. "You'd think people here would appreciate Japanese culture for more than just its monster-angel-robot-whatever cartoons. I don't like anime, for the record. Except for Studio Ghibli, but I don't think that really counts."

Millie decided not to mention how much she loved Pokémon,

Sailor Moon, Rozen Maiden, and the handful of other anime she had grown up watching.

Millie reached for the door but paused when Zuki stopped a few steps behind her. Her face was scrunched up in concentration. Or maybe it was a frown.

Millie's heart sped up, her mind racing backward to think of what she might've done wrong. "What's the matter?"

Zuki sighed, her shoulders falling. "I'm sorry if I talk too much. Everyone says I do. I just get excited and sometimes I don't know when to stop." A second passed before more words poured out of her. "You don't mind, do you? If you do, I can try harder not to say so many things. Charlie says it's annoying— not that he would even know, because I barely talk to him. Not since he called me 'Zucchini' in front of the entire class. But my parents are always telling me to be quiet, too, so I guess it must be annoying."

"You can talk as much as you want," Millie said with a shrug, mostly relieved she wasn't the only one worried about making a good impression. "I don't mind."

Zuki's face lit up again, her laugh resembling a hiccup. "Hey, let's swap numbers, okay? In case we have to talk about club stuff before next Thursday."

Fifteen minutes later, Millie was sitting on the late bus when she felt her phone vibrate. Her first instinct was to assume it was her parents.

Maybe they had called the school, or run into one of her

teachers, or used some kind of parental psychic connection to learn the truth. Maybe all of this was just too good to be true, and she'd never go to another J-Club meeting again.

But when she looked at her screen, it wasn't either of her parents' names that appeared. It was Zuki's.

And as Millie sent the very first text to her very first friend, she felt her heart sing.

CHAPTER EIGHT

Millie stepped off the school bus on Friday morning and it took her three whole seconds to realize it wasn't a coincidence that Zuki was standing at the front gate.

Zuki was waiting for *her*.

A smile stretched across Zuki's face, both rows of teeth on display. "Hey, stranger! I have something for you." She swung her backpack around and began rummaging inside. "Here." She thrust a fist in front of her, dropping something small and colorful into Millie's open palm.

It was a key chain with a string of blue, pink, orange, yellow, and white beads hanging in a row. When Millie looked closer, she realized the white beads each had a small black letter in the center, forming the word J-CLUB.

"I tried to make it match your backpack," Zuki said. She lifted her own bag and flicked an almost identical key chain dangling from one of the zips. Hers was pink and purple—Chiyo's favorite colors. "They're so we can promote the club," she offered gleefully.

Millie's cheeks reddened. The only presents she ever got were from her parents. She wasn't sure exactly what to say.

"Thank you. I love it," she said finally, and Zuki seemed pleased.

Millie hooked the key chain onto the front zipper of her backpack before swinging it back over her shoulders. She'd have to remember to remove it on the bus every day; if her parents saw it, they might have questions.

"What do you have for first period?" Zuki asked.

"I used to have Earth Science, but my schedule changed. So now it's Math."

"I have Geography, so I can walk with you to class. It's on the way!" Zuki half skipped toward the quad, pausing near the gate to make sure Millie was beside her.

Usually Millie was hyperaware of the crowd around her. The people moving in pairs, and the animated conversations she was never a part of.

But walking with Zuki made all of that go away. She didn't feel like people were staring at her or noticing all the things she was doing wrong. She practically forgot she was even *at* school until the first bell rang, and Mr. Kwan appeared in front of her desk.

"Tina, while I appreciate your newfound passion for math, you only have two minutes to get to your next class," he said, his eyes full of humor despite his serious tone.

"Sorry, Mr. Kwan. I'm going," Zuki squeaked, leaping out of

the chair she'd been temporarily borrowing. She waved at Millie. "See you at lunch?"

Millie smiled back, and Zuki disappeared through the doorway.

When Millie stepped into the cafeteria later that afternoon, Zuki had already saved a table for the two of them. They hurried in line to get their food, with Zuki talking in rapid-fire speed about her morning classes and the ranking of her favorite to least-favorite teachers.

"Chicken burger day is the best lunch day," Zuki said before falling into her chair and taking a massive bite of food.

Millie felt a trail of mayonnaise in the corner of her mouth and wiped it away with her knuckle. "Definitely better than pizza day."

Zuki widened her eyes as if to say, *I know, right?* before pointing at the notebook between them. "So"—she swallowed— "this is the updated playlist. I shifted these tracks around because I feel like number four is *always* a ballad, but I'm still not sure about number nine."

"I like it," Millie said, eating a fry like sitting at lunch with a friend was the most normal thing in the world. "I think it has a good balance. Plus, they're all amazing songs."

Zuki hummed thoughtfully and then sighed, returning to her burger. "We really need to recruit more members. We have the same taste—which is super cool—but, like, even Generation Love has Ryoko, who raps. We need a variety of talents in our club."

"I know what you mean," Millie said, which was only sort of true. It had never occurred to her that some people actually *liked* hearing different opinions. She was too used to her parents, who basically shared the same brain. "Plus, clubs should have more than two members."

"Exactly." Zuki pushed the notebook toward Millie. "You hang on to this until next Thursday. See if you can think of any way to make it better."

Millie set her burger down and pulled out her own notebook. She broke the pages apart, ready to set the playlist inside, when she spotted her Geography quiz. There it was, in bright red pen: 20%. She quickly flattened the playlist over the quiz and snapped the notebook shut before looking back at Zuki, who was too absorbed in her lunch to notice what had just happened.

Relief trickled through Millie's bloodstream. She didn't want Zuki to know how bad she was at school.

She didn't want to give her a reason not to like her.

"Do you know anyone in journalism? Maybe we could put an ad in the paper? Or film a video for morning announcements? How are you on camera? Do you have a camera?" Zuki asked, one question after the other like she'd stopped bothering with air.

Millie opened her mouth to say she didn't think being on camera was a good idea—public speaking of any kind was *the worst*—when Ashley Seo's voice distracted her.

Zuki must've heard it, too, because they both looked over their shoulders at the exact same time.

Ashley's short hair was wavier than Millie remembered, but their uniform had perfect creases in the pants and they wore the tie option instead of Millie and Zuki's matching bow ties. In a sea of students who preferred to individualize their uniforms, Ashley looked almost presidential in comparison.

Arms flat at their sides and eyebrows furrowed, they were talking gruffly to Luna, Ruby, and Annabelle.

"None of us care about Rainbow. We're not even friends with her," Ruby said in disgust, raising an eyebrow like that should've been obvious.

Ashley's voice was heavy and powerful, like they wanted it to mean something. "Then stop picking on her. She didn't do anything to you. *Any* of you." From Millie's vantage point, it almost seemed like Ashley was staring straight at Luna when they spoke.

Luna shifted uncomfortably in her chair but didn't reply.

Annabelle rolled her eyes. "It's not our fault she always sits by herself."

"That's because you chase her out of the cafeteria every time she comes in here," Ashley bit back.

"We were joking." Ruby snorted. "Your friend is just massively sensitive."

"She's not my friend," Ashley corrected. "I just don't like bullies. And you can call it joking all you want, but you literally go out of your way to make her feel bad. So maybe you're not as funny as you think you are if all your jokes involve picking on someone who can't stick up for themselves."

Ruby flinched and looked at Annabelle for backup. They might be mean, but maybe their meanness didn't extend to people who could potentially fight back.

Luna refused to bring her eyes up, letting her curls hang loosely at her temples like a shield.

"Whatever," Ashley said before leaving the cafeteria with the kind of calm resilience that even the popular kids couldn't compete with.

"Geez," Ruby hissed. "Where did *that* come from? All I asked was whether our vocab was due and they just started yelling at me."

"They need to take an anger-management class," Annabelle scoffed.

Luna tucked her hair behind her ear. Ruby and Annabelle feigned laughter beside her. They were clearly trying their best to recover from Ashley's words, and even though Luna hadn't actually said anything herself, it seemed like she was the most rattled of all of them.

It didn't make sense to feel bad for her, but Millie did anyway.

"Well, I know three people for sure who would *never* join J-Club," Zuki remarked with a snort.

Millie started to ask why the three of them were always so mean but changed her mind. Because it didn't really matter *why* they were mean. What mattered was that they were hurting people like Rainbow, and aside from Ashley, most of the school seemed okay with letting them get away with it.

It wasn't right.

"Maybe we should ask Rainbow to eat lunch with us," Millie offered. "I mean, if she's really all by herself . . ."

Zuki shrugged. "Maybe. But I think Rainbow *likes* being alone. One time in fifth grade, I asked if she wanted to be my partner for an English assignment. She started mumbling something about being sorry and then ran to the bathroom. I didn't see her until the end of class. Our teacher made me pair up with Daniel Rosewood instead, and Rainbow got to do the assignment all by herself. Which wasn't fair, because I would've *totally* rather done the assignment alone than with Daniel. All he did was write his name on the paper!" She sighed dramatically. "But, I mean, if we see her around, we could ask her to sit with us. Just don't be disappointed if she says no."

"Okay," Millie agreed, but it didn't make her feel any better.

Zuki smiled. "You're really nice. I'm glad because it would've been devastating if the only person to show up to the J-Club meetings turned out to be a soggy bag of spinach."

Millie laughed, and the two of them went back to eating their lunch and talking about new ways to find members for J-Club.

Maybe Zuki was right about Rainbow wanting to be alone, but Millie couldn't quite get her head around it. She hated being alone and couldn't imagine anyone else liking it.

Her eyes drifted back toward Ruby, Annabelle, and Luna, who were laughing together like the incident with Ashley had never happened at all.

Millie didn't understand it. Some people seemed to be able to collect friends like it was the easiest thing in the world, even when they weren't nice people. But other people—people like Millie and Rainbow—had a hard time finding even *one*.

It was a problem Millie had no idea how to solve. But she wanted to, just the same.

And maybe with Zuki's help, she could at least try.

CHAPTER NINE

At the next J-Club meeting, Millie and Zuki sat close together, eyes pinned to the latest Generation Love video. The pastel shades flashed across the screen and the group performed a series of choreographed dance moves. Millie tapped her foot in time to the music, while Zuki imitated some of the choreography with her free hand.

Having a real-life friend to share Generation Love with was a *trillion* times better than scrolling through online forums.

When the song ended, Zuki sighed dreamily. "I wish I could be in a J-Pop band."

Millie's eyes grew with excitement. "Imagine getting to be in a real music video."

"And the *outfits*," Zuki added with emphasis. She turned slightly toward Millie. "Would you want to be the lead like Chiyo?"

Millie hesitated. Chiyo had always been her favorite, but she knew Chiyo was Zuki's favorite, too. Besides, Millie had never craved the spotlight. In fact, she was usually terrified of it. "I don't know," Millie said. "Probably not."

Zuki nodded like she understood more than Millie did. "You seem more like Miyuki to me. She's kind of quiet and doesn't really like doing big solos, but she makes the group feel whole. I mean, it would be no good to have a group with just Chiyos and Ryokos and Hanas. They have such big personalities, you know? There needs to be someone to balance them out."

Millie bit the inside of her cheek. Zuki wasn't wrong—Millie *didn't* have a big personality. Sometimes she wasn't even sure she had a little one. But hearing it from someone else made her feel self-conscious.

Zuki grinned, oblivious to the shift on Millie's face. "I'd want to be the lead, just like Chiyo. It's fun being in charge—having the extra responsibility. And also, I mean, everyone always remembers Chiyo."

Millie didn't necessarily want to be remembered, but she also didn't want to be forgotten.

Stop worrying, her mind scolded. *Zuki is your friend. She doesn't mean anything by it!*

Millie did her best to brush the feelings away. "You'd definitely make a better leader than me," she said finally, because it was the truth.

Zuki flicked her thumb over the phone screen, searching for another Generation Love video to watch. "What's next on our playlist? 'Hearts on Fire'?"

"I think it was 'Stranger.'" Millie picked up her binder and flung it open to reveal a notebook. She'd almost reached the page where she'd scribbled her makeshift playlist when Zuki's voice interrupted her concentration.

"Is that your English essay for Mrs. Devon?" Zuki asked.

Millie followed Zuki's gaze to the stapled pages behind her notebook, the heading just peeking out in the corner.

Zuki frowned. "You didn't turn it in?"

"Mrs. Devon never asked us to. I just assumed they weren't due yet."

"You have to put your essays in the homework basket," Zuki said. "You're supposed to turn everything in at the beginning of class."

"I—I didn't know that." Millie's voice faltered and heat found her cheeks.

Zuki looked sympathetic. "Hey, don't worry. It's just one assignment. And I bet you could tell Mrs. Devon you were confused. She might give you a pass just this once."

Millie didn't say anything.

"It . . . was just this once, right?"

Millie felt her eyes well up and she hated that Zuki—her only friend in the world—was about to realize how completely unequipped Millie was to navigate Brightside Academy.

With a quick breath, she let the words tumble out of her. "I don't really understand how school works—what the rules are. I feel like everyone else knows what they're doing, and the teachers don't really explain things like it's someone's first time at school. They talk about stuff like we're already supposed to *know* everything, and when they do explain stuff, they do it so fast I can't always keep up. I'm missing assignments I didn't even know about, and whenever there's a test I feel like I have no idea what I'm supposed to be studying . . ." Millie's voice trailed off, and she shook her head like she felt too silly to say any more.

Zuki wrinkled her nose like she wasn't sure how to solve the problem, but she wanted to try. "Did you talk to your parents? Maybe they could call your teachers."

"They didn't want me to go to a school in the first place," Millie admitted. "If I tell them I'm failing, I know they'll say it was a mistake. They might not let me stay."

A few seconds passed. Millie genuinely wondered if Zuki had changed her mind about being her friend when suddenly her face lit up.

"Why don't you just sneak your essay onto Mrs. Devon's desk? If we do it now, it will look like it got left behind by accident. You'll still get a grade, and we can worry about the rest of your homework later." Zuki began packing her backpack in a hurry. "Come on, we still have twenty minutes before the late bus gets here."

"Won't we get in trouble?" Millie asked, wide-eyed.

Zuki snorted. "For trying to do the right thing? How could we possibly get in trouble for that?"

Millie wasn't sure about that, but with her place at Brightside Academy on the line, she decided it was better not to argue.

☆ ★ ☆

Locked. Of course it was locked.

Millie felt her insides shrink and shrink until she was sure they would disappear altogether.

Zuki shook the door handle again and peered into the slender window while Millie's eyes danced around the hallway in terror. What if a hall monitor saw them? What if they called their parents?

What if they called the *police*?

Millie's stomach churned. Clearly, she wasn't built for rule-breaking.

"The lights are still on, so Mrs. Devon must still be in the school." Zuki looked over her shoulder at Millie. "Maybe we could slip it under the door?"

"I think we should leave," Millie whispered nervously, twisting her backpack strap between her fingers. "What if she comes back and sees us here?"

Zuki poked at the glass. "We can't leave yet! Give me your essay." She held out a hand expectantly.

Millie bounced on her heels twice before quickly unzipping her bag and sliding out her homework. Before she could argue, Zuki snatched it from her grip and knelt to the floor. In a few clumsy motions, she tried and failed to stuff the pages beneath the door, crumpling the edges in the process.

"Almost there," Zuki hissed, though Millie could plainly see she was nowhere *near* almost there.

Millie curled her hands into fists. "It's not going to work. Let's just go before we get into trouble."

Zuki's voice was strained. "I'm so close. I just need to twist it so—"

"What are you two doing?" The low, clipped voice made Millie practically jump out of her skin. Even Zuki shot to her feet with military precision.

Ashley Seo was watching the two of them carefully, arms folded across their chest.

Millie opened her mouth, but no sound came out. Zuki not-so-subtly moved the essay behind her back.

Ashley lifted a brow. "I didn't peg you for the breaking-and-entering types."

Zuki rolled her eyes. "We're not trying to break in." Accepting defeat, she let her arms fall to her sides. "We just need to put this essay on Mrs. Devon's desk. Millie was confused about when it was due, and if she fails her class, she won't be allowed to come back to J-Club. And I can't let that happen. She's the vice president—I need her!"

The words stung. Zuki was making it sound like her main concern was *J-Club*, not Millie.

Millie knew with absolute certainty that she'd still want to be Zuki's friend, even without J-Club. But would Zuki feel the same?

She hoped so. Priorities aside, Zuki was still risking a lot to help her. That had to mean something.

Millie didn't want Zuki to get into trouble on her account, so she gathered up her courage and turned toward Ashley. "It wasn't Zuki's fault. It was mine. If you're going to tell on us, you can just blame me." Millie looked at Zuki apologetically. "My parents would've eventually found out about my grades, anyway. But thanks for trying."

Ashley frowned, their voice turning gruff. "What makes you think I'm going to tell anyone?"

Millie and Zuki exchanged glances.

Ashley was self-assured, mature, and never seemed to care what anyone thought. It wasn't normal for an eleven-year-old to be so confident. Or at least, it wasn't normal to Millie.

But Ashley wasn't known for being a tattletale, *and* they'd stood up for Rainbow in the cafeteria.

So maybe Millie had made the wrong assumption.

"Well, if you aren't going to tell on us, at least stand watch by the door," Zuki blurted out, severing the awkward silence. "I only need another few seconds." She had started to kneel back down when Ashley's voice cut in.

"That's never going to fit."

Zuki shot them a glare. "Do you have a better idea?"

Ashley stood silently for a moment and then motioned their head to the side. "Actually, I do. Follow me."

CHAPTER TEN

Ashley led them down the hall and around the corner to another row of classrooms. Millie was pretty sure it was one of the seventh-grade halls she'd gotten lost in on the first day of school.

When Ashley stopped in front of one of the doors and grabbed the handle, Millie's breath hitched. She couldn't help it; they weren't supposed to be wandering around the school unsupervised, and they *definitely* weren't supposed to be sneaking into random classrooms.

But Ashley didn't seem to care about getting into trouble. They simply pulled the door open and walked inside. After a short pause, Millie and Zuki walked in after them.

Zuki peered around the vacant room, her brow set in deep concentration like she was trying to solve a mystery. "Are you in detention? Is that why you're hanging around an empty classroom after school? Rosie McDonald from orchestra—she plays cello—had detention for a whole week last year because she wouldn't stop talking in class. But she said her teacher just gave her a homework packet that was full of crossword puzzles.

I like crossword puzzles. Did you get a crossword puzzle? Do you get detention a lot?"

Ashley blinked. "First of all, it's called detention, not solitary confinement."

Zuki moved her hands around impatiently. "And second of all . . . ?"

Ashley sighed. "Doesn't matter. It's not worth explaining." They moved across the room, just out of earshot of Millie and Zuki.

"They didn't answer my question about detention," Zuki whispered.

"I think there'd be a teacher here if it was detention," Millie whispered back.

"Maybe they had to go to the bathroom?"

"Should we leave before we get caught?"

"Come on," Ashley interrupted. "I don't have all day."

Millie looked up and saw Ashley standing in front of a shared closet that doubled as a corridor to another classroom. The three of them stepped inside, and when they emerged through the other door, they were standing in Mrs. Devon's room.

"Cool trick," Zuki mused, clearly entertained by their brief moment of rebellion. "I feel like I'm in a heist movie. It's kind of exciting, isn't it? It feels like . . . like a glowing orange marmalade!"

Ashley frowned. "A what?"

"The mood," Zuki replied simply. "It's a mix of terror and exhilaration."

"But why—" Ashley started, but shook their head. "Never mind. I don't want to know."

"You're definitely a duck-egg blue," Zuki said. "Understated and cool."

"Whatever is happening in your brain right now, please leave me out of it," Ashley said like a warning.

Zuki looked too excited to care.

Not wanting to waste any more time, Millie took the essay back from Zuki and set it on Mrs. Devon's desk. She stared at it for an extra second before turning it over. She stared at it for another two seconds before pushing it a few inches to the left. And she stared at it for another half of a second before straightening it again.

She turned around to look at Zuki and Ashley. "Does that look okay?"

Zuki frowned. "Maybe you could hide it underneath something? You know, to make it look like Mrs. Devon accidentally left it there?"

Ashley rolled their eyes, stomped over to the desk, and flicked the essay from the table. It sailed into the air for a moment before gently falling to the linoleum floor.

"What did you do that for?" Zuki demanded.

"You wanted it to look like Mrs. Devon accidentally left it behind." Ashley motioned toward the ground. "Now it looks realistic."

"Let's just go before someone sees us," Millie said, tugging at her sleeves. Zuki might enjoy a bit of espionage, but Millie was pretty sure she might actually be allergic to it. Her neck was itchy, her palms were sweating, and her head was spinning like a carnival ride.

The three of them headed back to the other classroom, making sure to close both doors behind them. The distance didn't do much to calm Millie's nerves, but at least she wasn't going to fail another assignment. And it was all because of Zuki and Ashley.

"Thanks for your help," Millie said gratefully.

Ashley shrugged. "No problem."

"What class is this?" Zuki looked around suspiciously. "And how did you know the supply closet connected to Mrs. Devon's room?"

"I guess people in detention know things," Ashley replied coolly.

Zuki's eyes widened. "So you *are* in detention."

"I think that was sarcasm," Millie said out of the corner of her mouth.

Zuki looked deflated. Whether it was curiosity or a need to be in control, she obviously wasn't happy about not knowing every detail.

The late bell rang as if on cue.

"We better go," Millie said, glancing at Zuki.

But just as they turned to leave, Millie noticed a dark green backpack on the floor near the teacher's desk. It was covered in colorful patches of cartoon characters and band logos. But one in particular stood out the most.

Big chunky letters—a *G* and an *L*—surrounded by a swooping rainbow heart. *Generation Love.*

Millie's heart fluttered. "You listen to Generation Love?"

Zuki froze when she heard the name, spinning to face Ashley again.

Ashley looked down at their backpack and grunted like it wasn't a big deal. "Yeah. So what?"

Zuki's face shifted completely, like a deep sense of understanding was dawning on her. She didn't look wary anymore; she looked positively jubilant. "It's kismet!" she exclaimed wildly.

Ashley made a face. "It's kiss what?"

"*Fate*," Zuki declared proudly. Excitement twinkled in her eyes. "It's why we ran into each other." She looked at Millie with a wide grin. "Don't you see? *This* is why we're here. To find our third member!"

Ashley held up their hands. "You're saying a lot of words I don't understand—"

"You have to join J-Club!" Zuki interrupted. "We meet after school on Thursdays. You'll love it! Technically it started off as a Japanese cultural appreciation club—that's the only way the school would approve it, because they said we needed an 'educational' aspect—but loving J-Pop *is* a form of cultural appreciation, so now that the club has been approved, we mostly just focus on music. And more specifically, our love for the *best group on the face of the planet.*" Her eyes looked like they were ready to swallow the world.

Ashley's hands dropped and their expression darkened. "Sorry, I'm not really a club kind of person."

Zuki wasn't deterred. "You *have* to come. At least once, just to see if you like it. Which I know you will, because how could you not? It's amazing! We get to hang out, and talk about Chiyo, and watch music videos, and—"

Ashley shook their head. "Look, no offense, but I don't see the point in clubs that are just for socializing. It's a waste of time, unless you're looking to make friends." There was a brief pause. "Which I'm not," they added, in case Millie and Zuki hadn't quite gotten the message.

"Pleeeeease?" Zuki begged, dragging out the word. "I even made key chains!" She pointed to the string of beads on her backpack desperately.

Ashley visibly cringed before stuffing their hands in their pockets. "It's just not for me," they said finally.

Zuki's shoulders sagged, heavy with disappointment.

Millie could feel the tension in the air and wanted to get away from it as fast as possible. "Come on," Millie said quietly, inching toward the door. "Or else we'll miss the bus."

Zuki nodded, and the two of them headed for the front gates without looking back. On the bus ride home, Millie couldn't stop thinking about Ashley. Something about their words just didn't add up.

Because for someone so adamant about not wanting friends, Ashley Seo sure had a knack for helping people they barely knew.

CHAPTER ELEVEN

Zuki didn't bring up what had happened after school the day before, so Millie decided it was best if she didn't either. But it was clear Zuki had taken Ashley's refusal to join J-Club as a personal rejection. Because for the first time since Millie met her, Zuki hardly said anything at all.

"Did you check the fan forums last night?" Millie tried when they were sitting together in the cafeteria. "Apparently Chiyo might be dating Jake Takeshi from that new singing competition show."

Zuki hummed noncommittally, fingers brushing over her rows of rainbow bracelets.

"There was a photo of them smiling backstage," Millie continued. "It didn't look like anything to me, but I guess people found an old Instagram post where he said Chiyo was his celebrity crush, so everyone is shipping them."

"Yeah, I guess," Zuki mumbled, eyes glued to her wrist.

Millie tried to think of something else to say. She remembered Zuki had said her parents were divorced, and that she split her time between two different houses. "Are you staying at your dad's this weekend? Maybe we could facetime and finish the new playlist."

Zuki's fingers stopped moving, but she didn't say a word.

When Millie was nervous, her voice had a tendency to squeak. She cleared her throat, just in case. "I was thinking for track five—"

Zuki sighed and shoved both hands in her lap. "It doesn't matter about the track. Not when J-Club isn't working."

Millie blinked. "What do you mean?"

For a moment, Zuki met her gaze, and her eyes darted back and forth like a bumblebee searching for somewhere safe to land. But when she couldn't find it, she turned away. "It doesn't matter right now. I'm supposed to be in the counselor's office in a few minutes anyway, so I have to go."

"What for? Are you changing your schedule?" Millie asked, suddenly feeling like she was saying all the wrong things.

Zuki hesitated before snatching up her bag. "I'll talk to you later, okay?"

"Okay," Millie said, and watched her friend disappear in the crowd.

When the bell rang a few minutes later, Millie could barely hear it over the worry ringing through her ears. She wasn't sure what to do. Friends should be able to talk to each other about anything, but Zuki didn't seem like she wanted to talk. And if there was a problem with J-Club, shouldn't they be discussing it together?

Unless Millie was part of what wasn't working . . .

After school she waited by the bus stop, but Zuki never showed up.

On Saturday, Millie's parents took her out for boba tea. It was sort of a family tradition—or maybe less of a tradition and more of a reward for being dragged around town running errands every other week. The tradition part was what they ordered, which was always the same: coconut boba tea, with extra tapioca balls.

Millie was studying the overhead menu when the cashier smiled at Scott. "What can I get for you today?" he asked politely.

Scott held up his fingers—he always did that before he'd say a number, like he was trying to limit any confusion. "Three coconut boba teas, please, with extra—"

"Wait," Millie cut in shrilly. "I—I want to try the Hokkaido milk tea instead."

Scott pulled back his face in surprise. Jane stepped forward and frowned.

"But," she said, scanning the menu like she was confused, "we always get coconut. I thought it was our 'thing.'"

"I know," Millie said, cheeks turning pink when she realized the cashier was watching her. "But I just want to try something new."

Scott and Jane exchanged a glance, and Millie immediately felt anxious.

It was already difficult enough to tell her parents how she was feeling on a normal day. But to break one of their family traditions? To change the *plan*?

She didn't want to disappoint them. But if she didn't say something now, it would be like the roast chicken all over again, and she'd be eating greasy chicken legs for the rest of her life.

Scott shrugged and faced the cashier. "Okay, three Hokkaido milk teas." He turned to Millie with a smirk. "With extra tapioca balls?"

Millie smiled back with relief and gave a series of quick nods.

The three of them sat at one of the corner tables. When her parents started talking about new tiles for the family bathroom, Millie took the opportunity to check her phone.

There hadn't been any texts from Zuki since Thursday—*before* their rebellious adventure outside Mrs. Devon's classroom.

Before Ashley basically said J-Club was pointless.

Millie didn't want to go the whole weekend without talking to Zuki, so she tried to think of something to say that had nothing to do with J-Club at all.

She snapped a quick photo of her drink and sent it to Zuki along with a text: Look what I'm finally trying! You said Hokkaido milk tea was the best, and you were right ☺

She stared at her phone for a while, waiting for the typing icon to appear. It didn't.

"What are you up to over there?" Jane asked, sipping her boba tea.

Millie shoved her phone into her pocket. "Nothing. Just texting."

Scott chased the tapioca balls with his straw, watching as they moved around the bottom of his plastic cup. "Hey, this is pretty good!"

"Better than coconut?" Jane lifted a brow, teasing.

Scott laughed. "Nothing is better than coconut. What do you think, Millie?"

Millie froze. She wasn't sure if disagreeing would hurt their feelings. She'd already broken tradition; maybe that was enough of a win for one day. "I like them both," she said finally.

Her parents smiled and carried on with their conversation about bathroom decor.

Millie retrieved her phone, drank big gulps of milk tea, and waited for a text that never came.

☆ ★ ☆

On Monday, Zuki was back to her old self. Except maybe *more* her old self than usual. Everything she did seemed to happen in double time. She was like a spinning top that had begun to wobble or bubble gum that had been blown too big. Millie wasn't sure what would happen if she nudged her the wrong way.

So she didn't bring up Ashley, or the weekend, or Zuki's previous comments about J-Club. Deep down, she hoped maybe they could pretend that none of it had ever happened.

When Millie walked into the orchestra room on Thursday, Zuki was pacing in front of a row of chairs. Her arms were folded stubbornly over her chest, hiding her rows and rows of rainbow-hued bracelets.

Millie made it all the way to the center of the room before Zuki looked up. When she did, her eyes rounded and her words burst out of her at full volume.

"Okay, so I've been thinking about what Ashley said—you know, about our club needing a bigger purpose?—and I think they might be right. J-Club needs something bigger to offer. Something more than just sitting around making playlists. I think we need a *hook*," Zuki explained quickly. "We're never going to find more members if we don't make the club more appealing. I mean, who wants to join a club just to listen to J-Pop for an hour?"

I'd join a club just to listen to J-Pop for an hour, Millie thought, instantly deflated. She couldn't help it; she'd only just found something she loved, and now Zuki wanted to change it. Besides, Millie *liked* making playlists. And what did a *hook* even mean?

She'd left Zuki to her thoughts, and now everything was going to be different. Zuki wanted new rules and new members, and maybe even new friends to eat lunch with.

Panic thundered in Millie's chest.

"I think we should start a band," Zuki said matter-of-factly.

Millie wasn't sure she'd heard her right. "A band?"

Zuki's smile grew. "We could start an imitation band of Generation

Love. We could learn the songs, practice all the dance routines, and perform them as a group. It would be perfect!"

Millie's voice cracked. "You mean you'd want me to be in the band, too?"

Zuki laughed. "Obviously! You're vice president!"

"Oh," Millie said sheepishly. "When you said you wanted to change things, I thought you meant . . ." She shook her head, feeling silly for getting so worked up over nothing. Maybe Zuki really had just needed some time to mull things over. "I think a band sounds great."

"Right? It's, like, the perfect solution to our problem!" Zuki exclaimed. "So many people are going to want to join J-Club when they find out we're starting a band. We'll probably have to hold auditions. You know, to make sure we find the best dancers and singers to fill the other roles."

"Roles?" Millie repeated.

"We should have five main members of the band, to match Generation Love. I'll be Chiyo Aoki, since I'm president, of course. And you can be Miyuki, if you want!"

"I've never really sung in front of anyone before," Millie admitted. She could sing in key, but she was hardly solo material. She didn't want Zuki's expectations to be too high.

"Miyuki mostly does backup, so you don't have to be nervous about singing on your own," Zuki assured her. "Besides, I've heard you humming along to the music videos before. You have a great voice!"

Millie could almost imagine it: a real band, with people who'd memorized every Generation Love song, who loved their dances and harmonies as much as she did. She thought of the way Chiyo acted with the other members of Generation Love. Like they were part of a family.

Was that what Millie had to look forward to?

Millie felt the excitement build in her chest. "How do we tell people about auditions?"

Zuki's eyes flashed with euphoria. "Easy. All we need is a really good flyer!"

☆ ★ ☆

Colored pencils were scattered all over the cream-colored carpet. Millie was resting on her elbows, eyes focused on the mocked-up flyer beneath her nose. Her first draft was crumpled up somewhere nearby. She'd originally drawn all the members of Generation Love, but realized halfway through the coloring stage that Bright-side was full of art majors who'd probably laugh at her amateur character art. It was best to leave the drawing to the professionals.

The newest draft consisted of big block letters with rainbow-colored hearts along the edges. She'd gotten as far as *J-Club Audition* when she heard footsteps coming from the hallway.

Millie pushed herself off the floor and shoved the flyer under a textbook, pulling her band folder in front of her just as her father opened the door.

She pretended to be flipping through her sheet music before glancing up at him.

Scott's eyes danced from colored pencil to colored pencil. "Wow. It sure is a mess in here."

Millie tried not to look guilty, especially when the lie slipped casually from her mouth. "I was working on a school project."

"You're supposed to be practicing your flute," her dad said gently. He was wearing a collared shirt and khaki pants, which seemed to be all he ever wore. He liked routine; so did her mom. Maybe that was why they wanted Millie to like it, too.

Did it make them less of a family if she didn't?

"I know. I'm going to do that now," she said, standing up and setting the sheet music on her stand.

He was still fixated on the colored pencils. "You know, you should really try to be better organized. Our brains work more efficiently when our workplace is clean."

Millie didn't know if that was something he'd googled or something he'd just randomly made up to win an argument. Because it felt like that sometimes—like her parents cared more about sounding right than *being* right.

Millie turned away from her dad to shield her annoyance. "I like being able to see all the colors. I'll clean everything up when I'm finished."

He continued as if he hadn't heard her. "Your mom and I were thinking about calling your teachers. Just to make sure you're doing okay."

Millie's heart was pounding. "I really don't think that's necessary, Dad. Progress reports come out soon anyway. I don't want to be the only kid at school whose parents have to check up on them for no reason. It's embarrassing."

"I'm sure you aren't the only kid with parents who care about them, Millie," he said with a careful tone.

"Well, like I said, progress reports come out soon anyway . . ." Her voice trailed off and she bit the inside of her cheek to hide how flustered she felt.

"It's really important you don't fall behind. Especially because you have so many new opportunities coming your way with flute. Solo ensemble won't be far away, and honor band, too," he said. Millie wished she could clap her hands over her ears just to stop hearing him for a second. "With enough practice, you could get a full scholarship to a university for music. For music! Imagine that—the dream."

No, that's your *dream*, Millie wanted to shout.

She picked up her flute off her bed, pressing her fingers against the keys anxiously. "I need to practice. And I still have homework to do."

Scott smiled. "Okay. Dinner's in an hour, all right?"

When he closed the door, Millie held her flute to her lips but couldn't stop shaking long enough to take a breath. She could barely remember a time when she didn't hate the flute, though she knew it existed somewhere in her memory. Flute used to be fun—before her parents got ahold of it and replaced *fun* with *pressure.* Now she felt like she was a failure for anything other than perfection. And she hated that part the most—that they'd taken something she liked and turned it into darkness.

When Millie was sure her dad's footsteps were far enough away, she set her flute on her bed, pulled the flyer from beneath the textbook, and got back to work on something that replaced that darkness with light.

CHAPTER TWELVE

Zuki was already sitting at the lunch table when Millie arrived in the cafeteria. She pulled the straps of her backpack anxiously before wading through the crowd and letting herself flop into one of the empty chairs beside her friend.

She'd been sent on a mission and she'd failed miserably.

Zuki looked up, wide-eyed. "I'm out of flyers. Are you out of flyers? I think I put too many in the Science hall. Not to stereotype, but I feel like the Science hall isn't the best place to waste our resources. I put six up near the choir rooms, but I totally forgot about the dance lockers. Dance majors love auditions, right? But I need more flyers. Do you have any? Did I ask that?" Her laughter hiccupped like her words were moving too fast for her to handle. "I'm so excited I can hardly think!"

Millie forced a grim smile before unzipping her bag and revealing the stack of flyers she still hadn't put up. She'd *wanted* to. But every time she found a good spot it felt like there were a hundred people around. And even though logically she knew she wasn't doing anything wrong, the fear that she *might* be was overwhelming.

"I tried, but—" Millie clamped her mouth shut. She didn't know how to explain such an irrational fear. Especially when Zuki was so unafraid in comparison. "I'm sorry. I guess I'm better at making flyers than sharing them."

She could see Zuki's brain going into overdrive. Her brow was furrowed, and her eyes were tick-tocking back and forth like an erratic clock. Millie braced for disappointment, but a few seconds later, Zuki's smile reappeared.

"Don't worry about it! I need more flyers anyway. We can hang these ones together after school, if you want?" she offered, scooping up the papers and tucking them into her own binder.

Millie made a face. "I have a flute lesson after school." She decided to leave out the part where her parents would never let her stay after school to hang up flyers. To them, it would be as silly as standing in a three-hour line just to try something like a cronut or brown sugar boba tea—a complete waste of time. They didn't understand trends *or* hobbies.

Music didn't count as a hobby, though. To Jane and Scott Nakakura, music was as necessary as oxygen.

To Millie, hobbies weren't supposed to be necessary; they were supposed to be fun.

"That's okay," Zuki said, undeterred. "I can do it myself. But you can come to the auditions, right? I don't want to judge on my own. I need your help!"

"As long as it's during the J-Club meeting, I can definitely be there," Millie said. "But . . . do you really think people will turn up?"

"For sure! These flyers look amazing," Zuki said enthusiastically.

Millie couldn't help but feel a little proud. It was nice to be good at something—especially something Millie *wanted* to be good at.

"Just think." Zuki's gaze danced around the cafeteria. "On Thursday, some of the people in this room might be in our club. In our *band.* How cool is that?"

Millie wished she had Zuki's impenetrable excitement. Sometimes Millie was afraid to be *really* happy, just in case it got taken away from her. But Zuki was never afraid to feel joy. She wasn't afraid to shine.

They still hadn't talked about why Zuki had disappeared for a whole weekend, but maybe it didn't matter anymore. Because Millie had her friend back.

And next Thursday, the rest of the school would finally get to see how special Zuki was, too.

Millie and Zuki turned up prepared, ten minutes early, with notebooks and pens in case they wanted to jot down notes. They pushed all the chairs to the side of the orchestra room to make an audition space and made sure their backpacks were hidden beside the instrument lockers. (Zuki said it would look more professional if they didn't have their bags out.)

And then they waited. And waited. And waited.

As the minutes passed, their giddy excitement disappeared, replaced by something horribly uncomfortable. Millie could feel it in the pit of her stomach, like a monster made of darkness that vacuumed up all the light around it. It made her jittery and squeamish, and when she looked up at the clock for what felt like the millionth time, she realized there were only a few more minutes left before the late bell would ring.

It had been over an hour. Nobody had turned up for the J-Club auditions. Not a single person in the entire school.

Millie was disappointed, but she was more worried about Zuki. She'd made the flyers, but this was Zuki's *idea.* Her brainchild. And Millie knew how precious ideas could be, and how awful it was when they didn't go to plan.

Zuki continued to stare at the door, completely unreadable.

Millie's shoulders sank. At least they could share the burden of rejection together, though something told her Zuki would take it much harder. And a bigger part of her worried Zuki might fall off the radar again and forget to be her friend.

Millie opened her mouth to point out the time but stopped short when the door was yanked open abruptly.

Startled, Millie looked up and found Luna Acevedo standing in the doorway. Her curly hair was pinned up in a tight, constricting bun, and she was wearing a turquoise dance leotard and a pair of baggy sweatpants.

"I'm so sorry," Luna said, her breathing uneven. "Our dance

rehearsal ran late—I got here as fast as I could." When neither Millie or Zuki responded, she frowned, reached into the bag hanging from her left shoulder, and pulled out one of the flyers. "Am I in the wrong place? For the J-Club audition?"

Millie blinked. Luna Acevedo, one of the most popular girls in school, listened to *J-Pop*?

She glanced at Zuki, who looked as if a bolt of electricity had just gone through her. Zuki sat up straight, placed her elbows on the table in front of her, and flashed a welcoming smile.

"That's right. Did you bring your own music?" Zuki's voice was melodic and steady, like she'd sat through a hundred auditions in the past hour and this was just more of the same.

Millie didn't know how to do that—how to pretend everything was fine when it wasn't.

Luna smiled briefly and stuffed the flyer back into her bag. "I hope it's okay if I play the music off my phone."

Zuki nodded patiently, an air of maturity in her posture. Millie felt like a wilted daisy next to a blossoming rose. She'd had no idea Zuki was such a good actor.

Luna made her way to the side of the room to set up her phone. "Do you want me to introduce myself first, or should I just start?"

Zuki hesitated and there was a slight crack in her composure as she reached for the notebook and pen beside her. She flipped to a new blank page for no reason other than to make it seem like the last one was full. "What's your name?"

Millie's cheeks turned red. Zuki had a good poker face, but was she taking it too far? Why on earth was she pretending not to know who *Luna Acevedo* was?

But if Luna thought it was strange, she didn't react. "My name is Luna Acevedo. I'm a dance major, and I'm in sixth grade." She folded her hands in front of her. "I'll be performing to 'Sugar Pop' by Generation Love."

Millie's mouth fell open involuntarily. It was one of her favorite songs. Even Zuki's eyes widened—but whether from alarm or excitement, it was hard to tell. Not when she was being so . . . constricted.

Luna took the silence as a cue to continue, so she tapped a button on her phone and hurried to the center of the room.

In an instant, the music took over, and Millie had to fight the urge to tap her thumb and shimmy her shoulders to the downbeat. And then Luna's smile flashed, and she started to dance in time with the pop song, imitating Chiyo Aoki's signature moves to perfection. When she started singing along to the vocals, Millie couldn't believe how seamlessly she blended into the sounds. Her voice was sugary sweet, but soft, too—and she could sing in key, which for most people was over half the battle.

But her *dancing*. Millie couldn't take her eyes off her. Luna moved with all the coolness of someone in a music video, but with a style that was all her own. She was in complete control of the audience. She had that thing everyone always talked about on reality talent shows—she had *it*.

When the song ended, Luna clasped her hands and let them

fall in front of her, rocking back and forth on her toes like she was still full of energy.

Millie looked between Zuki and Luna, wondering who was going to speak first, when all the professionalism from Zuki suddenly fizzled away, replaced by a smile that was too large for her face.

"That was *amazing*!" Zuki squealed. "I didn't know you liked Generation Love! 'Sugar Pop' is one of the best dance songs, too. I can't believe how good you are. You dance as well as Hana— did you see her dance solo in 'Parachute'? Oh my gosh, it's *so good.* And *you're* so good! When did you start listening to Generation Love? Millie, wasn't that amazing?"

Millie turned to Luna. "It really was."

"Best audition we've seen all day!" Zuki said.

Millie cringed. It wasn't exactly a lie, but it wasn't the whole truth either.

Luna smiled with relief. "I'm so happy to hear that," she said, tucking a barely there curl over her ear. "I'm always anxious about singing in Japanese because I can't actually speak the language. I just memorize the lyrics. I—I hope that's okay."

"Of course it is," Zuki said firmly. "Neither of us is fluent either, but that doesn't mean we can't love J-Pop."

It was hard to comprehend how Luna could be so nervous. Even if more people *had* shown up to audition, Millie was pretty sure Luna was one of the best dancers in the school.

"I've been a big Generation Love fan for a while, but none of my friends listen to them." Luna hesitated, suddenly conscious of her words. "I was really excited when I saw the flyers. I didn't even know there *was* a J-Club, actually."

Zuki nudged Millie and widened her eyes. "See?" she hissed. "I knew it was only a matter of getting the word out!"

Maybe it didn't matter that Luna was the only person who turned up to audition for the band or that Zuki was determined to pretend she wasn't. Everyone looked happy. Everyone was getting what they wanted.

And at least this way Millie and Zuki wouldn't have to deal with the awkwardness of turning anyone down.

"So . . . when will you post results for the band?" Luna asked.

Millie sensed that her question stemmed from more than just curiosity—for some reason, there was caution in her voice, too.

"There's no need—you're in for sure!" Zuki exclaimed, not even bothering to discuss it with Millie. "Unless you want us to post the results. We could do that, too, you know, if you want your name up on a flyer. It might be good to draw more attention to the band, actually. Plus, if people knew Luna Acevedo joined J-Club, they'd definitely want to join!" The twinkle in her eyes was turning into a full-blown fireworks display.

Millie tried to think of a way to reel her back in. She worried Zuki was already planning a second audition day, and she didn't want to be the one to tell her that was a terrible idea.

But Luna was the one to stifle Zuki's excitement. "Actually, I was sort of hoping I could keep my being here a secret?"

Zuki frowned. Millie shifted uncomfortably in her chair.

Luna waved her hands quickly like she was trying to stop

them from forming any conclusions. "It's only because my friends are . . . well . . . they don't really get J-Pop, you know? And I just thought it would be nice to have something for myself."

"You don't have to be embarrassed about J-Pop, you know," Zuki said, and Millie was certain she could hear a twinge of hurt in her voice.

J-Club was *everything* to Zuki. And Luna was practically admitting she was ashamed to be in it.

Luna crossed her arms protectively. "I get it if you don't want me to be in the band. But my friends can be kind of intense sometimes, and I just don't want them to make fun of me."

"I think if they were really your friends, they'd be happy if you're happy," Millie offered meekly.

Luna didn't say anything.

"It doesn't matter," Zuki said suddenly, her enthusiasm returning. "You're the best dancer we've seen all day, and we definitely want you in the band. Keep it a secret if you want to. You said it yourself—it's not like anyone knows about J-Club anyway."

Luna looked guilty, despite her smile. "Thanks for understanding."

Zuki hurried around the table and thrust out a hand. "I'm Zuki, and this is Millie. Welcome to the club!"

CHAPTER THIRTEEN

Kelly placed a folded piece of paper on Millie's music stand. For a brief second, she thought it was meant for her. But before her brain had time to process the anomaly, she caught Dia's impatient stare and quickly put the silly idea to rest.

Millie didn't have friends in band. Kelly and Dia had made that very clear.

She passed the note to her left.

Dia scribbled something on the paper and pushed the folded note back onto Millie's stand. Mr. Thomas was too busy running through the percussion section to notice what was going on in the front row.

Kelly bounced her knee like the message had a time limit.

Millie moved the note to Kelly's stand and picked up her flute, busying her hands with major scales and arpeggios. Her grades were still terrible, but at least she knew what she was doing in band.

And maybe being good at music would be enough to soften

her parents' disappointment when progress reports came out. Millie had mostly Cs in every class, but in band she had an A.

In a way, they should be *happy* her highest grade was in band. Wasn't that what they had always wanted? For music to be *the most important*?

Millie's heart sank like a baritone as her fingers moved down the scale. There was no point trying to twist the situation into anything other than what it was—a total and complete catastrophe.

Because it wouldn't be enough. Her parents wouldn't just be disappointed—they'd be furious when they saw Millie's grades. A single A in Wind Ensemble II wouldn't be enough to disguise the truth.

By her parents' standards, Millie was failing at school.

"Millie? Do you know where we are?" Mr. Thomas's voice broke through her thoughts like a crack of thunder.

She looked up, panicked. The rest of the flutes were already ten measures into the next section. She tried to mumble an apology before attempting to join in, but her face was burning with embarrassment and it was hard for her to form thoughts, let alone words.

Mr. Thomas raised an eyebrow like he wanted her to pay closer attention. He turned his eyes back to the rest of the woodwind section, his baton still ticking like a metronome in the air.

Millie fumbled note after note until she finally found her place, but by then there were hardly any more notes to play. She set her flute in her lap when the rest of the flute section did the same.

Dia's words were low but definitely audible over the French horns. "This is why a sixth grader shouldn't be second chair."

Millie stiffened. She knew how Kelly and Dia felt—she could tell by their stares and stifled laughter. But hearing it? Having confirmation?

That was so much worse.

☆ ★ ☆

"Just ignore them," Zuki said, chewing absentmindedly on a chicken strip. "If she wanted second chair, she should've practiced harder. She's got nobody to blame but herself."

"You make it sound so simple," Millie replied, fiddling with her sleeve under the lunch table. Kelly and Dia didn't have the same lunch hour as her, but she still felt like they could be watching nearby.

"It *is* simple," Zuki argued. "Because people like that aren't going to change. She's already made up her mind to be mad. But you don't have to let her get to you. You can choose to ignore it. They're a horrendous shade of pea-soup green. Don't let them darken your marigold."

"Is that what you do? Ignore it?" Millie secretly wished a bit of Zuki's confidence would jump across the table and into her own brain.

For some reason, it took Zuki an extra beat to answer. It was barely there, but Millie caught it—the faltering in her eyes.

What was she not saying?

Before Millie could ask, Zuki found her laughter again and snorted. "Of course! What's the point in letting some random person I don't even care about ruin my day, you know?" She took a sip from her water bottle and scrolled through a playlist on her phone.

Millie adjusted her bangs self-consciously, wondering if she should dye her hair with colorful streaks like Zuki. Could something as simple as hair be the thing that gave a person superpowers?

Because not being affected by the things people said—especially in sixth grade—was most *definitely* a superpower.

Millie would happily dye her hair every color of the rainbow if it meant she'd never again worry what people thought of her.

"I heard Luna Acevedo joined J-Club," said a voice nearby.

Millie stiffened. Zuki practically choked on a mouthful of water.

Ashley Seo was standing at the other side of the table, hands tucked casually in their pockets and their tie straightened to perfection. But something was different about their face. Normally they looked unbothered by the world, but today Ashley's frown wasn't one of indifference; it looked a lot like concern.

Millie and Zuki exchanged a look before eyeing Luna's table on the other side of the cafeteria. She was too far away to hear, but that didn't matter. Millie and Zuki had made a promise: nobody could know about Luna joining J-Club.

"We don't know what you're talking about," Millie said finally, and Zuki nodded in agreement.

Ashley rolled their eyes. "Not that I would believe you, because you're a terrible liar, but I literally saw her leave the audition room."

Millie's voice went up an octave. "People see things all the time. It doesn't make any of it true."

"So she auditioned and asked you not to tell anyone?" Ashley sighed. "Typical."

"No—she didn't—I didn't—" Millie sputtered.

Ashley shook their head. "Remind me to never trust you with a secret. Ever."

Millie felt like her face had been set on fire.

Zuki frowned, eyes pinned to Ashley. "Wait. How do you know Luna?"

"That's a big question. I don't answer big questions," Ashley replied.

"Why do you always stay late after school?" Zuki tried instead. "And what were you even doing near the orchestra room? Because it's starting to seem like you're spying on us."

Ashley grinned smugly. "I *have* to stay late—I don't have a choice. So I wander around campus, and sometimes I see things. It's a side effect of boredom."

"If it's just boredom, then why do you care whether Luna is in J-Club or not?" Zuki asked. She plucked at the bracelets on her left wrist.

"Just because you keep asking questions doesn't mean I have to answer them," Ashley pointed out tersely, their own eyes falling to Zuki's bracelets.

Zuki immediately tucked her hands beneath the table like she was hiding them from Ashley's gaze.

"Well, we can't talk about J-Club to people who aren't actually *in* J-Club," Zuki said, flattening her mouth.

Ashley's eyes found Luna again, and Millie realized it wasn't concern written all over their face; it was longing.

"You could still join, if you wanted to," Millie started, slowly weaving her thoughts together.

Ashley's eyes sparked. "I told you, I don't do clubs."

"I know. I just thought maybe you'd changed your mind." Millie lifted her shoulders. "We're more of a band now than a club anyway. Plus, you know, we have more members."

Zuki scrunched her face with confusion, but Millie only nudged her with her shoe. She wasn't telling anyone Luna had joined, *exactly*. She hadn't broken any promises. She just didn't want to miss an opportunity to recruit a new member when it was clear the only reason Ashley was curious about J-Club was because of Luna.

Zuki must've sensed the greater good, too. "Millie's right. You can always stop by, if you're bored."

"What about auditions?" Ashley asked.

Millie opened her mouth to confess they didn't go very well, but Zuki's upbeat voice stopped her. "We invited you to be in J-Club before the auditions." She looked at Millie with a bright smile before turning back to Ashley. "So technically you still have a place, if you want it."

Millie was relieved they wouldn't have to sit through any

more auditions. "That's true. And we already know you like Generation Love."

"You're a theater tech, right?" Zuki's momentum started to build. "Can you sing? Your backpack is covered in musical groups, so I bet you can. What about dancing? Is that how you know Luna? Did you use to dance together?"

Ashley made a face. "No, we didn't—" They sighed. "I'm not making any promises, but I'll think about it," was all they said before exiting the cafeteria.

Zuki stuffed the last bite of chicken in her mouth and failed to hide her growing smile.

Millie's chest filled with hope. "I think we just got another member."

A squeal erupted from Zuki's mouth and she threw her hands in the air. "I know, right? This changes everything. Now we're only one person short of having a full imitation band! Do you think Ashley will turn up to rehearsal? I mean, I'm sure they will. I don't know what that was about Luna, but clearly Ashley wants to be around her. I wonder if they know each other? They don't seem like they'd hang out in the same circle. But oh my gosh, we have a new member!" She took a breath and let it heave out of her again like the weight of her joy was too much to carry.

And for a moment, Millie forgot all about progress reports and the awkwardness of band. All she could think about was how their little world had just gotten a little bigger.

CHAPTER FOURTEEN

After school each day, Millie spent hours practicing her flute, doing her homework, and trying her best to avoid answering too many of her parents' questions about Advanced Studies. It didn't feel good to lie. Millie didn't like how it made her feel as if there was a gremlin in her chest, shaking at her rib cage harder and harder until she thought she might burst.

But if she told her parents the truth, they'd make her quit J-Club. And if they found out about her grades, they might even make her quit school.

So she focused on trying her best in all the ways she still could. And of course there was still the next J-Club meeting to look forward to.

Millie couldn't wait to get to know Luna and Ashley better. They were going to be a real band. A real *group*. She was nervous and hopeful and excited all at once. Was that how Generation Love felt the first time they met?

Generation Love had always said their chemistry was instant. That they bonded over cute animal stationery and a particularly adorable dorama and had been best friends ever since. One of their most popular singles, "Forever Love Song," was even inspired by their friendship.

Maybe J-Club could be like that, too.

Millie fell asleep dreaming of J-Pop, and friend groups, and what it would feel like if J-Club had their very own theme song.

And when she woke up on Thursday morning, she was already beaming.

CHAPTER FIFTEEN

Ashley and Luna sat across from each other in the orchestra room, arms crossed and backpacks at their feet.

Millie felt the tension crash against her, and her whole body wanted to recoil. It reminded her of home and the arguments with her parents.

She took a breath. J-Club was a safe space. She refused to let her worlds overlap.

So instead, she forced a smile and walked into the room. "You made it!"

Ashley looked up, their brows scrunched together. "You're late. Where's Zuki?"

Luna kept her eyes pinned to her candy-pink fingernails.

Millie tried not to be offended by the lack of enthusiasm. "I told Zuki I had to stay after class to talk to my teacher. Wait, she's not here yet?"

"Obviously not," Ashley said, looking around the empty room for emphasis.

Millie twisted her mouth, feeling the weight of her backpack grow heavier. It was unusual for Zuki to be late to anything, but especially J-Club. Maybe she had to stay behind to talk to a teacher, too.

Ignoring the weirdness brewing between Ashley and Luna, Millie took a seat and squeezed her phone. This was usually Zuki's job—the organizing and the leading.

Millie wasn't sure she'd be any good at it.

"How about we watch some Generation Love music videos, and figure out which one we could learn the choreography to?" Millie offered.

Luna nodded. "Sounds fine to me."

Ashley shrugged.

Halfway through the first song, Millie realized nobody was actually watching the video. Luna was staring at the floor, and Ashley was trying not to stare at Luna. And Millie was so self-conscious about having to lead the group that she could barely concentrate.

"Um. Is everything okay?" Millie finally asked, breaking the steel barrier separating the other two.

Luna looked up, eyes wide like she'd been caught cheating on an exam.

Ashley crossed their arms. "Why wouldn't it be?"

Millie shuffled in her seat. "It's just . . . Have you two met before?" She assumed they already knew each other, but maybe they didn't. Maybe *that* was why it was so awkward.

Ashley snorted, and Luna cast them a scowl that took over her entire face.

"Why is that funny?" Luna demanded.

"We've been pretending to be strangers for so long, I think maybe we finally are. Strangers, that is." Ashley lifted their shoulders. "What? It's kind of funny."

"No, it's not," Luna hissed.

Just then, Zuki burst into the room like she'd been thrown from a tornado, eyes jubilant and a wide smile stretched across her face. Her cheeks were more pink than usual, as if she'd been running across campus. When she spotted Ashley, she squealed.

"You're here!" Zuki raised a small stack of papers in the air, high above her head. "And I made a personality quiz!"

Luna raised an eyebrow. Ashley looked like they'd just been delivered terrible news.

Millie breathed out a sigh of relief. "I didn't know what to do, so we've just been watching videos. Where were you?" *And please don't leave me in charge of J-Club ever again*, she wanted to add.

Zuki handed a quiz to each member before taking a seat next to Millie. "The school counselor wanted to talk to me. It's not important. Anyway, I made these last night, and I think they'll help us all get to know each other better and figure out which Generation Love member we're most like. Does anyone need a pen?" A hoard of glittery gel pens appeared, and she held them out to the group like a bouquet of flowers.

Millie took a pen and frowned. "The school counselor? Again?" The only time she'd ever spoken to the counselor was when Mr. Thomas moved her to Wind Ensemble II and she had to rearrange her schedule. Why would Zuki need to go more than once?

Zuki waved a hand. "It's not important. Come on, I want to know what your answer to number seven is!" She flashed a bright smile before gluing her eyes to her paper.

Millie didn't think it was normal for school counselors to want to talk unless it *was* important, but Zuki didn't seem to think it was a big deal. So maybe it wasn't. Maybe Millie was just too overly paranoid about being in trouble all the time.

Besides, if something was *really* wrong, Zuki would tell her. They were friends.

She uncapped the purple gel pen and focused on the questions instead.

"I'm not answering these," Ashley said suddenly. When everyone looked up, Ashley was holding the quiz in the air. "Number nine says 'What is your favorite cupcake flavor?'" The room was quiet for three whole seconds. "Do I look like someone who has a favorite cupcake flavor?"

Zuki blinked. "I'm sorry, I don't understand the question."

"That's exactly my point," Ashley quipped.

"You could just write that you don't like cupcakes?" Millie offered.

"That's going to be their entire quiz—that they don't like anything," Luna muttered under her breath. Except in the quiet of the orchestra room, it came out a lot louder than she'd intended.

Luna stiffened, cleared her throat, and focused intently on whatever it was that she was scribbling.

Ashley was at a loss for words.

"This is supposed to be fun! Nobody has to take the questions too seriously," Zuki intervened with a bubbly laugh. "Just write whatever feels honest to you. Also, for the record, my favorite cupcake flavor is vanilla with fluffy pink frosting and rainbow sprinkles."

"Of course it is," Ashley grumbled, but returned to filling in their answers all the same.

Millie found most of the questions easy to answer.

What's your favorite animal? **Sea otter.**

If you could visit anywhere in the world, where would it be? **Japan, to visit the actual Pokémon Center in Tokyo.**

Do you prefer a song you can dance to or a song you can chill out to? **Both, depending on my mood.**

But then she got to question twelve.

If you could trade your parents for any two people from history, who would you pick?

Millie didn't know what to write. Even when her parents made her feel like she couldn't breathe, she never wanted to trade them in for someone else. She loved her mom and dad. And she knew they loved her, even if they weren't very good at listening.

But wanting parents who were a little bit different wasn't the same as wanting different parents *completely.*

She glanced at Zuki. The questions were supposed to be fun. Lighthearted. Millie wanted to write that she would keep the same parents she already had, but she worried it would hurt Zuki's feelings. And she couldn't figure out why.

So she wrote **I don't know,** and moved on to the next question.

When the late bell rang, everyone hurried to jot down the last of their answers before giving their papers to Zuki.

"Thanks, everyone," Zuki sang. "I can't wait to read your answers."

Luna paused by the door. "See you next week," she said finally, and disappeared into the afternoon sun.

Ashley slung their backpack over their shoulder. "I could only answer half the questions. I guess that means I don't really have a personality."

Zuki tutted. "No way. You have a great personality!"

Ashley flinched. So did Millie.

Zuki didn't seem to think she'd said anything strange at all. "You just have to open up to people more. Don't be so afraid of rejection."

"I'm not afraid of rejection," Ashley growled. "I just don't think a person can be summarized by a personality quiz. Especially one written by somebody who thinks bubblegum-pink is a mood."

"Colors can be moods," Zuki countered. "People can feel blue, can't they? So why not raspberry red? Or dazzling turquoise? When I walked in the room today and saw you'd joined J-Club, I was feeling fluorescent lemon!"

Ashley blinked. "We don't speak the same language."

"But you'll come back, right?" Zuki asked quickly. "Next week?"

Ashley shoved their hands in their pockets, staring sourly at the place where Luna had disappeared. "I don't know. Maybe."

Millie rocked back on her heels, searching for a way to break through the silence. She felt like someone should at least *ask* about the figurative elephant in the room. Because this wasn't just a normal elephant—this one had wings and was painted in neon colors and wouldn't stop singing Broadway tunes.

Nobody in the world could sit beside Luna and Ashley and not realize something major had gone down between them.

The words tumbled out of Millie in one quick rush. "What's with you and Luna?"

Ashley looked at the vacant doorway, eyes hardening. "I don't know what I was thinking. I thought joining J-Club might have been a sign, but . . ." Their voice trailed off.

"A sign of what?" Millie asked patiently.

Ashley just shook their head. "It doesn't matter. I have to go—and you two will miss the late bus if you don't hurry."

For a moment, Millie wondered if it was the last they'd see of Ashley Seo. But when they reached the corner of the street where their paths would sever, Ashley lifted their hand in a half-hearted wave.

"I'll see you tomorrow at lunch," was all they said before turning for the classrooms.

CHAPTER SIXTEEN

"You're in a very good mood today," Scott noted from the driver's seat. He flicked his finger against the turn signal.

Millie liked the sound it made. It was a gentle, lazy click. If sounds were animals, she imagined it would be an enormous bullfrog sitting in the mud, counting the seconds until another fly passed by.

She grinned at the thought. "Yeah, I guess I am."

"Did something happen in school?" her dad asked, eyes focused on the road.

Millie gripped her flute case in her lap. She'd had a *great* day at school. Ashley had officially joined their lunch table, and they'd even started talking about songs they could all learn to perform together. Millie was so happy, even her flute lesson had been bearable.

A big part of her wanted to tell her dad how she was feeling. But telling her parents things didn't feel natural anymore. They always thought her interests were silly or somehow turned the conversation back to band. That led to talking about chair placements or flute scholarships to universities Millie hadn't even considered yet.

J-Club was just for her. It was something she had to protect.

Millie breathed through her nose. "School was fine, same as always."

Scott tapped his thumb against the steering wheel. An instrumental soundtrack was playing through the car speakers—something from an Oscar-winning movie Millie had no interest in seeing. "Here comes the flute solo!" he announced suddenly, beaming from ear to ear as the sound filled the car. And then he was waving a hand in the air like he was Mr. Thomas conducting Wind Ensemble II.

Millie laughed in spite of herself. Her dad loved music in a way that probably wouldn't make sense to most people, besides maybe her mom. Maybe that was why they were so perfect for each other.

And even if Millie didn't love it in the same way, she could still understand it. She knew what it was like to have music transport you to another world, or help you make sense of your feelings. It was why she adored Generation Love so much.

"That could be you one day, with a big solo in the London Philharmonic," Scott said, voice full of pride although it was barely even a dream.

It certainly wasn't Millie's dream.

She shuffled in her seat, no longer laughing. "I don't really want to keep playing the flute my whole life. I'd rather do something else in college."

Scott's hand moved to the stereo and he turned the volume down. "What are you talking about? Flute lessons are an investment—it's how you'll get *into* college. You could get a full scholarship and go to an amazing school. And if you want to study something else, maybe you could double major. There are so many possibilities, Millie."

She shrugged. "That all sounds like the same possibility to me."

Scott frowned. "I know you hate practicing, but nobody really likes practicing when they're a kid. Wait until you're older. You'll be so glad we made you stick with music and didn't let you waste your potential."

Millie made a face. Didn't she still have potential even without music? Or did music really have to be *it*?

Maybe she hadn't really settled on a dream yet. She didn't have a plan, the way her mom and dad had when they were younger and wanted to perform in the London Philharmonic. But even their plans changed. Instead of music degrees and flying across the Atlantic Ocean, they'd had Millie.

Why was it so important for Millie to share a dream that never came true for them in the first place?

"Hey, we should stop by Chinatown. Isn't there a store you really like that sells erasers that look like hamburgers? Maybe we could get a few of them for school," Scott offered, oblivious to Millie's sunken shoulders.

"Maybe another time. I have homework." She didn't want to go to her favorite place when she felt so frustrated.

"Okay, kiddo," Scott said, and turned the volume back up on the stereo.

The car filled with growling timpani and whispering violins. It was tension all the way through. The complete opposite of what J-Pop felt like.

The complete opposite of what Millie wanted.

She stared out the window and counted the passing trees until her head spun.

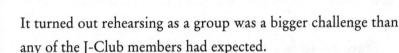

It turned out rehearsing as a group was a bigger challenge than any of the J-Club members had expected.

Millie had never sung in front of anyone before, and her nerves got the better of her. Luna and Ashley spent more time looking embarrassed in front of each other than actually singing. And Zuki was so focused on Chiyo's solo riffs that she barely noticed when the rest of the room had gone quiet.

The rehearsal was a disaster. Yet for some reason, it seemed to be the very thing that united the group. After enough failed attempts at the same song, everyone found themselves in an unstoppable burst of giggles.

"I'm sorry." Luna hiccupped. "I laugh when I'm uncomfortable."

"This is *so* awkward," Millie said as her eyes began to water.

"You realize we sound terrible, right?" Ashley mused.

Zuki managed to smile and grimace at the same time. "No,

we don't! We just need to practice more. Besides, I thought it was really good for our first day of singing. Generation Love's first recording session went so bad they were afraid they were going to get fired. So they practiced outside their normal hours and came back with a vengeance and blew the whole studio away!"

"Well, at least we don't have to worry about getting fired," Millie offered like a sad consolation prize.

Ashley rolled their eyes. "Of course not. Zuki isn't going to fire anyone when this is basically the first time in years anybody actually turned up to J-Club. I'm surprised she didn't make us sign contracts to keep us from leaving."

Luna sucked in a quick breath of air, and for a moment the room fell silent. Everyone turned to Zuki.

And then the laughter exploded like a tuba.

Zuki clutched her sides. Millie wiped her eyes with her sleeve. Even Luna and Ashley exchanged a humorous glance.

"Well, the point is, we have plenty of time to practice," Zuki managed to say. "And I just know we'll get better and better. Maybe we could even practice outside of school sometime!"

The laughter quickly dulled, and Luna shifted in her seat.

Ashley sniffed. "Yeah, I doubt that's going to happen. What if someone sees us all together?"

Luna looked hurt. "What's that supposed to mean?"

Ashley lifted a brow. "Wasn't that your rule? That J-Club had to be a secret?"

"Yeah, but the way you said it . . ." Luna shook her head. "Never mind. Forget it."

Millie reacted immediately, searching for a way to smooth things over. "We really don't mind. You told us when you joined how you felt, and it's really not a big deal. Right, Zuki?"

Zuki waited a beat too long. "We're just happy you're in the band."

Luna bit her lip, flustered. "It's not what you think. I like being in J-Club. But sometimes it's nice to keep something you love to yourself."

"I—I know what you mean," Millie said, her voice faltering. Everyone turned to look at her, and she swallowed the lump in her throat. "I don't really talk to my parents about Generation Love, or J-Pop at all, because I know they wouldn't understand. They'll think it's silly or a waste of time. And it takes away some of the joy, when people don't get you. I guess sometimes I feel like I love J-Pop so much that I want to protect it, even if that means keeping it to myself."

Luna relaxed. "Yeah. Exactly."

Ashley stared at their hands, jaw clenched, but didn't say anything.

"That's the whole point of J-Club," Zuki said, gazing around the room. "We have a space just for us, where we can be ourselves." She grinned toothily. "How about we make that our rule?"

"I don't think we need any more rules," Ashley mumbled dryly.

"Not a rule then," Zuki countered. "More like a club philosophy. When we're in J-Club, nothing else matters. We get to be the person we really want to be, and not the person anyone expects us to be."

"I like the sound of that," Millie admitted.

Luna smiled softly. "Me too."

Ashley ran a hand through their hair. "Yeah, okay, whatever. But if this is some kind of club 'moment' you're all having, please know in advance that I'm not hugging any of you."

"Fine. No hugging," Zuki said, rolling her eyes. "But let's promise to always be there for each other, if we ever need it."

"'Always and forever,'" Millie added, quoting one of Generation Love's songs.

Zuki beamed. "Exactly."

Luna opened her mouth to reply, but Ashley stood up suddenly, frustration pooling in their eyes.

"Where are you going?" Millie asked, puzzled.

"The bell is about to ring. And I don't want to stick around making promises none of us are going to keep," Ashley said simply. As if on cue, the ding of the late bell sounded, and Ashley left without another word.

The others gathered their belongings in awkward silence until Luna paused near the doorway, turning sharply on her heels.

"Don't listen to Ashley. I like your club philosophy. And—" She bit her lip. "And I don't think you should feel bad about loving what you love. Because hiding it feels so much worse. Trust me."

She left Millie and Zuki alone in the orchestra room, and for all the time it took to get to the school bus, Millie couldn't stop wondering whether Luna's message had been meant for them at all.

CHAPTER SEVENTEEN

On Saturday, Millie and her parents went to Chinatown for lunch. Their favorite ramen restaurant was right inside the mini-shopping mall, between the bakery and one of three boba tea shops scattered around the complex. And upstairs was Millie's favorite store in the whole world—Pop Cute.

It was filled with adorable key chains and stationery, and stuffed animals that ranged from pocket size to *bedroom* size. But the best part was the back of the store, which housed an entire wall of J-Pop albums, posters, and fan trinkets.

It was the only place in Oregon that sold the limited edition Generation Love CDs. Anyone could order them off the internet, if they were willing to pay a small fortune for shipping. But Millie had always felt like there was something special about being in a store and holding the CD in her hands. It was kind of like finding a hidden treasure out in the wild. It was *memorable*.

Scott and Jane were still in the restaurant, but they'd said it was okay for Millie to visit Pop Cute on her own, as long as she didn't leave the shopping center. Millie was staring at a pack of animal-shaped highlighters when she heard the bell above the shop door ring. It didn't occur to her to look up—not until the newcomer made a beeline for the CD shelf, and Millie caught a glimpse of coffee-colored hair.

She blinked. "Luna?"

Luna looked like a deer caught off guard. Her brown eyes were wide and alarmed until recognition set in. And then, relief. "Oh, Millie! What are you doing here?"

Millie moved away from the stationery shelves and took a few steps closer to Luna. "Just looking around, mostly. Me and my parents just finished eating lunch at the ramen place downstairs."

"I love that restaurant!" Luna exclaimed, tucking a curl over her ear. She was wearing purple leggings and a loose T-shirt. Her dance school's shiny gold logo was printed across the chest.

Millie couldn't hide her surprise. "You like ramen?"

"My mom was stationed in Japan for a while—she was in the navy before I was born—and she still makes ramen all the time. And chicken katsu curry, which is my favorite."

"That's so cool," Millie said. "My parents cook curry all the time, too. And corn chowder on rice, but that isn't really Japanese. I think only the rice counts." She paused. "I guess it's half Japanese, like me."

"Well, that's half more than I am." Luna laughed at first, but her smile slowly faded. She fiddled nervously with her silver charm bracelet. "Sometimes I get embarrassed about loving J-Pop so much." Her eyes widened and she quickly added, "Not because J-Pop is embarrassing or anything! It's just sometimes I don't feel like I'm *supposed* to like it, since I'm not Japanese."

"You don't have to be Japanese to like J-Pop."

Luna lifted her shoulders like she wasn't so sure. "I used to go on the fan forums all the time to talk about new albums, and videos, and rumors. You know—all the fun stuff. But then one day someone called me a weeaboo. I know it was just one person, but after that I started to feel really self-conscious. Like maybe *everyone* was thinking that, and I just had no idea. So I stopped telling anybody about the kind of music I like." Luna's hands dropped to her sides. "It felt safer to keep it to myself."

"That's ridiculous for someone to call you that," Millie said, defensive on Luna's behalf. "*Anyone* is allowed to like J-Pop. Music is supposed to be a universal language. It's about how it makes people *feel.* Liking it has nothing to do with how someone looks or what last name they have."

Luna half smiled. "When you say it like that, it makes sense. But I don't know . . . People on the internet can be mean, I guess."

Millie lifted her brows. "People can be mean in real life, too."

Luna hesitated, probably imagining Ruby and Annabelle and how they'd react if they saw her in Chinatown shopping for CDs at Pop Cute. After a moment, Luna tightened her jaw like she didn't like imagining it at all.

Would they call her names if they knew she liked J-Pop, too? Was that why she didn't want to tell them about J-Club?

"You know, it really shouldn't matter what they think," Millie said quietly.

"Maybe it shouldn't, but that doesn't mean I don't care." Luna looked around at the J-Pop posters and sighed. "Sometimes I feel like I just don't fit neatly into a box. Like there are too many different pieces of me that won't make sense to other people. But sometimes what I really want more than anything is just to feel like I *fit in*, you know?"

Millie had never imagined that anyone as popular as Luna could actually be lonely deep down, but maybe she was. Maybe she'd been as lonely as Millie, even if she wasn't technically alone.

"It hasn't always been easy making friends," Luna admitted sadly. "I know that might seem silly to you because you and Zuki are so close."

"It's not silly at all," Millie said. "I'd never even had a friend before Zuki. So I get it. I get why it's so important for you to feel like you fit in. But you have J-Club now, and we don't care what kind of box you come in or whether you have a box at all. We just want to be your friend."

Luna stared at the floor. "I seem to be better at losing friends than keeping them."

All Millie wanted was to make her feel better. "I'm sorry people are making you feel bad. But it's not your fault. You're amazing! And I think it's really cool that you like J-Pop." She offered a grin. "Everyone is so obsessed with K-Pop these days. I feel like J-Pop is kind of underappreciated."

The tension in Luna's face began to fade. "Generation Love is a million times better than any K-Pop group."

"Definitely," Millie agreed, smiling brightly.

Luna stared up at the nearby posters and brushed a strand of curls away from her face. "So," she said, "how many of these groups have you listened to?"

They spent the next few minutes gushing about their favorite solo artists and bands and about all the rumors of Chiyo and Jake Takeshi breaking up until Scott and Jane arrived with a pink box Millie recognized from the bakery and said it was time to go home. They even said a quick hello to Luna, who, thankfully, knew better than to mention anything about J-Club.

On the drive home, Millie ate a coconut bun in the back seat while her parents chatted about work, and thought about how she and Luna had more in common than she'd ever imagined. More than simply a love of J-Pop.

It turned out they were both afraid of losing their friends. And maybe what they wanted most of all was just to feel like they belonged.

CHAPTER EIGHTEEN

When the bell rang, everyone grabbed their backpacks and hurried for the door. Mr. Holland had just finished wiping away the notes from the whiteboard and set the magnetic eraser in the far corner. "Millie, could we talk for a moment?" he asked.

She paused, immediately worried. One of her classmates started to push past her, so she stepped out of the way and ended up right in front of Mr. Holland.

He waited until the other students left before he spoke. "I want to talk to you about your grades."

Millie dropped her eyes. "Oh," was all she could think to say.

"You're barely hanging on to a D. And it might be too late to change that before progress reports come out, but you still have time to bring your percentage up before final report cards." Mr. Holland waited for Millie to reply, but she didn't. She *couldn't*.

She felt like a statue, unable to move.

Mr. Holland looked serious. He was usually full of jokes, so that wasn't a good sign. "I expect every student to spend at least fifteen minutes reviewing the material when they get home each night. That's really not asking a lot."

Millie frowned. She easily spent twice that amount of time studying. Not to mention her other classes *and* flute practice.

He continued. "I'd like to see you start making more of an effort—and not just with homework. Class participation is also part of your grade, you know. You haven't raised your hand once so far."

Millie's heart was shriveling up like a prune. Now she had to worry about public speaking, *too*?

When Millie still didn't say anything, Mr. Holland sighed. "I give every student the grades they earn. And yours aren't going to improve unless you start trying harder."

Millie managed to nod twice and mumble something that sounded a lot like okay, before making her way out of the Science room and toward the cafeteria.

The fizz of Zuki's soda bottle caught Millie's attention, and she watched as Zuki quickly screwed the cap back on to keep it from bubbling over.

"Ugh, seriously? Why does this always happen to me?" Zuki said with a comical groan. She snatched up a napkin from the lunch table and wiped her hand.

Ashley's gaze stretched across the cafeteria. "Does it not

bother you two that she basically pretends she doesn't know us?" they asked, oblivious to the mess Zuki had made.

Luna was sitting at her usual table, surrounded by her dance-major friends. Their table always seemed to be laughing over a never-ending inside joke.

Zuki tossed her napkin on her tray. "We should find a choir major to join J-Club. Do either of you know any choir majors? Haley Corral is in Choir II, and she's in my Science class. But she says she hates pop music, so I don't think that's going to work. I don't know how anyone can hate pop music. In a way, almost *everything* was pop music at some point, right? Even Mozart!"

Ashley didn't seem to hear her. "I mean, it's like we don't even exist outside of J-Club. It's *rude*."

"It doesn't *have* to be a choir major. A theater major could be good, too," Zuki said from far away, her thoughts dancing in her eyes. "But someone who's a strong singer. You know, to help with the harmonies. Maybe we could even sing 'Lost Star' a capella, the way Generation Love did on that radio show last month!"

Zuki and Ashley clearly weren't listening to each other. Millie wanted to respond, but she wasn't sure what to say. Discussing Luna seemed unfair when she wasn't there to defend herself, and finding a fifth member for J-Club seemed like too big a problem for Millie to solve alone—especially since she didn't know any choir *or* theater majors.

So instead, she changed the subject altogether.

"Today might be my last J-Club meeting for a while," Millie said in a hollow voice.

Ashley snapped their mouth shut immediately.

Zuki looked panicked. "What do you mean?"

"My progress report has a lot of Cs," Millie admitted. "And a D in Earth Science. There's no way my parents won't ground me." It didn't matter if they didn't know about J-Club. Staying after school at all, for any kind of club, would be out of the question.

Getting a D would've probably been enough for her to be grounded from a *flute* club, if that was even possible.

Ashley made a face. "How do you have a D in Earth Science? All you have to do is turn in the homework. The answers to the tests are basically the same thing."

Millie opened her mouth to explain how confusing she found school, but Zuki interrupted. "You can't miss J-Club! You're the vice president. Maybe you can just promise your parents you'll get your grades back up? Or just not show them the progress report?"

"They know that they come out this week. And I can't lie," Millie said. Not again. Not when J-Club *was* the lie.

Ashley stood up suddenly. "I have an idea. I'll see you both after school."

"But what about your—" Zuki started, but Ashley was already gone. She looked at the plate of fries Ashley had left behind before shoving a few of them in her mouth. "What?" she asked when she saw Millie staring at her. "I don't want them to go to waste."

"It's not the fries." Millie frowned, desperately trying to find the right words. "It's—is school hard for you?"

Zuki picked up another fry. "No, not really. Math is hard sometimes. Or having to remember all the rules for it, anyway." She paused. "Didn't you have to learn the same stuff when you were homeschooled?"

"My parents mostly wanted me to focus on music, but I had workbooks and science projects, and sometimes they'd even make me write essays." Millie tilted her head back thoughtfully. "But even if the work was hard, I was never confused about what I was supposed to be *doing*."

"You can always ask the teacher for help," Zuki offered.

"But I feel like I'm the only one who needs extra help. And I feel like I'd be bugging them."

"That's their job."

Millie squeezed her hands into nervous fists. "Then why do they always assume I'm being lazy or forgetting to do my home-work? How come none of my teachers ever ask if I understand what homework to *do*?"

"Well, because it's not that hard to figure out," Zuki said like it was the simplest answer in the world.

"That's what I mean," Millie said exasperatedly. "It *is* hard for me. I feel confused all the time. And I'm not saying it's because homeschooling is bad or anything like that, because my parents tried really hard to teach me stuff. But it's different."

"Maybe it's like going to school in a foreign country," Zuki mused. "Like in Japan, the rules are different. Did you know everyone eats lunch in their classroom? And they have to clean every day. They don't even have janitors!"

"Is that true?" Millie asked.

Zuki lifted her shoulders. "That's what the internet said."

The internet had the answers to a lot of questions, but it didn't know everything. It couldn't make school easier for Millie or get her parents to stop pressuring her.

It couldn't change her grades.

Millie sighed, took a fry from Ashley's plate, and wished there was a way to make all her problems disappear.

At the J-Club meeting after school, Ashley stood in front of Millie with their arm outstretched, a piece of white paper stamped with the school's logo in the top corner. It was a progress report. A *blank* progress report.

"Where did you get that?" Millie asked with wide eyes.

Ashley shrugged impatiently, like what they were handing over wasn't a big deal at all. "You can fill this one out and change the grades. That way your parents won't get mad at you."

"I *knew* you were a delinquent," Zuki hissed, half playful, half serious. "Did you steal that from a teacher?"

Luna watched Ashley curiously but didn't say anything.

"It doesn't matter," Ashley grumbled. "Just take it."

Millie did, and felt her hands begin to shake. She may have lied to her parents about J-Club, but forging her teachers' signatures? Changing her grades? That was a different level of lie.

Zuki snatched the paper out of Millie's hands before she could think. "I'll do the signatures. I'm pretty good at copying them."

"And you think *I'm* the delinquent?" Ashley asked dryly.

Zuki compared Millie's real progress report, scribbling in pen like she was following a pattern. "My parents always forget to sign stuff. I've had practice," she replied. Millie expected her to elaborate, but she didn't. When Zuki was done writing, her sunshine smile returned. "There. Perfect."

Millie couldn't even tell the difference.

"Now for the grades," Zuki began, bringing her pen back to the page.

"Don't do all As," Luna said in a rushed voice. She looked at everyone in the room—even Ashley—like she was apologizing for jumping in. "It's just, if you put in all As, it looks obvious. At least put one B."

"Good point," Zuki said. "Okay, Millie, you have a B in Earth Science."

Millie opened her mouth and closed it again, like a confused guppy. Was she really going to do this? Was she really going to lie to her parents about something so enormous?

"All done," Zuki said with a grin, handing the progress report to Millie for inspection.

She looked at the new grades as if they were the truth and not a lie at all. She expected to feel guilty. She thought being part of such a big deception would crush her.

Instead, she felt relieved.

"Thanks," Millie said finally.

Zuki smiled. Luna nodded. Ashley crossed their arms like they were bored.

They'd helped her. Maybe even saved her. And the truth was, she was happy to let them.

"Now, about the choreography . . ." Zuki's voice trailed off before erupting with ideas for J-Club.

And since there was nothing else Millie could do but wait, she joined in with her own ideas, too.

☆ ★ ☆

Millie had barely stepped through the door before her parents asked about her progress report. With the real one crumpled up somewhere in the bottom of the orchestra room trash can, Millie gave them the fake version. The version she hoped would keep her from being grounded.

Their eyes scanned the piece of paper, and Millie searched them for doubt. But she couldn't find any. Because Jane and Scott Nakakura weren't expecting a lie. They trusted their daughter. They believed she'd always do the right thing.

That was the part that stung most of all.

She'd been so worried about disappointing her parents that

she didn't think about what it would feel like to be disappointed in herself.

"You're doing a great job." Her mom smiled warmly. "Just try to work on that B, okay?"

Her dad hummed. "You still have time to fix that before report cards come out."

"Okay, I will," Millie said, burning her stare into the floor.

It was one more lie to add to the rest.

CHAPTER NINETEEN

"Did you see it? Isn't it amazing? And the poster is huge!" Zuki bounced on her toes several times before taking a seat at their usual lunch table.

Millie slid her tray closer and picked up her fork. Macaroni and cheese, and definitely no coleslaw.

Ashley was already there, eating a packet of chips. "How could anyone *not* see it?" they pointed out dully. "It's practically the whole length of the courtyard."

It was true—the poster was impossible to miss. Brightside Academy wasn't shy about advertising their school performances, and Pop Showcase was by far their biggest. It was the only performance that was open to every major and every grade in school. More than that, it was the only show where students got to have full creative control over their performance. They got to pick their song, outfits, choreography . . . They even got to talk to the tech majors about what kind of lighting they wanted.

As long as the student could sing, they had a shot at being in the show.

Millie was almost afraid to ask. "Are you thinking about auditioning?"

Zuki held up her hands like the answer was obvious. "*We are* auditioning!"

A knot tightened in Millie's stomach. More secrets. More lies. She felt queasy.

"This school is full of choir and theater majors. Our little imitation band—if you can even call it that—doesn't stand a chance," Ashley pointed out.

"So? All of us can sing," Zuki argued. "*And* Luna is the best dancer in the school."

"But none of us can *sing* sing." Ashley looked doubtful. "Not the way choir majors can."

Zuki was unruffled. "That doesn't matter. Besides, Chiyo always sang most of the solos, and everyone else sang backup. We don't need everyone to be as good as the lead."

"I'm assuming you're talking about yourself?" Ashley asked, and it sounded more like an accusation than a question.

Zuki prickled, even though she kept smiling. "I mean, I *am* the president of J-Club."

Inside, Millie felt like she was prickling, too. The thought of having to keep another secret from her parents was making her panic. How could she possibly tell them she was auditioning for Pop Showcase when they had no idea J-Club even existed?

"We're still a member short, in case you've forgotten," Ashley pointed out, and Millie felt a pang of relief.

She wondered if it made her a traitor to want Zuki's plan to fail before it even got off the ground.

Zuki hardly reacted. "There's still time. Besides, lots of groups have four members. We could make it work."

"Are you sure you'd even have four?" Ashley asked, eyeing Luna across the cafeteria. "We all know Luna will never agree to a public performance. It would jeopardize her popularity."

Zuki's shoulders fell a little. Millie hated how much her heart felt like it was returning to safety. Zuki was her friend—she should be on her side.

But her heart and her brain weren't on the same page.

"We don't *have* to audition for Pop Showcase." Millie tangled her fingers together. "We can still be an imitation band, even if the rest of the school doesn't see us perform."

"You don't know Luna would *definitely* say no," Zuki countered, glaring stubbornly at Ashley. "It's not like you two are even friends."

"We used to be," Ashley said coolly. "But then she found other friends."

Millie could hear the rawness in their voice, but Zuki didn't seem to notice at all. There were more important things to talk about.

"She'll say yes," Zuki argued. "I'll talk to her later. I'll convince her to do the audition with us—you'll see. She won't let us down. She likes us."

"Kind of a big assumption to make, don't you think?" Ashley said, unconvinced.

"It's not an assumption." Zuki was unfazed. "Millie and Luna even hung out together outside of school."

Millie sucked in a breath. She wasn't sure Chinatown really counted as hanging out, even if they did have fun talking. It was brief. It wasn't planned. And Ruby and Annabelle weren't there.

Maybe the rules were different outside of school.

Ashley snorted. "If you're so sure you know Luna better than me, why don't you go and ask her right now?"

Zuki instantly squared her shoulders, like she was ready to face any dare head-on. Millie's eyes pleaded with her to reconsider. It didn't feel right to put Luna on the spot. Especially when her only rule was that nobody else found out she was in J-Club.

But Zuki ignored her.

"Go on—ask her in front of her friends. You'll see what I mean," Ashley challenged.

"Fine," Zuki practically barked before moving across the cafeteria.

"Wait—" Millie started, but it was too late.

Zuki stopped in front of Luna's table, and Ruby and Annabelle glanced up at her curiously. Luna looked positively terrified.

"Um, do you need something?" Ruby asked, eyelashes fluttering with annoyance.

But Zuki was confident. Maybe too confident. "Hey, Luna!"

Annabelle stifled her laughter and turned to Luna. "Is this a new friend of yours?"

Luna looked up at Zuki, eyes registering for only a flash of a second before her face went stoic. "No. I don't know her."

Even from several yards away, Millie could see Zuki's heart break.

The other girls muttered words Millie couldn't hear, but the laughter in their eyes spilled into the room. It wasn't the kind of laughter that made you feel warm and safe. It was the sticky kind, black as tar, that latched on to your heart until it smothered it whole.

Millie got out of her seat and started to take a few steps toward Zuki when she heard her voice again, a little shakier than it was before.

"I was just wondering if you had the page numbers for tonight's English homework. I forgot to write them down and we're in the same class." Zuki's fists were balled at her sides.

Luna's gaze seemed to land everywhere except on Zuki. "Oh. I—I must've forgotten to write it down, too."

"It's fine. Sorry to have bothered you," Zuki said, her voice clipped and quick. She spun around and marched back toward Millie, who tried to stop her.

"Are you okay?" Millie whispered.

"Totally fine," Zuki said, brushing past her and sinking into her seat.

Millie could hear the lie. She was becoming familiar with them. But she sat down beside Zuki anyway, trying to think of something to say to make her feel better.

But she couldn't think of anything, and when she looked at Ashley, there wasn't any satisfaction in their eyes.

There was only sadness.

CHAPTER TWENTY

Luna stepped through the orchestra room doors, her dance bag hanging from her shoulder. She ignored Ashley, who looked surprised to see her, and took a seat beside Zuki instead. "I'm really sorry about what happened in the cafeteria."

Zuki forced a smile. "It's fine. We don't have to talk about it. I'm just glad you're here." If it weren't for the edge in her voice, Zuki could have convinced anyone she had recovered completely. But Millie knew her giveaway—it was like playing a note on the flute and knowing it was just a little sharp. Someone untrained might not notice, but Millie wasn't untrained. At the flute *or* at being Zuki's friend.

"You didn't have to pretend like you didn't know her," Millie said quietly. "That was really mean."

Even though Luna looked guilty, she kept her posture straight. "I know. But I did ask you all to keep this a secret. I thought you understood."

"You told us not to tell anyone about J-Club. We didn't think you meant *we* were part of the secret, too," Millie pointed out.

"And you did it in public. In front of the whole cafeteria. Friends don't treat each other like that."

Zuki barely reacted. If she was grateful for the support, she was hiding it well.

"You caught me off guard, that's all," Luna argued. "I hadn't even had a chance to—to—" She opened her mouth, clamped it shut, and then opened it again, like she just couldn't find the words.

"Had a chance to warn your friends about us?" Ashley challenged. "Are you really so ashamed of us that you need to give them a disclaimer?"

"It's not like that," Luna huffed, frustrated. "It's got nothing to do with any of you personally. But you don't understand. Ruby and Annabelle . . . We do everything together. We all go to Brightside, and the same dance school, and all the same competitions. I know they can be mean sometimes, but they're not like that *all* the time. They're still my friends. And I don't know how they'll react if they think I'm hiding something."

"But you *are* hiding something," Ashley pointed out forcefully. "You're hiding the fact that you listen to J-Pop. You're hiding the club. You're hiding *us.*"

Luna flattened her mouth and turned to look at Zuki. "I really am sorry."

But Zuki didn't get a chance to reply.

"Why can't you just admit you're embarrassed of the group?" Ashley looked as if someone had dented their armor. "Then at least we'd all know where we stand."

Luna's eyes blazed. "Why are you always trying to make me look bad? What did I ever do to you?"

"You're making *yourself* look bad," Ashley replied. "You care more about your image and your popular friends than you do about your friends in J-Club. Or maybe Zuki and Millie aren't actually your friends at all."

"You mean *you're* not my friend," Luna shot back. "That's what this is about, isn't it? Believe me, I *know*, okay? You don't have to keep reminding me. Besides, at least I have friends, which is better than what you do, which is not have friends at all!"

Something shifted in Zuki's eyes, like a switch turning off all the lights. She looked . . . absent, somehow. At first, Millie thought it was because of what Luna had done. But then she realized it was something else.

Zuki didn't like the fighting.

"Um, Luna? Ashley? I think maybe we should lower our—" Millie started.

But Ashley was already too out of orbit to hear her. *"I'd rather have no friends than fake ones!"*

Luna's eyes glistened. The hurt was building and building and building.

If someone didn't do something soon, Millie was afraid they'd both explode. And there'd be no going back.

And maybe Zuki sensed it, too, because barely half a second passed before she was on her feet with her fists balled tight. "ENOUGH!" her voice boomed.

Ashley and Luna blinked. Millie felt like all the air had been sucked out of the room.

Zuki's shoulders shook. "You two *have* to stop fighting."

"I was sticking up for you," Ashley grumbled.

Luna scoffed. "More like using it as an excuse to attack me. *Again.*"

Zuki began waving her hands in the air before either of them could get another word out. "I already said I was fine, and I really don't want to talk about it anymore. But the way you two act around each other is not good for J-Club." She glanced at Millie for backup.

Even though she didn't want to hurt anyone's feelings, Millie felt like it was important to be honest with them, too. "Maybe you two could talk things over?" She looked between Ashley and Luna. "You know—for the sake of the group?"

"Ashley doesn't want to be my friend. What else is there to talk about?" Luna folded her arms across her chest.

"I never said that," Ashley countered.

"You just called me fake," Luna bit back.

Ashley looked away. "I didn't mean it like that. I was just mad."

"But *why*?" Luna demanded. "I know you don't like Ruby and Annabelle, but do you have to hate me, too?" She shook her head. "It's not fair. If you're going to be mad at me all the time, I'd rather we didn't talk at all. And maybe—maybe it's better if I left J-Club."

Zuki's eyes looked wild. "What? You can't quit!" She turned to Ashley like she was shouting *You need to fix this.*

But Ashley wasn't paying attention to Zuki. They were only looking at Luna. "That's not what I want. Besides, you joined first. If anyone has to leave, it should be me."

"Well, that's not what I want either," Luna said quietly.

Zuki was barely holding herself upright.

Millie remembered what she'd said about Miyuki, and how she made Generation Love feel whole. Maybe that was what J-Club needed. Someone to be the glue that kept them all together.

Millie lifted her eyes slowly. "What about a truce? For the sake of the club?" Everyone turned to look at her, and her voice became the only sound in the room. "You both could agree to put your differences aside. Even if you can't be best friends again, maybe you could at least learn to get along?"

Luna looked at Ashley seriously. "I don't want to fight with you."

Ashley stuffed their hands in their pockets. "I'm fine with a truce. But you can't pretend like you don't know us. We deserve better than that."

"I know you do," Luna said with a nod. She looked at Zuki. "And I really am sorry."

Zuki mostly looked relieved J-Club wasn't going to lose any members. "I accept your apology. And I did almost break our promise about keeping J-Club a secret, so I guess it's not totally your fault."

Luna frowned. "What do you mean?"

Zuki sighed and let her arms fall to her sides. "I was going to ask you about Pop Showcase, but it doesn't matter. Ashley was right: we don't have enough members."

Luna's face fell. "I—I can't audition for Pop Showcase. Not with . . ."

"I know," Zuki said curtly. "Let's just pretend it was never a thing. Besides, I was thinking we could work on the choreography for 'Love Bright' today. I was watching their video, see, and I thought . . ."

And just like that, she turned back into Zuki—the Zuki who talked fast, and laughed with excitement, and had a thousand ideas going on at once. The tension was still in the room, hovering over the air like a blanket, but it was thin. And with Zuki gushing about dance routines, it was almost easy to pretend the tension didn't exist at all.

Millie was glad there was a new truce in place, but part of her wondered if arguments were like cracks in a vase. If you didn't mend them, they'd get worse over time. And eventually, the vase would break.

All she could do was hope that J-Club was a lot stronger than ceramic.

CHAPTER TWENTY-ONE

Millie's dad gripped the steering wheel the way he always did—like he was a bus driver making his way down a crowded, narrow street. He did most things that way: hyperfocused and maybe even a little impatient.

Millie stared out the window, drumming her fingers against her flute case in time to a Generation Love melody. She was still worried about her friends.

She had suggested a truce because she wanted to stop the fighting and keep the group together. But had she made the right choice? Would it have been better to actually *talk*?

Not to mention Luna was still keeping J-Club a secret. And if Millie was learning anything about secrets, it was that they only got harder to carry with time.

"What's on your mind?" her dad asked, slowing the car at a stop sign.

Millie's fingers went stiff. It wasn't like him to notice when something was bothering her. "My friends had an argument at school, and I don't know how to fix it."

"Ah. Is that why you were so distracted during your flute lesson?" Scott asked.

Millie frowned. "Well, maybe, but—"

"You have to pay attention to your flute teacher. Lessons are expensive, Millie. It doesn't help anyone to have you stand there for an hour daydreaming about your friends."

"I wasn't daydreaming. My friend was upset and—"

"If you're going to challenge the first chair flutist, you need to focus. You still have so much to learn, and Brightside Academy is going to offer you a lot of opportunities."

"I don't want to challenge anyone, Dad!" Millie said too loudly. "I'm happy where I am."

Scott frowned, turning a corner and gripping the wheel tighter. "I'm not saying second chair isn't something to be proud of, but I know you can do better. You have it in you— you're so talented. And part of the agreement with going to school was that you were going to work harder at the flute. Otherwise we'd be better off homeschooling you so you'd have fewer distractions."

"I can care about more than one thing, you know," Millie said stiffly. "My friends matter, too."

"Letting your friendships get in the way of your real life is just as bad as someone not turning up to work because they had a fight with someone. You have to prioritize what's important."

"My friends *are* important. And they are my real life."

Scott sighed. "I know it feels like that now because it's new and you're young, but you're at school to learn. And if your friends are getting in the way of that, we're going to need to sit down and have a serious talk."

He was threatening to take her out of school. She could hear it in his tone, like he was gripping the edges of a rug and was prepared to pull it out from beneath Millie's feet.

So Millie did the only thing she could think of to end the conversation. She agreed.

"I'll practice harder," she said, her voice numb.

"I'm glad to hear it," Scott said.

Millie put in her earbuds and turned the volume up on her phone, trying to drown out the pounding in her head with the sound of Chiyo's voice. She practiced the dance routine in her mind, mimicking the choreography with her toes where her dad couldn't see.

And all the while, she tried her best not to cry.

CHAPTER TWENTY-TWO

The cafeteria rattled with noise. Millie and Zuki sat in their usual table at the edge of the room and were halfway through their lunch when one of them asked the obvious question.

"Where do you think Ashley is?" Millie stared at the empty chair.

Zuki stuffed her mouth with fries. "No idea." She spoke through the corner of her mouth. "But I saw them in class this morning." She swallowed her mouthful of fries. "Maybe they're sneaking into empty classrooms again. I mean, it's kind of their thing at this point."

Millie watched Zuki reach for another few fries, admiring the colorful new addition on her friend's wrist. "I can't believe you made that out of Starburst wrappers," Millie said, full of awe. It matched the rest of Zuki's bracelets, all rainbow-hued and attention-grabbing.

Even though it wasn't like her to be embarrassed, Zuki immediately tucked her hand into her lap. It took two whole seconds before her smile returned. "It's pretty easy. I can show you how to do it later, if you want," Zuki offered. "But we need more Starburst. If you get any from the vending machine, don't throw the wrappers away."

Millie didn't know what to make of the long pause, so she decided to ignore it. "My parents don't give me extra money for vending machines," she admitted. "So it might take a while."

Zuki reached into her pocket and pulled out a dollar. "Here, take this!"

Millie froze. "Oh, I didn't mean I needed money or anything. I just meant my parents only give me enough to cover lunch."

"My parents always give me extra. So take it—I want to make you a bracelet, too!" Zuki said.

Even though it made her uncomfortable, Millie took the dollar, mostly just to stop Zuki from waving it in front of her face. "Thanks."

"No problem." Zuki grinned and turned back to her lunch.

"It's kind of cool that your parents give you money like that," Millie said. Her parents only gave her spending money for very special occasions, like if they went to an arcade or an amusement park.

Zuki stiffened. "Huh? Oh, yeah, I guess." A fragile laugh tumbled out of her. "I guess they do it because they feel guilty."

"Guilty about what?" Millie asked quietly.

"Oh, nothing. I didn't mean anything by that." Zuki adjusted her bracelets like she was preoccupied, but Millie could see there was something else bothering her.

Before she could ask what it was, Ashley appeared with their hands stuffed in their pockets. For all Ashley acted like they didn't care about anything, their uniform was always immaculate. Millie could never keep her bow tie straight, and her skirt was always a little wrinkled by the end of the day. But Ashley looked like they'd just stepped out of a catalog.

"I think I found us a fifth member," Ashley announced.

It took Millie and Zuki a moment to process what they'd just said.

"You mean someone else wants to join J-Club?" Millie's excitement was already growing.

Zuki fired question after question. "Who is it? What did they say? What's their major? Can they sing?" She clapped her hands. "How do they feel about pastel color schemes?"

Ashley rolled their eyes. "I'm not a recruiter. I'm just saying I think I know someone. Just—follow me, okay?"

Millie and Zuki put their lunch trays away and followed Ashley in a blur.

Ashley led them to the other side of campus, past the orchestra and band rooms and all the way to the end of the street until they reached the theater. The parking lot was empty and all the doors were shut, but Ashley made their way up the stairs anyway.

"Are we supposed to be here?" Millie whispered to Zuki. "It looks like it's closed."

Zuki giggled. "Of course it does. There's no performance on today, and the only people who have a class here are the tech majors."

"So we won't get yelled at for going inside?"

"I mean, maybe. But how else are we going to know who wants to join J-Club?"

Millie wanted to point out there were at least three solid alternatives. She couldn't help it—overthinking was just part of her personality. But she also envied the way Zuki and Ashley moved through spaces like they belonged there. Like they were totally and completely comfortable living in this world.

She wished she could be more like them.

So she did the next best thing and followed them inside.

The sound of someone singing carried through the auditorium doors and filled the foyer. Whoever it was sang beautifully, with perfect pitch and an earthy tone. They sounded relaxed, which was probably the first indication that they thought no one could hear them.

Millie followed her friends into the theater until she had a clear view of the stage. Sitting in the center, with her half-eaten lunch at her side and headphones planted on her ears, was Rainbow Chan.

And she was singing a Generation Love song.

Ashley looked over their shoulder at Millie and Zuki and pointed to the stage. *See?* they mouthed.

Zuki was beaming from ear to ear. She rushed to the stage before Millie could stop her. "You are amazing!" she said, but with the acoustics it sounded like she was shouting.

Rainbow jolted to her feet, tearing off the headphones like she'd been caught in her hiding place. With saucer eyes and two messy braids hanging from her shoulders, Rainbow folded her arms in front of herself protectively.

"We're sorry," Millie said quickly, sensing Rainbow's discomfort. "We didn't mean to sneak up on you."

"It's okay," Rainbow mumbled noncommittally. She sounded like someone who said those words at least fifty times a day just to make everyone else feel better.

"You have a really good voice," Millie offered.

Rainbow froze but didn't bring her eyes back up. There were a few plastic containers near her feet, filled with brown rice, tofu, and something the color of beets.

"Do you always eat your lunch in the theater?" Millie tried again.

"I don't—there—um—there's usually nobody else in here," Rainbow said, her voice a nearly inaudible squeak.

Ashley looked around the auditorium. "It's a good hiding place. I bet the hall monitors never check it during lunch."

Rainbow's face turned bright red.

"We're not here to get you in trouble," Millie said quickly.

"No, definitely not. We want to know if you want to join J-Club!" Zuki exclaimed. "Did you see the posters we put up a while ago? We were auditioning for a Generation Love imitation band. And you're fantastic! We could really use another singer. Another member, really. We meet on Thursdays in the orchestra room after school. You could eat lunch with us from now on, too, if you like. Ashley does—oh, you must know Ashley Seo, right? They're the one who told us you were here!"

Rainbow looked confused.

"We don't know each other," Ashley corrected. "I'm just observant. And also, I left my backpack in the tech room earlier and came back to get it. That was when I heard Rainbow singing."

It was the second time Ashley seemed to be looking out for Rainbow. For someone who claimed not to care about anything or anyone, Ashley was clearly more friend than enemy.

But why hide it? What was so wrong with people knowing they were kind?

Maybe Ashley simply preferred being backstage, in the shadows, where they could work without people watching their every movement. They were a tech major, after all.

Millie guessed some people liked being onstage, and some preferred to build the stage. Rainbow scratched her arm nervously.

Zuki smiled. "So what do you think? About J-Club, I mean. Will you come to the meeting on Thursday? I promise it will be fun!" It was like she didn't even notice how uncomfortable Rainbow looked. All Zuki ever saw was the possibility of something wonderful. The details didn't matter.

For a while, Rainbow didn't say anything at all, but then a small smile tugged at the edge of her mouth. "You said it was a Generation Love imitation band?"

Zuki nodded too many times. "We even have someone to help with the choreography! And with another member, we could probably try out for Pop Showcase!" Her excitement was like a cartoon snowball rolling down a hill, getting bigger and bigger until it was unstoppable.

But for the first time, Rainbow didn't seem to *totally* mind. "Okay," she said timidly. "I—I'll be there on Thursday."

When Millie and Zuki cheered, the acoustics made the entire room cheer right back. And they didn't care who heard.

Because J-Club finally had its fifth member.

CHAPTER TWENTY-THREE

Luna was sitting on the floor with her legs crossed, studying the choreography to one of the easier Generation Love routines on her phone. Millie and Zuki had pushed all the chairs to the edge of the orchestra room to clear as much floor space as possible. It wasn't exactly ideal, but it was better than nothing.

Ashley leaned against the podium. "Wouldn't it be better to rehearse somewhere with mirrors? Like, I don't know, in one of the dance rooms, for example?"

Luna looked up from her phone, jaw tensed.

Zuki's face brightened. "Is that something you could ask about, Luna? Could you get permission? I was going to do it myself, but I don't really know the dance teachers. But it would be so much better to rehearse in a dance studio. We wouldn't have to waste so much time recording ourselves with our phones, or taking turns watching the rest of the group practice to look for mistakes. And we'd have so much more space!"

Luna hesitated. Millie knew what she was thinking, even if Zuki was too excited to piece everything together.

"She'd have to say what it was for," Millie said quietly. "And then the other dance majors might find out about J-Club." Millie had a feeling most of the dance majors wouldn't care at all—the majority of them were perfectly nice people—but she could think of two in particular who would care a whole lot.

Luna's eyes fell to the floor.

"Would it really be so terrible if Ruby and Annabelle knew?" Millie asked. "Even if they think J-Pop is silly, or if they get mad that you have a secret hobby, they'd get over it eventually. They wouldn't just stop being your friend because of something so small."

"But what if they did?" Luna argued. There was genuine fear in her eyes.

Ashley stiffened. Even Zuki didn't seem to know what to say, which was a rarity.

So Millie lifted her shoulders and answered for all of them. "Then you'd still have us, and it would be Ruby and Annabelle's loss."

Luna opened her mouth just as the orchestra door fell shut. Everyone looked toward the noise and found Rainbow Chan and her big red glasses and argyle socks standing near the doorway.

She was staring right at Luna, her face devoid of color.

"Rainbow!" Zuki said with a smile. "Come on in! We were just about to start learning the choreography."

Rainbow hesitated. "If—if this is a joke . . ." Her eyes started to water. "And if you're just trying to make fun of me . . ."

"It's not!" Zuki and Millie blurted out in unison.

"It's really not," Luna agreed quietly. "Ruby and Annabelle don't even know I'm in J-Club."

Rainbow took a few slow steps into the room like she was still debating whether fleeing would be a safer choice.

Ashley watched Luna curiously. "I don't know why you're so scared about them finding out. They're sixth-grade bullies. They have no real power."

Luna scowled. "I'm not *scared.*"

"I am," Rainbow said quietly.

Everyone turned to look at her, which only made her shrink into herself more.

"Well, you don't have to be scared here," Zuki said almost triumphantly. "J-Club is a safe space. And we're happy to have you."

Rainbow shuffled her feet. "Um. Thanks."

The silence stretched on and on and on. Millie had been so excited about finding a fifth member that it hadn't really occurred to her Rainbow might not have joined if she knew who else was in the club.

Maybe it would've been better to prepare Rainbow—and Luna.

Eventually someone spoke. But to everyone's surprise, it was Rainbow who broke the silence.

"You say they don't have power, but they do." Rainbow tugged at her shirt. "Otherwise the whole school wouldn't still be making fun of me for something that happened in first grade."

Millie frowned. "What do you mean?"

Rainbow lifted her eyebrows. Maybe she wasn't used to being around someone who hadn't heard the story.

"Sorry," Millie added quickly. "You don't have to tell me if you don't want to."

"It's—it's not that. I just don't like being the center of attention." Rainbow averted her gaze. "And everyone is staring at me."

When Millie looked up at the others, they all cast their eyes down sheepishly. Zuki even threw her hands over her eyes for emphasis.

"Would it help if we all turned around?" Ashley asked. Somehow they sounded dry and earnest all at the same time.

"It's okay." Rainbow's cheeks flushed. "I didn't mean—"

"We don't mind!" Zuki declared, like it was the most ordinary request in the world, and spun around. "Okay, go!"

Rainbow blinked. Millie smiled encouragingly, but turned to face the wall as Luna and Ashley did the same.

Rainbow took a deep breath. "It—it was all because of my birthday party. My parents told me to invite everyone in my class. I was never very good at making friends, and I guess they thought it would help. I hadn't been with them long—I'm adopted—and they really wanted me to feel at home." She paused like she was trying to figure out how much of the story to tell. "The party didn't go very well. My family is vegan, and Ruby and Annabelle complained about the food being gross—even though it wasn't gross at all—and then none of the other kids would even try it. Not even the birthday cake. They made fun of all the games, so nobody wanted to play them. And then, in front of every-one, Ruby announced that everyone's parents made them come because they felt sorry for me."

"That's awful," Millie said, still facing the wall. She could sense Luna's guilt beside her.

"Yeah," Rainbow agreed sadly. "I thought it was going to be one bad day that we'd never have to talk about again. But by Monday afternoon, *everyone* at school was talking about how weird my parents were, and how my house smelled funny, and how I had thrown the worst party in existence. And it just never stopped from there—the laughing and the mean jokes. And I don't know, maybe because I'm a little weird it makes it easier for people to laugh . . ."

"No," Millie said adamantly. "You didn't do *anything* wrong."

Rainbow's voice sunk. "Well, there was also that one time I threw up onstage . . ."

Ashley and Zuki shuffled nearby. Clearly they'd heard about that particular incident. Maybe even seen it.

"*Still*," Millie insisted. "That isn't a good reason to be targeted by bullies." She didn't think there was *any* good reason to be targeted by bullies.

It was quiet for a long time, until Rainbow cleared her throat. "Um. You can all turn around now. That was the whole story."

Millie and the others turned to look at Rainbow, who adjusted her glasses self-consciously.

"I'm sorry you had to go through that," Zuki said. "But we have a rule in J-Club: this is a place where we get to be ourselves, and nobody gets to judge us."

"I thought it was a philosophy, not a rule," Ashley pointed out tersely.

Zuki ignored them. "You don't have to worry here. The last thing we'd ever do is laugh at you."

Rainbow chewed the edge of her lip. "I just—I don't want to join a club if it's going to make things worse."

"It won't," Millie said, very sure of herself. "We won't let Ruby and Annabelle bother you again. Right, Luna?"

"Right," Luna agreed without missing a beat.

Rainbow looked like she desperately wanted to believe her.

And Luna must've really wanted to reassure her, because she added, "If they give you any trouble again, I'll make them stop."

Ashley scoffed. "How are you going to manage that when you still won't even acknowledge any of us in public?"

Luna narrowed her eyes. "It's *complicated.*"

"It's *not,*" Ashley argued firmly. "But you don't want to be seen with people that might make *you* a target. You don't want to be treated like Rainbow, and you'll abandon your friends if it means protecting yourself." There was a sadness in their voice that flashed like an exploding star, bright and loud, before vanishing like it had never been there at all.

Luna recoiled. Maybe she was trying to figure out where the sadness had come from, too. "That's not fair."

"Maybe not, but it's true," Ashley replied.

"No." Luna's voice shook. "*I'm* not the one who abandons my friends."

Ashley's forehead crumpled with confusion. But Luna had already shifted away from them, breaking the eye contact. And because they were both stubborn, neither made an effort to repair what was clearly broken between the two of them.

Millie wished she could make everything better. She could see they both cared, deep down. But how could she make them see that?

Whatever had happened between the two of them wasn't going to be fixed in a day. Maybe not even in a week. But maybe, with enough practice, they could at least learn to stop hurting each other.

Millie kept thinking about what her mom would say when she'd scrape her knee or graze her elbow. *That's never going to heal if you don't stop picking at it.*

Maybe broken friendships were the same.

"Annabelle and Ruby pressure Luna to be someone she's not. And that isn't fair," Millie said slowly. Carefully. She looked around at the others. "And if we're doing the exact same thing, that isn't fair either. Luna has just as much right to feel safe in J-Club as the rest of us. Even if that means keeping it a secret."

Luna wiped her eyes and looked around the room. "I love J-Club. It's the only place where I can actually be myself."

Millie offered a smile. "Me too."

Ashley was unreadable at first, but then their face softened.

"Okay," they said finally. "I mean, I still think you should be honest, but Millie has a point."

"It's not that I don't want to be honest," Luna said. "But telling everyone about J-Club . . . I'll be making a choice that will change everything. If I start being honest about existing in my new world, I'm not sure I'll be able to keep existing in my old one."

"What's so great about a world where you can't even be yourself?" Ashley's voice was strained.

Luna's eyes watered. She blinked the tears away. "I—I don't know. But for a long time, it's the only one I had. They're the only *friends* I had."

Ashley flinched.

"Wait. Does that mean you might not keep J-Club a secret forever?" Zuki asked suddenly, breaking through the tension. Her eyebrows went up, up, up like she was a balloon racing for the clouds. "Because we have five members now. We could do it, if we wanted to."

Rainbow looked puzzled. "Do what?"

Millie didn't have to ask. She could see the yearning in Zuki's face. The *hope*. "Pop Showcase," she said softly.

Luna's face fell. "You want to audition? But—but the performance is—"

"—in front of the whole school," Zuki finished. "I know. But the final show would still be months away, and that's if we even make it through auditions. Which I totally think we will, for the record. And by then who cares what Ruby and Annabelle think?

You'll be in Pop Showcase! How could they possibly make fun of that?"

"I don't know . . ." Luna's voice trailed off. "Can't you just audition without me?"

Zuki shook her head stubbornly. "We're supposed to be imitating Generation Love. It's either all of us or none of us." Energy seemed to crackle all around her. "But I really think we could do it."

Rainbow's nerves were making her fingers twitch. "The last time I was on a stage alone . . ."

"You won't be alone," Zuki insisted. "We're a club. And clubs stick together."

A smile appeared at the corner of Rainbow's mouth.

Millie raised a hand. "I'm in, definitely."

"I mean, I've got nothing else to do," Ashley said with a sigh.

Everyone looked at Luna and waited.

"You're allowed to say no," Millie pointed out gently. "We all get a choice, and we're still your friends no matter what."

"That's true," Zuki agreed. "Friends no matter what."

Luna stared at her hands and then found Zuki's eyes. "Okay," she said finally. "I'll do it. But until I'm ready, J-Club still gets to be my secret, okay?"

Zuki stuck out her hand. "It's a deal."

CHAPTER TWENTY-FOUR

A breeze moved through the courtyard, sending a scattering of fallen leaves across the concrete. The autumn colors were starting to appear, leaving the trees flecked with crimson reds and walnut browns.

Millie liked the way the air smelled, like apples and firewood. It was her favorite time of the year.

"I don't think I can do this," Rainbow said. The cafeteria doors were only a few feet in front of her, but they may as well have been a thousand. She wasn't going to budge.

"It will be fine. We won't let anyone pick on you, I promise," Zuki urged. "And we'll take turns getting our lunches so you won't have to sit at the table alone for even a second. Just pretend they aren't even there!"

Rainbow shook her head.

Millie looked up at the bright blue sky. There were only a few fluffy clouds scattered below the sun, and it was the warmest it had been all week. "We could eat outside," she offered. "There are plenty of tables out here."

Rainbow looked up and her forehead wrinkled anxiously. "Really? You'd—you'd do that?"

Millie remembered what it felt like to have nobody to sit with. She never wanted to go through that again, and she didn't want it for Rainbow. "How about under the tree over there?"

Rainbow, Zuki, and Ashley looked to where Millie was pointing, and then they all shuffled over to one of the tables in the courtyard. Zuki swiped at the stray leaves on the surface and took a seat.

"You know," Ashley started, sitting between Zuki and Rainbow, "you need to work on your armor."

Everyone looked up curiously, but especially Rainbow.

"What do you mean?" she asked.

Ashley shrugged. "I mean you have to protect your heart, even if it means wearing armor like you're going into battle. You always look vulnerable—bullies like vulnerable."

Rainbow's cheeks turned pink. "It's not that easy."

"I know," Ashley agreed, to everyone's surprise. "It's really hard, and it feels unnatural. Like you're pretending to be someone you're not. But I used to get picked on, too, a long time ago. And the only thing that ever made it stop was sticking up for myself and pretending like I was totally unaffected by what people said. 'I don't care what you think' goes a long way. And the more you say it, the more you start to believe it."

Millie couldn't hide her shock. Ashley was always so tough and unbothered by other people. It had never occurred to Millie that it was something they'd had to work at.

Ashley noticed the surprise. "Brightside may be more accepting than most schools, but I used to be the only first grader here who openly talked about gender identity," they explained. "It's not exactly what you'd call a universal experience."

Zuki folded her hands beneath her chin. "I remember reading an interview with a Japanese fashion model—you know, the one from Generation Love's very first music video?—and they said they didn't come out as nonbinary until their twenties because they were still figuring out what label felt right for them."

"That's the thing—everyone is different. I'm only one person with one experience. Not every nonbinary person is going to look like me, or dress like me, or even think like me. But I don't believe there's a time limit on anyone figuring out their gender—*or* their sexuality, which is a totally different thing," Ashley explained.

"Did you always know you were nonbinary?" Millie asked, and then immediately frowned, hoping she wasn't saying the wrong thing. She cared about Ashley. The last thing Millie wanted to do was make a mistake with her words.

Ashley let out a short laugh. "You don't have to look so scared. It's just gender and pronouns, right?"

"I don't know if I'm using the right language," Millie admitted bashfully. "It was just me and my parents growing up. I'm not scared of gender, but I'm worried I don't know the right way to talk about it."

"Nobody knows everything," Ashley said. "We're not computers! I think it matters more that people are respectful. And if you mess up, just apologize, correct yourself, and carry on, instead of making the focus all about how bad you feel, you know?"

Millie relaxed. "Yeah. That makes sense."

"But to answer your question," Ashley continued, "I remember on the first day of kindergarten, the teacher had asked all the students to line up outside the door—one line for girls and one line for boys. And I remember hesitating. It seemed so easy for everyone else to just get into line without thinking about it. But for me? I guess that was one of the first moments when I thought, 'Why do I have to choose? Why are there only two options? And why do neither of them feel right for me?'" Ashley leaned back. "My mom saw me hesitate, and we talked about it. And I guess after a while, I just figured if it wasn't a big deal to me or my mom, then why should it be a big deal to anyone else? So when I started first grade, I told my teacher 'they' and 'them' were the pronouns that made me feel good about myself."

"I think it's great you were able to tell the teachers about your pronouns," Millie said. "I'm too scared to correct them even when they say my name wrong."

"Standing up for yourself is like anything else—it takes practice." Ashley turned to Rainbow. "But it gets easier."

"Not for me," Rainbow said sadly. "My parents always say I'm extra-sensitive, and maybe I am. But when people are mean to me, I just want to disappear and never come back. Because the words—the meanness—it follows me around all the time. It becomes a permanent voice in my mind, playing on repeat." She shook her head. "I don't know how to turn that off."

"You shouldn't care what a few jerks think," Zuki offered. "One day, when we all graduate, you'll never have to see them again for the entire rest of your life."

Ashley nodded. "You just have to make the decision. That you're not going to let their words get through your armor."

Rainbow forced a thin smile, but her eyes were tired. Because they didn't get it. They didn't understand.

"It's not that easy," Millie said, and when Rainbow smiled gratefully, the words rushed out of her. "Because sometimes when people are mean, it makes you feel like you don't belong. Like someone is slamming a door in your face, and you have no idea what you even did. It makes you feel like you aren't welcome. And it's worse when you don't have any friends because there's nobody to tell you otherwise." She swallowed the lump in her throat, remembering her first week at Brightside Academy. Maybe it was easier for people to stand up for themselves when they had people behind them. A safe space to return to. But not everyone was lucky enough to have that kind of support. "Besides, being sensitive isn't necessarily a bad thing."

Ashley sniffed. "I'd rather protect my heart than risk someone hurting it, but that's just me."

"That sounds kind of lonely," Millie said. And she considered herself somewhat of an expert on being lonely.

Ashley shrugged like they didn't care. "What's the point in making friends when one day they'll ditch you for someone else anyway?" They shook their head. "They might even ditch you for people they don't even *like.*"

The others exchanged a glance. Luna wasn't there, but it was obvious who Ashley was referring to.

"I think of you as my friend," Millie offered.

Ashley raised an eyebrow.

"So do I," Zuki said, nudging them with her shoulder. "And Rainbow, too. Being in J-Club means we're automatically friends. Those are just the rules. And before you say anything about not liking rules or philosophies or *people*, for that matter, I'd like to remind you that I'm president. I can do what I want."

"That's not what a president is supposed to do," Ashley grumbled while everyone else laughed. "And if we're friends, then we're the most random bunch of friends in the history of the world."

Millie smiled. "I'm okay with that."

"Me too," Zuki said.

"Me too," Rainbow agreed.

And even though Ashley rolled their eyes, they didn't stop smiling.

CHAPTER TWENTY-FIVE

Millie's grades were terrible. Even though she'd gotten used to the routine of homework, it was too late in the quarter to bring her grades back up in any significant way.

She knew her parents would find out eventually. She knew it was only a matter of time before all her lies unraveled.

But she was so happy having friends and being in J-Club that she didn't want to think about report cards. The truth would come out eventually.

For now, Millie wanted to pretend everything in the world was as it should be.

CHAPTER TWENTY-SIX

"Repeat after me: *I don't care what you think.*" Ashley's hands were lifted up in front of their face. It reminded Millie of the way Mr. Thomas looked when he was conducting band.

Rainbow teetered in place like she was about to lose her balance. "I—I don't care what you think," she half mumbled, half whispered.

Ashley tutted. "No. You have to say it like you mean it. Like you're going into battle."

Rainbow cringed. "I don't want to go into battle."

Millie tried not to giggle, even when Ashley raised their hands higher and growled, "*I don't care what you think!*"

Rainbow took a deep breath and closed her eyes. "I. Don't. Care . . ." She wrinkled her face and chirped, "What you think?"

Ashley dropped their arms. "This is going to be a challenge."

Luna poked her head up from the front of the orchestra room. She and Zuki had been going through Generation Love videos to find choreography they wanted to mimic,

and until that moment, neither of them had even acknowl-
edged Ashley's mission to teach Rainbow how to stand up
for herself.

"You should try pretending you're talking to someone else.
Like instead of speaking to someone you're scared of, imagine you're speaking to someone you feel indifferent to." Luna
paused. "Like a cartoon troll who won't stop telling you weird
jokes."

Ashley looked offended. "That's *terrible* advice."

Luna pouted. "I'm only trying to help."

"If you want to help, why don't you tell Rainbow what Ruby
and Annabelle's weaknesses are? Everyone has one. And you're
on the inside," Ashley said.

Luna scowled in response. "I am not on the *inside*."

Ashley turned back to Rainbow. "Okay, one more time."

Rainbow's entire body wilted. "Please don't make me say it
again."

"You have to learn how to defend yourself," Ashley said
matter-of-factly. "And no offense, but you don't look like the
fighting type."

"Those aren't your only options," Luna interjected just as
Rainbow started to turn a panicked shade of carnation pink.
"You can also choose to ignore people."

Rainbow adjusted her glasses. "I—I'd probably be better at
that. I'm not really good at confrontation."

"But they won't leave you alone if you don't stick up for
yourself," Ashley argued gruffly.

"You're not leaving her alone either," Luna pointed out.

"She's scared," Ashley said. "I'm trying to help her overcome that."

"By making her do something she doesn't want to do?"

"*Someone* has to stick up for her."

"She can stick up for herself!"

"No, she can't!"

"Yes, she *can*!"

Luna and Ashley went back and forth with their words, again and again, and then they were talking over each other and Millie could barely differentiate between what was being said. All she knew was that neither of them was going to back down.

And then Rainbow *shouted*. "Stop talking about me!"

Everyone froze. Even Zuki looked up from her phone in alarm.

Rainbow's shoulders were shaking, and her eyes were as wide as full moons. "Please?" she added like an afterthought.

Ashley smirked. "See? I knew you had it in you."

Even though Rainbow was on the verge of tears, she let out a strained laugh. "I don't think I've ever shouted at someone before."

"I'm sorry," Luna said guiltily. "I didn't mean to upset you."

"Neither did I," Ashley admitted. "But I'm proud of you for using your voice."

Rainbow tugged at her sweater-vest. "Thanks. I—I think I'd be happier if I didn't have to use it again anytime soon, though. I feel a little light-headed."

"But now you know you *can* use it," Ashley pointed out, "if you ever need to."

Rainbow glanced at Millie nervously. "Is J-Club always so intense?" she whispered.

Millie snorted. "Honestly? Yes." And then she grinned. "But I kind of love how alive it makes me feel."

Warmth flooded Rainbow's eyes. "I think maybe I do, too."

"I've got it!" Zuki exclaimed like she'd just been catapulted from another world. "Okay, check this out. I think we should use the main choreography from the music video but combine that with the opening sequence from this live show." She pushed her phone out into the center of the room, and everyone gathered around to watch.

When the video ended, Millie beamed. "I love that idea!"

"I could work on coming up with some transitions as well," Luna said. "We obviously don't have all the extra backup dancers, so we'll need something a little cleaner for just the five of us."

Everyone began talking over top of one another, eager to provide input to make their new routine as strong as possible.

They may have been different pieces of the wrong puzzle, and maybe none of them quite fit the way they were expected to, but there was something bigger bringing them together. And it was more than just J-Club.

All Millie had wanted for years were friends who felt like family.

And maybe—just maybe—the universe had finally answered.

CHAPTER TWENTY-SEVEN

Pop Showcase auditions weren't far away, and J-Club was practicing harder than ever.

Millie was still fumbling over some of the dance steps, but that was mostly nerves. Because she *did* get nervous, even if she was around her friends. Playing the flute in front of people made her feel the same way—like messing up once would be the end of everything.

But Luna was a patient teacher. She made learning the steps feel like *she* was learning them, too, even though she was clearly the best dancer by miles. Millie didn't know how someone could be so talented and still have zero ego, but Luna managed it. She was nothing like Ruby and Annabelle. She was *kind*.

Millie wished the rest of the school could someday see that kindness, too.

"Try to keep this pose clean," Luna said, holding up her hands to show everyone. "It has to be sharp—like this."

They ran through the song two more times before taking a break to grab their water bottles.

"We should record the next run-through on my phone," Zuki suggested. "So we know what we need to work on, vocally." She looked at Millie seriously. "I think you need to sing just a little bit louder."

Millie's shoulders fell. "Sorry. I only used to sing Chiyo's parts at home. I'm still trying to remember the background parts."

"It's okay, you'll get there! Just don't be shy about it. It's probably way easier singing the background anyway since you're doing it with three other people." Zuki motioned to herself. "I have to sing lead, which means I'm under the most pressure. It's like Chiyo at the Sugar Flower Stadium. Do you remember when she was sick, and she still had to go onstage and perform in front of thousands of people? Everyone talked about how phenomenal she was for months!"

"That was one of the greatest live performances of all time," Rainbow said dreamily.

Ashley made a face. "But you aren't sick, so how is that the same thing?"

Zuki ignored them and focused on practicing her dance steps instead.

Luna took another sip of water. "Well, I'm *very* glad I don't have to do any solos. I can't imagine an entire auditorium listening to my voice." She shuddered.

"You dance in front of people all the time," Zuki pointed out, halfway through an eight-count.

"Yeah, but it's different. Singing is scary." Luna sighed. "I don't know how you do it, Rainbow. You're the shyest theater major I've ever met."

Rainbow shrugged awkwardly. "I never get picked for lead parts anymore, so it's not so bad when you're in a group. People are never watching me directly."

"You *should* get picked for a lead," Ashley said. "You're an amazing singer."

"Yeah," Millie and Luna agreed.

Rainbow blushed. "I always used to dream of singing a solo on a big stage. But it didn't go so well last time . . ."

"You threw up *once*," Ashley pointed out, waving their hand like it wasn't a big deal. "It's not a recurring thing. You were nervous."

"Other people get nervous," Rainbow squeaked. "What happens to me is more like an atomic bomb going off inside my chest."

"Oh, that reminds me!" Zuki exclaimed, clapping her hands. "I compared all of our personality quizzes and decided we each should take on a persona from Generation Love. It makes sense since we're an imitation band."

Rainbow looked confused. "Personality quiz?"

"Don't worry," Zuki said with a short laugh. "You weren't here when we did it, so I just filled out a form for you and guessed what your answers would be."

Ashley snorted. "Because that's not supercontrolling *at all*."

Zuki continued, oblivious to Ashley's remark and Rainbow's discomfort. "So obviously I'm Chiyo, and then Ashley is most like Ryoko—you both have short hair. And Rainbow is definitely Miyuki, who is like a quiet bookworm. And Luna is like

Hana, because she's outgoing and funny and she can dance. And Millie, you can be Asuka!"

Millie's heart pinged. "I thought you said I was Miyuki?"

"Huh? Oh, yeah, I changed that because Rainbow is way more shy than you are," Zuki explained.

Asuka was the supertrendy one who always wore pink and loved stuffed animals. She wasn't like Millie at all.

But Millie got the feeling the personas weren't up for negotiation. Zuki had already made the plan; everyone else was just supposed to follow it.

"Why am I Ryoko? Just because I have short hair?" Ashley argued. "Seems more like a physical thing than a personality thing."

"I think this will really help us practice. Because now when we watch the videos, we'll know who we're studying!" Zuki said enthusiastically.

"Well, I'm fine with Hana, even though I'm not sure anyone actually thinks I'm funny," Luna said.

"I don't mind if Millie would rather be Miyuki," Rainbow offered.

"No, it's fine." Millie smiled, too, just to make everyone feel better. "I'll be Asuka."

Zuki squealed. "Perfect! Should we run through the routine again?"

Everyone stood up, and when the music started and Luna counted them in, they performed in unison, voices blending in harmony while Zuki attempted to outsing everyone. She sounded pretty good—she only got the pitch wrong once during the chorus—and with the backing track, it was hardly noticeable.

But would it be enough to get them through the audition?

Millie hoped so. She wanted to believe they stood a chance. Because after all their hard work, J-Club was finally starting to fall into sync.

CHAPTER TWENTY-EIGHT

Millie's report card sat on the kitchen table, like evidence being displayed in a court case. Jane was sitting across from it, with heavy frown lines around her mouth and her forehead wrinkled with confusion.

Millie couldn't move. It felt like there was a rock lodged in her throat, and she couldn't get rid of it, no matter how many times she swallowed.

Scott closed the front door and hung up his keys. "I can't believe the traffic today. There must be a game on or something at the high school. I felt like we were at that stop sign for years!" When he turned the corner, his face fell. "What is it?"

Jane eyed the table, then Scott, then Millie.

Millie silently begged the universe to freeze time. Maybe even indefinitely.

"Millie's report card came in the mail today," Jane said. She stared at Millie with hard, serious eyes. "When were you going to tell us you were failing two of your classes? And getting Ds and Cs in almost everything else?"

"What?" Scott asked, flabbergasted. He marched over to the table and picked up the report card, reading it again and again like he didn't understand. "I thought you were getting mostly As?"

Millie's voice wobbled. "I just get confused about what I'm supposed to be doing sometimes. And I think I missed a few homework assignments."

"You haven't been doing your homework?" Jane asked. "I don't understand. Why on earth not?"

"You don't get Fs by missing a few homework assignments, Millie," Scott corrected. "This is unacceptable. What happened? How did your grades fall so much since progress reports?"

Tears pooled in Millie's eyes. "I—I don't know. School is just really hard. But I'm working on it. It's just an adjustment."

"An adjustment?" Scott shook his head. "You never missed assignments when we were homeschooling you. And I don't remember you ever telling us you were confused."

Jane sighed. "I'd say I'm glad you at least have an A in band, but I'm not sure anything on this report card deserves praise. This is terrible, Millie. We didn't raise you to just blow off doing your homework."

"That's not what I did," Millie tried to argue. "But the teachers don't always make it clear what we're supposed to do. They write assignments down on the board, but they don't tell you to look there—they just expect you to *know*. It took me a while to figure it out, and by then it was too hard to bring my grades up."

"But you had As," Scott said, holding up his hands. "So how does this happen? And how could your teachers not let us know you were failing so many classes?"

Millie burst into sobs. "Because I wasn't getting As. I—I just didn't want you to be mad at me."

Jane and Scott fell silent.

Millie was certain the temperature in the room had dropped.

"Did you forge your progress report?" Jane asked.

Millie nodded, tears streaming. "I'm sorry. But I didn't want you to be disappointed in me. Because I really am trying. I just needed more time to get the hang of school."

"We don't lie in this house, Millie." Scott clenched his jaw and shook his head. "How are we supposed to help you if we don't even know there's a problem? How are we supposed to *trust* you?"

Jane sighed. "Maybe Brightside Academy wasn't the best idea. I don't think Millie was ready for that kind of responsibility."

"No!" Millie blurted out. "My grades will be better next quarter. I *am* ready for school. I just needed some time!"

Jane and Scott exchanged a glance. They were having a silent conversation, which was the worst kind. It meant whatever they decided would be final, and Millie didn't get a say at all. She didn't even get the courtesy of listening to them work it out.

"You're grounded," Scott said finally. "No more Advanced Studies sessions until you get your grades up. Clearly you can't handle the extra workload, and I want you home every day after school, sitting at this table so we can all do homework together."

Jane's mouth was a thin line. "And if your grades don't improve, there will be a serious discussion about whether leaving you in school is the right thing."

"Okay," Millie managed to say between floods of tears. Her heart was sinking, sinking, sinking.

"And by grounded, we also mean no computer and no phone," Scott clarified, holding out his hand.

Millie handed him her phone, feeling like she was being torn from her friends—like she was one half of a discarded photo being tossed in the fire. Like her feelings didn't matter at all.

Millie knew she'd lied. She knew she'd done something wrong.

But right then, she felt like she had been wronged more than anyone in the world.

CHAPTER TWENTY-NINE

It was nearly lunchtime, and Millie still hadn't told any of her friends what had happened. Because she knew what was at stake.

She knew how much she'd be letting them down.

Millie stuffed her math textbook into her locker and bit the edge of her lip to keep it from wobbling.

"Um, Millie? Are you okay?" a quiet voice said from behind her.

Millie turned to see Luna. It wasn't unusual—most of the students stopped by their lockers before lunch to swap out their morning textbooks for their afternoon ones. But usually Luna was with Ruby and Annabelle, pretending nobody else in the world existed.

Except the other two were nowhere to be seen. It was just Luna, her brows knotted with concern even as her body language suggested she was on a time limit.

Millie shuffled her feet. She'd have to tell Luna and the others eventually. But maybe she could at least wait until there were fewer people around, just in case saying the words out loud caused Millie to burst into tears. "I'm fine. It's just . . . grades and stuff."

Luna smiled sheepishly. "Oh, right. I thought you were crying. I—I was worried something bad had happened."

Millie didn't know how to point out something bad *had* happened. She'd failed Math and Earth Science. Her parents had found out she'd lied about her progress report. And she'd been grounded quite possibly until the end of time.

But worst of all, she'd have to quit J-Club.

Luna had opened her mouth to say something else when a few students laughed nearby. She practically jumped in response until she realized they weren't looking at her. Still, she tightened her arms around herself and lowered her voice. "You know, you can always try asking your teachers for extra-credit assignments if you need to boost your grades."

Millie blinked. "The teachers will do that?"

"Not all of them, but some of them are happy to help if they know you're trying," Luna explained.

"I wish I'd known that last quarter," Millie admitted sadly. Why didn't teachers ever announce things like that? Were the students just expected to know? Was it some kind of *secret*?

Millie needed to do better in school. And she was going to try her best.

But wouldn't it be more helpful if someone at least gave her all the right tools, and pointed her in the right direction? Preferably *before* she failed any classes?

Luna looked thoughtful. "Hey, don't be too hard on yourself. If you do better this quarter, your semester grades will average out. And finals make up a huge percentage. You can still turn it around."

"There you are!" Ruby groaned. Annabelle was beside her looking extremely bored. "We've been waiting outside for like a million years."

Luna spun so quickly her hair nearly hit Millie in the face. "Sorry! I—I just had to check on something," she mumbled, flustered. She moved toward Ruby and Annabelle and hesitated, looking back over her shoulder. She held up a shaky hand, waving slightly, before the three of them hurried down the hall.

Millie tried not to let it bother her. She knew Luna was trying to balance two very different worlds. And deep down, Millie knew they were friends, even if it was a secret.

But Millie didn't want to be someone's secret friend. She wanted to be someone Luna was *proud* to call a friend.

Even though in that moment, as she stared into her locker and thought of her grades, and failing, and having to let everyone down, she didn't feel like someone who had all that much to be proud of.

With a heavy sigh, she collected her thoughts, shut her locker door, and headed to the courtyard for lunch.

Halfway through her plate of fries, Millie found the courage to tell everyone the truth.

"But what about Pop Showcase?" Zuki asked immediately. "Will they at least let you audition? The show is still months away. You'll be able to get your grades up before the performance."

"I don't think so," Millie said sadly. "They still don't know about J-Club. Maybe you all could audition without me?"

Zuki considered it.

"What happened to 'either we all do it or none of us do?'" Ashley pointed out grimly. "Besides, even if we make it through the audition, there are still rehearsals. If Millie can't stay after school, how are we supposed to be ready for the final performance?"

Rainbow gave Millie a weak smile. "I'm sorry you're in so much trouble, but don't worry about J-Club. We'll still be here when you aren't grounded. And if you need help getting your grades up, maybe I could help." She turned bright pink. "My grades are okay."

Ashley snorted. "Aren't you at the top of our class?"

The pink darkened to purple. "Oh," Rainbow said. "Yeah, I think so."

Millie was too sad to smile, but she tried anyway. "Thanks for the offer. I'd appreciate the help, but I don't know when we'd be able to study together. If I'm grounded from staying after school, I'm sure inviting you over to my house is out of the question." She looked around. "I'm really sorry, everyone."

Zuki blinked and sat up straight, like an actual light bulb had gone off above her head. "What if we rehearse during lunch?" She waved her hands excitedly. "It's perfect! It's not like any of us are stuck in class. And this way Millie won't be breaking her parents' rule."

Millie frowned. "Doesn't Ms. Jimenez have an orchestra class during our lunch hour?"

"We have somewhere even *better*." Zuki looked at Rainbow. "We could rehearse in the auditorium. Rainbow was eating lunch there for weeks, and nobody found her. We'd have total privacy!"

"*You* all technically found me," Rainbow pointed out.

Zuki rolled her eyes and laughed. "But the hall monitors didn't. It's genius!" She turned to Millie. "You won't be grounded forever. And even if we don't make the audition, at least this way we can keep J-Club going."

"That . . . could work," Ashley said with a slow nod.

Rainbow flashed a tiny smile. "I did always like hanging out in the auditorium."

Millie's heart flooded with relief. "Okay. Let's do it. Let's rehearse during lunch."

The leaves whistled overhead in response. Maybe everything was going to be okay after all.

Everyone exchanged a glance.

"Luna," they said quietly.

She'd never choose rehearsals over lunch with Ruby and Annabelle. Not when it would risk blowing her cover.

"I'll text her," Zuki said, typing quickly on her phone. "I'll tell her it's an emergency—that J-Club is depending on her."

Even though the read receipt showed that Luna had seen the message, there were no dots to show she was typing. No icon to indicate what she was thinking.

She seemed a world away from them, and Millie felt her heart sink. If Luna refused to come to rehearsals, everyone else would blame her for the death of J-Club. And that wouldn't be fair.

Because it was Millie's fault. She'd ruined J-Club, just like she'd ruined the Pop Showcase audition.

She'd let everyone down.

CHAPTER THIRTY

The weather shifted once again. Frost appeared on the glass in the mornings. Millie started to wear her thick coat to school—the one with the furry hood. And it was too cold to sit in the court-yard for very long.

But with J-Club meeting in the theater during lunch every day, Millie didn't have to worry about the cold. She did, how-ever, have other things to worry about. Her grades were improv-ing, but not fast enough for her parents' liking. Luna was only making it to one or two rehearsals a week, which made it diffi-cult to practice as a group. And the Pop Showcase audition was days away.

It was looking less and less likely they'd make it.

But the worst part was seeing how much it was affecting Zuki. She'd been so hopeful at the start that everything would sort itself out. But she'd underestimated Millie's parents and Luna's loyalty to her dance-major friends.

Millie had never thought of Zuki as someone who wore armor,

the way Ashley did. But she was starting to think she'd been wrong—and that maybe Zuki's armor had started to crack, just as it had all those weeks ago when Ashley had implied J-Club didn't have a purpose.

She'd lost her friend for an entire weekend back then. Would it be the same this time around? And was there anything Millie could do to stop it?

"Is your arm okay?" Rainbow asked softly. Almost too softly for anyone else to hear.

Zuki was adjusting one of her layers of bracelets. When she realized Rainbow was looking at her, she yanked her sleeve down.

"Yeah, it's fine," Zuki mumbled, moving across the stage to where she'd left her phone. "Let's run through the routine one more time."

Millie frowned. "Did something happen to your arm?"

"I just bruise easily, that's all," Zuki said quickly, before forcing her face into a smile. "Okay, from the top?"

Ashley stared up at the clock. "The bell is going to ring soon."

"We have enough time to run through it again," Zuki repeated. "I need to make sure the intro vocals are perfect. It has to be right."

"What does it matter?" Ashley shrugged. "We all agreed we're not doing the audition without Millie. And we keep messing up the choreography without Luna here. The only point of doing this was to have fun. It's not supposed to be this serious."

"It is to *me*," Zuki snapped.

Ashley's eyes widened in surprise.

Zuki looked flustered. "You're acting like none of this matters anymore, but it does. You don't know what's going to happen on Friday. Or any day! Maybe we *will* make the audition. Which means we have to keep practicing. We can't just give up. So stop acting like a—a—" She paused. "Like a shriveled-up burnt marshmallow!"

Ashley blinked.

The bell rang, and Zuki threw her arms in the air. "Forget it!" She snatched up her phone and her orange backpack and marched out of the theater without even waiting for Millie.

Ashley held up their hands innocently. "I didn't do anything."

"I don't think it's you," Rainbow said slowly. "Zuki's been on edge all week." She seemed to be wrestling with her thoughts. "Which parent did she stay with last weekend?"

Millie frowned. "Her dad, I think. Why?"

Rainbow looked embarrassed. "Oh. Um, no reason, I guess. She just . . . always seems a little more stressed when she's at her dad's."

Millie opened her mouth to argue but realized she had nothing to say. Maybe it *was* true.

Was she a bad friend for not noticing it sooner?

Millie pulled her backpack onto her shoulders. "I'll go and talk to her."

She hurried out onto the sidewalk, casting her eyes toward the crowd of students moving across the street. She squinted, searching the cold landscape for her friend, but she couldn't find her.

☆ ★ ☆

Millie could tell something was wrong during band, because Kelly and Dia didn't pass each other a single note. When everyone started putting their instruments away and Mr. Thomas appeared in front of Millie's music stand, she finally found out why.

"Dia has filled in a form to challenge you for second chair," he explained. "The audition will include two scales and a selection from our band repertoire. Make sure you're both practicing all your music, because you won't know what I've picked until the audition. Can you make it after school on Friday? It shouldn't take long."

Millie's stomach somersaulted. Dia was beside her, packing her backpack and not making eye contact. She wasn't technically doing anything wrong—everyone had the right to chair challenges. But that didn't make them any less awkward. Because they involved taking something from someone else; and regardless of who succeeded, both people still had to sit next to each other for the rest of the year.

At least with sports, kids were taught to be gracious at winning and losing. Band felt positively ruthless in comparison.

Millie hated auditions, and playing in front of people, and the possibility of failure. She hated it so much that she wished she could just hand over the chair and forfeit.

But what would her parents say?

Millie remembered Mr. Thomas was still staring at her. "Friday is fine," she said.

The band director nodded. "Great. Thanks, Millie."

Dia and Kelly stood up and walked toward the lockers, their mouths moving in rapid-fire like they'd been waiting the entire class to finally speak.

Millie didn't share their excitement. The worst had yet to come.

Because Millie still had to tell her parents the news.

Millie managed to make it all the way through dinner without mentioning band. It wasn't easy—especially when Jane and Scott kept talking about flute lessons, and band concerts, and a new solo book they'd ordered in the mail.

After dinner they put on a movie—something with subtitles—and her parents made an enormous bowl of buttered popcorn and sprinkled it with M&M's. It was another one of their family traditions.

Millie should've found the salty-sweet combination comforting, but instead she couldn't get the thought of Friday out of her head. When the credits appeared on the screen, she found the courage to speak.

"The third-chair flutist challenged me in band," Millie said as her parents were shuffling off the couch.

Jane looked up, immediately engrossed. Why was her interest only ever reserved for music? "How are you feeling? Are you nervous?"

"I know you'll do great, Millie. These things happen, but you'll be able to keep your chair," Scott said reassuringly.

Millie bit the inside of her cheek. "I have to stay late on Friday for the chair challenge. Mr. Thomas says he's going to pick a random section and have us both play it."

Scott slapped a hand against his knee. "Well, that's perfect! You know all those pieces by heart. You'll be fine."

Jane smiled. "We could go out to celebrate afterward. Get ice cream sundaes at the outlet mall?"

They were so confident she'd do well. So sure she wouldn't fail.

There was no room to make any mistake at all.

"I guess so," Millie said.

"Maybe you can challenge the first chair flute after this. It's good to take this kind of thing seriously—one chair could make the difference between getting a solo or not," Scott pointed out.

Jane looked elated. "It would be great to go to your first band concert and hear you featured. Wouldn't that be so fun?"

"Sure," Millie said, tugging at her pajama bottoms. "I'm going to bed. I'm pretty tired."

Jane stood up and gave Millie a hug. "I love you. See you in the morning."

Scott did the same and kissed Millie on the forehead. It made it so much harder to be angry with them, but Millie had to be. Because if she wasn't angry, why did she feel so unhappy?

She spent hours staring at the ceiling, thinking about Friday and how much her heart was already racing. Two more days. Two more days until she'd give her parents another reason to be proud or disappointed.

There was no in-between. There was no room to breathe.

But somewhere, in all the darkness, a little light appeared in her mind. Because Friday was also the Pop Showcase audition. And Dia may have inadvertently just given her the perfect excuse to make it.

Maybe losing her chair could be the thing to solve all her problems.

Millie desperately wanted to text Zuki, but she still didn't have her phone back *or* access to her parents' computer. So instead she watched the shadows flicker across the room and daydreamed about how happy her friends would be when she told them the next day that their band had been saved.

CHAPTER THIRTY-ONE

"Whenever you're ready," Mr. Thomas said.

Millie's heart was going to burst out of her. It felt like a roar of thunder building in her rib cage, ready to explode at any moment. Her palms had gone clammy, and her fingers were trembling like the room was freezing, even though she felt like she was burning up at least a million degrees.

Somehow, she managed to take a breath. She played the first note. It came out clear, which was a good start. Halfway through the song, Millie wondered if maybe she wasn't doing too bad.

But then her nerves caught up with her. A high note cracked, her breath faltered, and then her fingers fumbled to fix what couldn't be undone. She tried to keep going—that was a rule in auditions, to make a mistake part of the song—but the tempo was off, and she'd missed a sharp, and her heart was racing so fast that her playing had become panicked.

When the song ended, she knew. She could see it in Mr. Thomas's face.

She'd messed up.

"Thanks, Millie. I'll post results on Monday," he said with a patient smile.

Millie left the office and spotted Dia in the band room, concentrating on her sheet music in silence.

"Dia, come on in," Mr. Thomas said from the doorway.

Millie took her flute apart and managed to squeeze the case into her backpack, and on her way out the door, she heard Dia begin to play.

She sounded flawless.

But Millie didn't have time to be disheartened. She raced across the campus as fast as she could, toward the choir room where everyone was waiting to audition for Pop Showcase.

Zuki's face flooded with relief. "Oh, thank goodness! We thought you weren't going to make it."

"There are three auditions in front of us," Luna said. She spun her curly hair into a bun and tied it into place. "Maybe we could run through the routine one more time?"

"Please, no," Ashley moaned. "This is how people psych themselves out. We know the dance. We've practiced a million times."

"We haven't gone over it together all week," Luna pointed out.

"That's because you won't come to lunch rehearsals," Ashley quipped.

Luna clamped her mouth shut. She'd been pretty good at not acknowledging how infrequently she attended rehearsals. Maybe she was hoping if nobody brought it up, her problem would suddenly vanish.

Millie knew the feeling.

"How did your audition go?" Rainbow asked quietly.

Millie sighed. "Terrible. I definitely flubbed it. I just hate performing in front of people."

Ashley lifted their shoulders. "Really? You say that *right before our audition*?"

Everyone laughed.

"This is different," Millie promised. "I'll be with all of you."

Zuki was beaming. "We've got this, everyone. I know we do. I feel it in my bones!" She held out her hand in front of her, palm down. "On three?"

Ashley groaned. "Hard pass on the secret handshake."

Millie put her hand over Zuki's, and Rainbow and Luna followed suit.

They looked at Ashley expectantly.

"Fine," they muttered, and clapped their hand over the others'.

"One, two, three . . . ," Zuki started.

"J-Club!" they all shouted at once.

CHAPTER THIRTY-TWO

The Pop Showcase announcement sheet was hanging from the choir room doors on Monday morning. There was a crowd around it, like honeybees swarming to a single flower.

It made Millie nervous to see so many people, all desperate for the same good news. Because there were only so many spots on the list.

So many people in the crowd would walk away feeling disappointed. And Millie didn't want that for her friends. *Or* for herself.

When the path cleared, they inched closer to the posted results. Zuki grabbed Millie's hand and squeezed hard. She heard Luna take a breath. Rainbow and Ashley were so still she wasn't sure they were breathing at all.

At first, everyone simply stared in silence. Millie didn't know what to look for, exactly.

But then she saw it. One line, two rows from the bottom:

J-Club — "Sugar Pop" by Generation Love.

Zuki shrieked. Millie and Rainbow hugged. Ashley smirked.

And Luna jumped up and down, as if it was impossible for her to contain her joy.

"We're in!" Zuki raised her hands and smiled as wide as the sky. "I knew it, I knew it, I knew it!"

The group fell into a chorus of laughter and congratulatory squeals—with Ashley mostly trying not to smile with their teeth, even though sometimes they couldn't help it. Even Luna wasn't afraid to celebrate in public.

They'd wanted this. They'd worked hard for it.

"We have to rehearse every day at lunch," Zuki insisted. "We have to make our performance *spectacular*!"

Luna relaxed slightly. "I—I'll try my best. But I don't know if I can make it every day."

The energy dimmed just a little. And when Millie remembered the results for her flute audition would be posted nearby, too, the energy fizzled out completely.

"Does anyone want to come with me to the band room?" she asked gloomily.

"Of course we will," Rainbow said, and the others nodded to show their support.

The five of them made their way around the building until they found the band room doors. The updated chair placement list was taped up for everyone to see.

Millie Nakakura—third chair.

She'd known it was coming. Her audition had gone horribly wrong in every way possible. But seeing the words in print felt like someone had sucked all the air from her lungs. All she could see was her parents' faces and the word *failure* flashing above them.

"It's okay," Rainbow said. "It's just one chair. You could always challenge them back."

A weight pressed down on Millie's shoulders. "You don't understand. When my parents find out, they're going to put even more pressure on me. Because now on top of my grades, I'm doing badly in band, too. I'll be grounded for the rest of the school year." *If they even let me stay in school*, she thought.

After a few seconds, Ashley piped up. "How do your parents feel about after-school tutoring?"

Millie frowned. "I mean, they made me quit my imaginary Advanced Studies club . . ."

"But that's not the same as tutoring. Tutoring would help with your grades, not give you extra work," Ashley clarified.

"I can't tell them another lie," Millie said.

"It wouldn't *be* a lie." Ashley shrugged. "There'd be a teacher there and everything, three days a week. I could make sure you fixed your grades in time for Pop Showcase."

"I could help, too," Rainbow offered.

"It would have to be official," Millie said slowly. "In a classroom. With someone my parents could talk to if they wanted to. And even then, they still might not agree to it."

Ashley looked like that wasn't a problem at all. "My mom is a teacher here. That's why I'm always around after school."

So *that* was how Ashley had been helping them all this time— they had someone on the inside.

"This explains so much," Zuki said with huge eyes.

The morning bell rang, and Luna lifted her hand in a wave. "I'll see you later!" she said before hurrying away toward the dance rooms.

Rainbow waved, too. "I have Geography first. I'll see you at lunch?"

"I'll walk with you," Zuki said, falling into step beside her. "And cheer up, Millie! We're in Pop Showcase!" She waved both her hands, her rainbow-colored bracelets dancing against her wrists.

Millie smiled despite her heavy heart and watched the two of them walk away. She turned to Ashley. "Thank you. For always trying to help. Sometimes it feels like you're secretly a superhero." Ashley laughed, but Millie continued. "You try hard to be kind, even though you say you don't want friends or that you don't like clubs. And I don't know why that is, but I just want you to know you mean a lot to me."

"I guess I kind of forgot what it felt like to have friends," Ashley admitted. "But J-Club—and all of you—you're making me feel like it's okay to let my guard down once in a while."

Millie smiled. "See you at lunch?"

Ashley threw a thumbs-up. "See you later, friend."

CHAPTER THIRTY-THREE

Mrs. Seo taught journalism, and although Millie had never had an interest in newspapers, she was actually looking forward to being tutored by Ashley's mom. Because it turned out she was the nicest teacher at Brightside Academy.

"You must be Millie," Mrs. Seo said with a big smile. "I've spoken with your parents, and they said you'll be coming Mondays, Wednesdays, and Fridays. Is that right?" When Millie nodded, Mrs. Seo motioned to a Tupperware container on her desk. "I made brownies, if you need a snack—they're vegan and nut-free!"

Millie took one of the brownies and found a seat at the front of the class. It seemed weird to sit anywhere else since Millie was the only student in the classroom.

Most teachers talked to Millie while they were looking down at her. It always made her feel small, and like she was being scolded. But Mrs. Seo sat on the chair beside her and rested her chin on her fist.

"So. Having a tough time with homework, huh?" Mrs. Seo

scrunched her nose. "I remember the feeling. I used to really struggle with math when I was your age, and it took me years to finally tell the teacher I needed extra help."

Millie lifted her eyebrows. "Really?" It seemed too weird to think teachers weren't always great at school. At *learning*.

"Oh, absolutely. But you're smarter than I am because you're not waiting years to ask for help. And I'm really proud of you for that."

Millie stared at the brownie on her desk and relaxed into a smile. "Thanks."

"How about we go over your classwork, starting with first period, and see what we need to put more focus on? Does that sound okay?" Mrs. Seo asked.

Millie pulled out her binder. When she opened it to her homework section, she paused. "It's—it's not always the material I need help with. It's more the rules."

"What do you mean?" Mrs. Seo asked gently.

"Well, sometimes the teachers don't explain things very well. I feel like there are a lot of things the other kids just *know* about. Maybe because they've always gone to school. Things like how to write your name on the top corner of every page, with the date and class and assignment, and how you have to look for homework assignments on the board even if the teacher doesn't tell you about them. And how you have to turn in your homework into the baskets without being asked in some classes, but in other classes you have to hand them to the teacher when they ask for them." Millie pushed her brownie around nervously.

"And I feel like the teachers assume that I'm just not trying hard enough, so they look at me like I'm a bad student. It makes me embarrassed to say anything."

"I'm sorry you've been feeling that way for so long. I'm sure that's been really hard. But I want you to know that you should *always* say something," Mrs. Seo said. "If you're struggling or feeling uncomfortable, or just don't understand what's being asked of you—speak up. I know that's hard at your age—it's hard for grown-ups sometimes, too—but learning to advocate for ourselves is so important. You should never feel embarrassed to look after yourself."

Millie sat with her words for a moment. "I guess that makes sense. I just don't want to get in trouble."

"Your teachers are here because they want to help you learn." Mrs. Seo offered a smile. "And I don't think there's a single teacher I know who would be mad at a student just because they asked for help. Maybe try it next time, even if it's scary? And if it's still too hard, you can always come and talk to me. I'll sort it out."

"You'd really do that?" Millie asked. "Even though I'm not in journalism?"

Mrs. Seo folded her hands into her lap. "My door is open to any student who needs it. And speaking of students . . ." Her eyes trailed toward the doorway. "Are you two here to study, or because you heard about the brownies?"

Millie followed her gaze to Ashley and Rainbow, who were standing several yards away. Ashley's hands were tucked firmly in their pockets, their backpack hanging from one shoulder. Rainbow was tugging at the edge of her sweater and staring at anything and everything *but* Mrs. Seo.

"We, um—to study?" Rainbow turned a deep shade of magenta and pushed her glasses up the bridge of her nose.

Ashley was so used to Rainbow's nerves that they barely reacted anymore. "We're here to help Millie."

Mrs. Seo lifted a brow. "Oh? I didn't know you were interested in tutoring."

Ashley strode through the classroom with Rainbow close behind. "I'm not. But we have most of the same teachers, so it makes sense to do our homework together if we both have to be here anyway."

Mrs. Seo looked at Millie knowingly. "I'm happy to see Ashley's making some new friends."

Ashley rolled their eyes, but the hint of a smile appeared at the corner of their mouth.

Mrs. Seo curved her neck and smiled at Rainbow. "Welcome! Just take a seat and make yourself comfortable, okay? Millie and I were just about to get started."

They worked through Millie's classes one by one, and Rainbow and Ashley generously chimed in whenever Millie had questions about assignments or class rules. Mrs. Seo seemed more concerned about Millie herself than about her grades, which somehow made all the difference in the world. And by the end of the tutoring session, Millie felt more informed than she'd been since the start of school.

Even though it wasn't J-Club, it was still something she had to look forward to.

☆ ★ ☆

Tutoring carried on three times a week, and it didn't take long for Millie to notice the changes. School felt easier. She stopped missing assignments. She understood the *rules.* And if she had a question about homework, she had people she could ask for help.

It felt like the safety net she'd always needed. And the best part was that she still got to see her friends.

Ashley and Rainbow rarely missed a session. Sometimes Zuki came by, too. She wasn't as interested in tutoring, but she did like the snacks, and it gave her a chance to do her homework. It also seemed like she was never in a hurry to get home. Millie hadn't noticed it before—Zuki was always so excited and happy—but there was something about the way she'd watch the clock and her shoulders would sink as the hour got later that made Millie wonder why Zuki seemed to dread leaving school.

Rainbow nodded encouragingly as she read over Millie's answers. "This looks great! You'll have no problem on the test."

Millie smiled. "Thanks, Rainbow."

"You're a really fast learner," Zuki pointed out, and Millie couldn't help but latch on to the compliment. "I bet that's because you were homeschooled. There's a kid in seventh grade—Jeremy

Cortez—who was homeschooled until fourth grade, and he was the same. He's our age, but they moved him up a year because all his classes were just too easy for him."

"Oh yeah," Rainbow agreed before Millie could say anything. "I have a cousin who is homeschooled, too. He's way smarter than me, *and* he's two years younger. I think his parents are going to let him graduate superearly." She smiled at Millie. "You never know, after all these tutoring sessions, the teachers might decide to move you up a grade, too!"

Millie didn't want to switch grades. All her friends were in sixth grade, and it had taken her long enough to find them. Besides, she doubted Jeremy Cortez and Rainbow's cousin had made as many mistakes as Millie had.

Maybe homeschooling had never been the problem. Maybe it had been Millie all along.

But Mrs. Seo had told her that every student learned a little differently, so maybe it didn't really matter where the problem came from, as long as Millie was able to solve it.

And with tutoring, she felt like she finally was.

"I'm happy where I am," Millie said truthfully. "I only just got to school—I don't want to rush it and miss out on spending time with my friends."

Rainbow sighed. "Sometimes I wish I was homeschooled. I bet it's nice not to have to see people you don't want to."

"I guess." Millie could see the benefit of avoiding people like Ruby and Annabelle. But still. She liked going to school and seeing people and being a part of something bigger than her own little world. "I always thought being homeschooled was kind of lonely, though."

"Didn't you go to any homeschool clubs?" Ashley asked.

Millie frowned. "What are those?"

Zuki jumped in. "Oh, Jeremy used to talk about them all the time when he first started Brightside! He went to one for volleyball and another for reading. I think there was even one for video games, which seems totally weird. But I guess they have to come up with different ways for them to socialize."

"I had no idea something like that even existed," Millie said, trying to hide the sadness in her voice. Maybe she would've enjoyed being homeschooled more if her parents had given her a chance to meet other kids. But to them, socializing just wasn't a priority.

And maybe some kids, like Rainbow, weren't as bothered about meeting people. But Millie craved it. It was why she loved to read the Generation Love forums so much. She liked what it felt like to have something in common with someone else. She liked the connection.

Millie felt guilty for thinking it, but the truth was, she had never liked being homeschooled. She'd spent most of her time feeling like she was missing out on the real world. She'd felt cut off from people her own age. Maybe people like Jeremy Cortez loved it, and were supersmart and made friends easily. But that wasn't Millie's experience.

"All I know is that I was homeschooled for six years and I never want to go back," Millie said firmly. She looked between

Zuki, Ashley, and Rainbow. "And hopefully, if I keep my grades up, I won't have to."

Ashley kept their eyes pinned to Millie. Rainbow and Zuki smiled.

And Millie didn't know how, but she could feel what they were thinking. It was why they were going out of their way to help her.

They didn't want Millie to leave Brightside Academy either.

CHAPTER THIRTY-FOUR

At lunchtime, Millie hurried to the courtyard to meet her friends.

"Sorry I'm late." She motioned behind her, even though the classrooms were out of sight. "I forgot one of my textbooks and had to run back to get it." She looked between Rainbow and Ashley and frowned. "Where's Zuki?"

Rainbow hesitated. "She, um, said she'd meet us in the theater."

Millie blinked. She wasn't *that* late. And they always walked together. Why wouldn't Zuki wait?

Ashley ran a hand through their hair, scuffing up the waves. "She said something about 'punctuality' and 'commitment' and ran off. I think she's in one of her moods."

"I know she's stressed out about Pop Showcase," Millie said carefully. "Maybe she's just worried about the performance?"

"That's months away." Ashley shook their head. "I think it's something else."

"What else could it be?" Millie couldn't imagine something being wrong and Zuki not telling her.

Rainbow scratched her arm nervously. "Maybe—maybe it's

something to do with her family?" She paused, seeming unsure whether she was saying too much. "She did have kind of a weird reaction when I asked if her parents were going to come to the performance."

Millie opened her mouth to ask what she meant when a nearby voice cut in.

"Rainbow! Is it true you auditioned for Pop Showcase?"

Everyone turned to find Annabelle, Ruby, and Luna standing a few feet away, dance bags hanging from their shoulders. Luna fidgeted with the strap like she didn't exactly know where to look.

Rainbow paled instantly. "Um. Yeah. I did."

Ashley crossed their arms, voice smooth as silk. "She didn't just audition. She got *in.*"

Ruby sneered. "Did someone feel sorry for you, or is there a bet going around about whether you'll vomit onstage again?"

"Come on, guys," Luna said, and her friends' eyes snapped toward her. She winced, but continued. "I'm hungry, and the line is probably getting long."

Ruby turned back to Rainbow, barely missing a beat. "I remember when you actually had to be talented to get into Pop Showcase. I guess they're just letting anyone in these days."

Rainbow trembled like an animal caught in the cold. Millie wanted to hug her, but she was afraid it would make it worse.

"Last I checked, I didn't see either of *your* names on the list," Ashley said coolly. "So I guess they still have *some* standards."

Annabelle scowled. "You think you're so—"

"Stop, seriously," Luna interrupted, shifting her weight from one leg to the other. "Let's just leave them alone."

Ruby scoffed. "Since when do you care about sticking up for these losers?"

"Yeah," Annabelle said, one hand on her hip.

Luna clenched her jaw. "I just—it's getting old, you know? And I'm—I'm—" She cast a look at Millie and her friends. "I'm *hungry*."

Ruby and Annabelle burst out laughing.

"*Hangry* is more like it, you grouch," Ruby said, and shoved Luna's shoulder playfully. Although Luna didn't look like she appreciated it very much.

Annabelle flicked her hair over her shoulder. "Come on then. Let's get you fed before you completely lose it." She stuck her nose up and peered down at Rainbow. "Otherwise next thing you know, you'll be the one telling us Rainbow Chan deserved to get in." She looped her arms through Luna's and Ruby's and guided them toward the cafeteria.

Just before Luna stepped inside, she glanced over her shoulder and offered a barely there smile. An apology. And then she was gone.

Rainbow's expression was cracked in half. There was sadness there and so much fear.

Millie touched her arm. "Are you okay?"

Rainbow nodded once, twice, and then a breath exploded out of her. "I hate this cafeteria so much."

Ashley was still. "I know."

"I'm sorry," Millie said.

Rainbow looked up meekly. "Can we go now? I—I'll feel better once we're rehearsing."

All of them stood up and hurried across the courtyard toward the theater. When they were safe inside and reunited with Zuki, they flooded the room with Generation Love and danced until their sides ached. Millie didn't even mind that Zuki was acting even bossier than usual. It was a good distraction.

Because Millie was struggling to push the image of Luna walking away from them out of her mind.

CHAPTER THIRTY-FIVE

Millie's fingers were sticky with glue. She wiped them on a paper towel; it left bits of paper stuck to her skin, but at least she could grab hold of the last Generation Love cutout without ruining the picture.

She smeared another few lines across the back of the photo with a glue stick and then placed the picture carefully over her binder. Pressing down, she counted to five and sat back to admire her work.

Her school binder was no longer covered in Pokémon. Instead, it was layered with stickers and magazine pictures of Generation Love (mostly Chiyo). In the center, surrounded by a rainbow heart identical to the one in Generation Love's logo, was Millie's name.

Zuki will love this, she thought, and wished she could send her friend a text.

There was a knock at the door, and Millie jumped up to turn the stereo down. It was her dad's old one, and even though it looked ancient, it was a lifesaver when she didn't have her phone for listening to music.

Jane poked her head through the doorway. "Hey, sweet pea. Your dad and I were thinking about watching a movie. I've got popcorn and M&M's ready to go. Want to join us?"

Millie's fingers felt tacky as she wove them together. "Actually, I was wondering if I could borrow your laptop? I wanted to practice a dance routine, but I need to see the music video to remember the steps."

Jane's mouth turned downward. "A dance routine? Is this for school?"

Millie shook her head. "No. It's just for fun." She waited for her mom to react with disapproval and to remind her that she was still grounded, but to her surprise, she didn't.

"Well, that sounds like good exercise. You can borrow my laptop. But make sure you bring it back downstairs when you're done with it." She paused, staring at the scraps of magazine pages and paper littering the carpet. "You really do love that group, huh?"

"Yeah," Millie said softly. "And so does Zuki. We both decided to redecorate our binders over the weekend." She motioned to the spare rainbow heart in the corner. "I was going to ask her if she wanted me to make one with her name, too, but I forgot I didn't have my phone. I might make it anyway and give it to her on Monday."

Jane leaned against the doorframe. "You've been really good

about keeping up with your homework. I think tutoring was a good idea."

Millie didn't say anything, but she felt her mom watching her, like she was mulling something over. Finally, Jane spoke again.

"Okay. You can have your phone back. But *only* over the weekends. And only as long as your grades stay up," Jane said.

Millie's smile grew and grew. "Really? I'm not grounded anymore?"

"You're not *not* grounded," Jane clarified. "But I think you've earned a few privileges back." She smiled. "It's in the drawer next to my laptop. And if you change your mind about the movie, we'll be downstairs in the living room."

As soon as Jane left, Millie ran to the office. She didn't bother with the laptop at all—she was too excited to have her phone back.

When she was in her room, she plugged her charging cable in and sank onto the edge of the bed. Swiping her thumb against the screen, she immediately started to type a message to Zuki, but then she hesitated.

It had been such a long time since she'd had the ability to communicate with her friends outside of school that she didn't want to just text. She wanted to *talk*.

So Millie hit the call button and waited for Zuki to pick up.

There was a shuffle on the other end of the phone. "Hello?" Zuki's voice sounded strange. It didn't have the energy it usually did.

"It's me!" Millie exclaimed, and waited for the familiar sound of her friend's voice. But it wasn't there. "Oh. Hey." Zuki paused, distracted. There was a lot of background noise that sounded like the television was on full blast on the other side of a wall. "You got your phone back."

"Only on weekends, but still," Millie continued. Maybe Zuki was just tired. She'd probably feel loads better once Millie told her about the binder. "Guess what I've been working on all day?"

Zuki shuffled again, like she was muffling the phone with her hand. It did nothing to hide the noise, but Millie didn't mind. She was thrilled to finally have a way to reach her friend.

When Zuki didn't reply, Millie couldn't hold it in any longer. "I decorated my binder! How does yours look? Did you cut out magazine photos? I used some, but a lot of the images were printed off the computer, because it's hard to get magazine clippings of Generation Love, and a lot of the magazines I have were ones I didn't want to ruin. And I was going to make you something, but you have to leave some room in the center of your binder, for your name!"

The background noise grew louder, like the tremors of a bass building at a concert. A sudden *thump* carried through the phone.

Millie frowned. "What was that?"

"Um," Zuki started, voice quivering. "It's not really a good time. Can I call you back later?"

Millie's heart sank a little. She'd thought Zuki would be more excited to hear from her. "Yeah, of course," she said. "But . . . is everything okay?"

"*Zuki!*" someone shouted from behind a wall somewhere.

"What did I tell you about locking this door?" The voice was guttural and loud. The person sounded angry. And Millie wondered if the background noise hadn't been a television at all.

"I gotta go. Bye," Zuki whispered, and the call went silent.

Millie waited for her to call back, but she didn't. She sent a text instead, but Zuki never replied.

After a while, Millie got back to work on the logo for Zuki's binder and hoped that when she gave it to her on Monday, everything would feel like it was normal again.

CHAPTER THIRTY-SIX

When Zuki didn't show up to school on Monday, Millie thought it was strange. She'd never been absent before. In fact, she was one of the only people Millie knew who *missed* being at school over the weekends.

When Zuki didn't show up to school on Tuesday either, Millie started to worry.

On Wednesday during lunch, Luna stepped onto the theater stage with a raised eyebrow.

"Still not here?" she asked.

Everyone shook their heads.

"My parents only let me have my phone back on weekends, so I can't text her." Millie squeezed her hands tight. "Do you think it's something serious?"

"I tried texting her—she hasn't replied," Ashley said.

"Should we ask someone?" Rainbow looked around. "I mean, if she's sick, maybe her teachers will know at least?"

"Doesn't she have, like, perfect attendance every year? She

gets one every time they give out those awards at assembly. I doubt a cold would keep her away from school." Luna frowned, dropping her bag near the others and sitting cross-legged beside Ashley. It wasn't the first time they'd sat next to each other, but usually there was at least four feet of empty space between them.

Judging by the way Ashley's shoulders stiffened, it hadn't gone unnoticed.

"Luna's right. Zuki loves being at school," Millie said. "Maybe it's something more serious? Like the flu?"

"Can't you still text if you have the flu?" Rainbow asked.

Luna and Ashley shrugged like they had no idea.

"We should at least ask her teachers for her homework so she doesn't fall behind," Rainbow said quietly. "Maybe we could drop it off at her house. Then we'd also be able to check on her." She turned to Millie. "Where does Zuki live?"

"I—I'm not sure," Millie admitted. Zuki had never invited her over before. In fact, she rarely talked about her home life at all. Was that strange?

Ashley hadn't told anyone their mom was a teacher, but Ashley had also made their stance on friendships and secrecy very clear. Zuki, on the other hand, was always an open book.

Except maybe she wasn't.

"I'll talk to my mom," Ashley offered. "Maybe she's heard something."

Nobody felt like rehearsing without Zuki.

It just wasn't the same without her.

Zuki didn't show up to school on Thursday or Friday either. But on Saturday night, Millie got a text.

Zuki: Hey! Did you hear that Chiyo is dating the lead singer from Hotaru? I'm OBSESSED!!!

Millie: Where have you been? Are you okay?

Zuki: Yeah, I'm fine. I'll be back on Monday! Okay, I'm sending you a photo of Chiyo and her boyfriend.

Zuki: THEY'RE SO ADORABLE.

Millie: But where were you all week? Were you sick? I was worried.

Millie watched as a photo popped up, and then another, and another. It pushed their conversation out of view.

Maybe that was the point.

Millie didn't want to keep asking about something Zuki clearly didn't want to talk about, so she gushed about Chiyo's new relationship with her and tried to forget all about it.

Zuki returned to school on Monday, just like she'd said she would, and things went back to normal. She didn't answer questions about where she had been or what had happened. And she didn't explain why she had to see the school counselor three times in one week.

But she was herself again. She seemed happy.

So Millie didn't push it.

☆ ★ ☆

In December, semester report cards arrived in the mail. Millie had a mix of As and Bs. She'd aced every single one of her exams.

Her parents said there was still room for improvement, but Millie tried not to care.

She was proud of herself. Prouder than she'd ever been when it came to flute.

Mrs. Seo said people needed to advocate for themselves. Maybe that meant being kind to themselves, too.

So Millie decided it didn't matter if there was room for improvement. In that moment, she let her heart celebrate how far she'd come. She celebrated the friendships she'd built along the way. And she celebrated how, secret or not, J-Club was still alive and well.

CHAPTER THIRTY-SEVEN

Christmas in the Nakakura house was a big deal. Millie's parents weren't just festive—they were the only people she knew who actually got excited to see winter holiday decorations on sale in September.

So by the time winter break came around, Jane and Scott were prepared.

The house flickered with colorful lights, strings of candy canes, and paper snowflakes that twirled from the ceiling. Ornaments hung from the tree and covered every surface, lined with stretches of forest-green garlands and frosted pinecones. Rows of nutcracker soldiers sat on the mantel, and below them were three stockings. And scattered around the living room were ornaments that moved: a miniature train carrying sacks of toys, a tiny sleigh pulled by cartoon reindeer, and a doll-sized elf hammering at a toy bench. Nothing matched, but that was part of the fun. Part of the *magic.*

Millie breathed in the smell of cinnamon and eggnog—another holiday staple in the Nakakura house.

Jane lifted her head from the couch and smiled. "Merry Christmas Eve!"

Millie smiled back and slumped onto one of the nearby chairs. "It smells good in here."

"Your dad is making French toast," Jane said. "Want to watch a movie after breakfast?"

Another Nakakura tradition was spending most of Christmas Eve watching movies. Usually old ones, too, like *The Sound of Music*, *My Fair Lady*, *Chitty Chitty Bang Bang*, and *The Witches*. And of course they always watched at least one classic James Bond film, which Jane was forever arguing was not a proper holiday movie.

Scott's voice carried through from the kitchen. "I vote for *Dr. No!*"

Jane rolled her eyes and laughed. "I vote for anything that isn't James Bond!" She glanced back at Millie. "You can be the tie-breaker."

It was a weird feeling, being given a choice. It was a weird time of the year in general—her parents always eased off pressuring her to practice flute. Instead, they spent time singing along to holiday music and baking way too many sugar cookies.

Maybe it would be too much to wish her parents would be like that all the time, but she wished there could at least be a happy middle.

Millie's phone buzzed. When she looked at the screen, she saw an incoming call from Zuki.

"Hang on just a second," Millie said before hurrying to the next room and pressing the phone to her ear. "Hello?"

"Hey!" Zuki's voice burst through the speaker. "I was sitting here watching music videos, and I realized that it's been like a whole week since we had a rehearsal. Isn't that weird? It feels like it's been months! Anyway, what are you doing today? Want to come over for a sleepover?"

Millie couldn't understand the casualness in Zuki's voice. "It's—it's Christmas Eve." Maybe Zuki celebrated a different holiday. Or maybe she didn't do winter holidays at all.

"Huh? Oh, yeah, I forgot about that," Zuki said with a forced laugh.

Millie thought back to the words everyone in J-Club had exchanged before parting ways for the holiday break. Rainbow's family didn't celebrate any particular holiday, but they still spent the break visiting family. Luna went to Disney World every year. Ashley's mom always had a big family dinner. But Zuki never said anything about plans.

Now Millie wondered if it was because she didn't have any.

"Do you not celebrate Christmas?" Millie asked.

"I do, usually," Zuki said, her voice distant for a moment before snapping back. "But I think my parents got confused this year. I take turns—one year with Mom, one year with Dad—but I think they assumed it was the other person's turn. My mom is on vacation with her boyfriend, and my dad never came to pick me up. So there's no tree up or anything. Luna's so lucky—I wish I could go to Disney World for Christmas!"

"Wait. You're home alone?" Millie asked, suddenly alarmed. How could Zuki's parents just *forget* about her like that? It was terrible even on a normal day, but on Christmas?

"It's fine," Zuki said lightly. "I had money for pizza, and there's still a ton of leftovers. Plus, ramen is supereasy to make, and we have a *ton*. Mom always buys them in bulk from Costco." She paused. "Besides, it's just three days, and then she'll be back. I like having the house to myself."

"But . . . isn't that kind of scary? And illegal?" Millie asked.

Zuki laughed. "No way! About the scary part, not the illegal part. It probably is illegal. But it's not scary! I'd rather be here than at my dad's anyway."

Millie frowned. "Why?"

"Oh, a lot of reasons, I guess. I can play the music as loud as I want when it's just me. And nobody hogs the TV," Zuki explained.

Millie didn't want to ask the question, but she felt like she had to. "Has this happened before? Your parents forgetting about you?"

"Sometimes. I don't know. It's not a big deal." Zuki sighed like she wanted to hurry along the conversation. "Anyway, you're obviously busy. Sorry I forgot about Christmas! Call me if you get bored, okay? I'll be home all day."

Before Millie could reply, Zuki hung up. When Millie returned to the living room, her mom was crouched near the TV, rummaging through their DVD collection.

"Your breakfast is on the table," Jane said, looking up at Millie. "Who was that on the phone?"

Millie folded her arms around herself. It didn't feel right to leave Zuki alone. It didn't feel *safe*. "That was my friend Zuki."

Jane smiled softly. "Is she enjoying her break?"

"Not really," Millie said slowly. "I think—I think her parents kind of forgot about Christmas. She seems lonely." It was sort of true. Maybe they hadn't forgotten about Christmas *entirely*, but they'd definitely forgotten about it when it came to their daughter.

They'd forgotten *Zuki*.

But if Millie told her parents that part, they might get involved. Zuki could get in trouble. And that was the last thing Millie wanted.

"Oh dear," Jane said with a genuine frown.

Millie's parents had always told her the holidays could be hard for a lot of people and that it was especially important to be kind. Maybe it was because everyone always associated winter holidays with family. It made people without families—or with difficult families—feel like they were missing something important.

Millie didn't know what was worse—to have a bad family or none at all.

"Would it be okay if she came over?" Millie asked meekly. "Maybe she could sleep over, so she'd at least have people to celebrate with tomorrow?"

Jane paused, and Millie was certain she was going to say no. Except she didn't.

"I don't see why not, as long as it's okay with her parents," Jane offered.

Millie blinked. "Really?"

Jane set down the DVD case. "People should try to be kind around the holidays. You never know what people are going through." She frowned. "Why do you look so surprised?"

"No reason," Millie blurted out quickly. She didn't want to give her mom any reason to change her mind. "I'm going to call Zuki back right now." And then she hurried to her room to tell Zuki the good news.

When Millie let Zuki into the house, Zuki closed the door quickly and marched straight toward Jane and Scott and thrust out her hand. "Hi, I'm Zuki! Thanks for letting me stay! I was just going to eat cold pizza for dinner, so this is really nice of you. I couldn't find my sleeping bag, but I'm fine sleeping on the floor. Do you need help with anything? Oh, and Merry Christmas! Well, for tomorrow, anyway. Oh, wow, I *love* your tree!"

Scott shook her hand, eyeing the door behind her. "Er—thank you, Zuki. Did your parents want to come in and say hi?"

"No, they're not those kinds of parents." Zuki laughed like she'd told a joke.

Millie tried to keep her face from revealing anything. She knew Zuki's parents weren't outside. They didn't even know she was here.

Zuki had explained on the phone how she was going to take a bus all the way to the park near Millie's house and then walk the rest of the way with her overnight bag. Millie didn't even know it was possible to take a bus like that without your parents. But Zuki had laughed like it was something she'd done a million times before.

Jane smiled. "Millie, do you want to show Zuki where your room is? Dinner will be ready in a couple of hours."

Millie tugged at Zuki's arm to pull her away, and when they reached her bedroom, she lowered her voice.

"I didn't say anything about your parents not being home, so it might be a good idea not to mention it," Millie said.

Zuki nodded, but her eyes were scanning the room. "Oh my goodness, I love all your posters! I have that one of Chiyo, too—did you get it with the deluxe edition CD?"

Millie fidgeted with her sleeves. Zuki looked so happy. Maybe a little *too* happy. Millie would be absolutely devastated if her parents had left her home alone for Christmas, but Zuki was acting like she'd won a million dollars. Like being forgotten about was a *good* thing.

"Are you okay?" Millie asked. "Because you can talk about it, if you want to."

Zuki turned around. "Talk about what?"

"It's just . . . your parents . . ." Millie tried hard to find the right words. "I guess I'd be feeling kind of weird about it, is all."

Zuki waved a hand. "This is so much better than being home with them, honestly." When Millie didn't say anything, she sighed. "Okay, it bothers me a little. I mean, at home, I always try to be quiet and stay out of their way. I know, it's weird, right? Because I'm not quiet at school at all! But it's different at home. I think they *want* me to be quiet." Her shoulders sank, like it wasn't just her heart that felt heavy—it was everything. "But I guess maybe I was *too* quiet because they forgot about me altogether."

"I'm really sorry, Zuki," Millie said.

"Sometimes I don't know what to do differently. I'm loud at school, and it's so hard to make friends. I'm quiet at home, and I can't seem to get anyone's attention." She paused. "But maybe it's better that way. Maybe having their attention would make things worse."

"Worse?" Millie repeated.

Zuki's smile reappeared. "It's so cool that we're having our first sleepover! And at Christmas, too. Which reminds me—I have a present for you." She stuffed her hand in her bag and reemerged with a small frame. It was made of cardboard and paper, but it was covered in bright paint and splotches of glitter. There was even a small drawing of Generation Love in the corner, like they were tiny anime characters. And in the frame was a photo of everyone in J-Club.

A photo of her friends.

Millie didn't know what to say. It was perfect. "I—I didn't get you anything," she admitted sadly.

"That's okay," Zuki said with a grin. "I just like making things for people."

"You don't have to do anything differently, you know. You just have to be exactly the way you are." Millie looked up and found Zuki's eyes. "Because you *do* have friends. And you're my best friend."

She hoped that they'd stay friends forever.

"You're my best friend, too," Zuki said.

They stayed in Millie's room talking about J-Pop and school and how there were photos all over the internet of Chiyo and her new boyfriend, who were spending Christmas at a ski resort, until Millie's dad called them down for dinner. They spent the rest of the evening laughing with her parents, eating delicious food, and watching *My Fair Lady* until everyone was too tired to stay awake.

And in the darkness, with both girls camped out on the floor on a sea of blankets and pillows, Millie decided it was the best Christmas Eve she'd ever had.

CHAPTER THIRTY-EIGHT

Millie stared into the bowl of sticky white rice and watched as her mom flopped an over-easy egg on top. She reached for the jar of furikake and sprinkled the seasoning all over her food before stabbing the egg with her fork and letting the bright yolk soak into the rice.

She took a bite, smiling at Zuki as she did the same. It was Millie's favorite breakfast in the entire world, and now she got to share it with her friend.

Zuki was beaming. "This is delicious, Mrs. Nakakura!"

Jane poured some orange juice for the girls and took a seat beside Scott. "I'm glad you like it. I'm sorry it isn't anything fancy; Millie is usually in a big hurry to open presents."

Millie stopped chewing, aware of how it must look to Zuki, to see so many unopened presents under the tree and to not have any herself.

"I was thinking maybe we could leave them for a while?" Millie said slowly. "We could watch a movie instead."

Zuki swallowed a mouthful of seasoned rice. "No way! It's Christmas! You have to open presents."

Millie shrugged. "Yeah, but I can open them whenever. And you don't come over very often."

"I like watching people open presents. It's one of my favorite things." Zuki looked at Scott and Jane. "I like when someone opens a present that they really wanted, and there's this moment—a look of genuine *joy*, you know?" And then more to herself than anyone, she added, "I like seeing people happy."

But happy or not, it didn't seem right to open presents in front of Zuki. Her parents weren't there, and she had no presents under the tree.

Millie didn't want to rub it in.

Thankfully, her parents seemed to have the same thought.

"Maybe you could open just one present for now, and save the rest for later on?" Jane offered. "I think there might be something under the tree you'd both enjoy anyway."

Jane wasn't wrong. One of the gifts turned out to be a portable karaoke machine. Millie and Zuki were both so excited, it was sort of like sharing a present anyway.

They disappeared into Millie's room, spending most of the morning adding karaoke versions of their favorite J-Pop songs to a playlist. Millie's parents didn't tell them they were being too loud or to turn the volume down. They just let them *be*, which was something Millie yearned for more often than not.

"You have really cool parents," Zuki said when Millie was flicking through the list to find her next song. "They care about you a lot." There was a crack in Zuki's smile, and a rush of sadness seeped through.

"Your parents care about you, too." It felt like the right thing to say, but also completely wrong. Because they'd forgotten all about Zuki for Christmas. Because Millie didn't know Zuki's parents. Because Zuki rarely talked about them—and sometimes she actively *avoided* talking about them.

Maybe there was a reason for that.

Zuki dragged her fingers along the carpet, her eyes beginning to glass over.

Millie's heart sank. "I'm sure they didn't mean to leave you home alone. They're probably going to feel really bad about it when they come back."

Zuki let out a sad laugh. "Yeah. Maybe. I thought maybe they'd call today. You know, to say Merry Christmas or whatever. But maybe not all parents do that."

"How about I ask my parents if you can sleep over for another day? At least until your mom gets home?" Millie offered.

Zuki opened her mouth to speak, but her eyes suddenly went large like she'd seen something she shouldn't have.

Or maybe like she'd *said* something she shouldn't have.

"Millie, can I talk to you for a minute?" Jane's voice sounded from the doorway.

Whatever was in Millie's stomach seemed to disintegrate. Even her ears started to ring out of sheer panic. When she turned around, her mom was standing with her arms folded and her brows pinched together.

Millie was too horrified to look back at Zuki, so she followed her mom into the living room where her dad was already waiting.

"Millie, I want you to tell us right now what's going on," Jane demanded. "Do Zuki's parents know she's here?"

Millie felt the tears well up in her eyes. "No, not exactly."

Scott shook his head, the anger tense in his jaw but the disappointment practically pouring from his eyes. "We don't lie in this house. We've *talked* about this."

"But they forgot about her!" Millie blurted out. "She was all alone because neither of her parents remembered it was their turn to have her for Christmas. I couldn't leave her by herself. She's my friend."

Jane's face softened while she worked through her thoughts. Finally, she sighed. "*Of course* Zuki shouldn't be home alone. But right now, neither of her parents realize the other one isn't watching her. They have no idea she's *here*." Jane lifted her shoulders. "Millie, there are rules. Not just in this house, but in the world, too. And Zuki's a child—it's not right for us to have her over without her parents even knowing."

"Why not? She's safe here," Millie said. *Safer than she would be at home*, a small voice in the back of her head wanted to add. Millie had no proof, but she knew it was true.

She knew Zuki better than anyone, and it was obvious something about Zuki's home life worried her. Maybe even scared her.

"But her parents don't know that," Scott argued. "How do you think we'd feel if you were spending the night at someone's house without even telling us? We'd be terrified."

"But that's because you care, and Zuki's parents don't!" Millie said. "Zuki deserves better. She deserves to have a happy Christmas with someone who cares about her."

Jane and Scott exchanged a glance.

"I'm sorry, sweetheart," her mom said. "But I need to call Zuki's parents. They need to know where she is."

Scott's voice was firm. "Please ask Zuki for their number. And we'll talk about the lying again later, understood?"

Millie's lip wobbled, even as she made her way back to her room and tried to explain to Zuki what was happening. Zuki's face was devoid of any reaction at all. She looked like someone had sucked all the color out of her, and when she wrote down her dad's cell number, she didn't say a word.

Millie and Zuki sat in silence while Jane made a call from the other room.

They sat in silence while Scott explained Zuki's dad was on his way to pick her up.

They sat in silence when they listened to the doorbell ring and heard their parents' voices from downstairs.

And when Millie watched Zuki leave from the window, her eyes following the way Zuki's dad grabbed her arm too roughly and shoved her into the car, she was silent then, too.

It scared Millie, realizing how silent the world could be.

Nobody from J-Club heard from Zuki for the rest of winter break.

CHAPTER THIRTY-NINE

Brightside Academy came into view, framed by soft gray clouds and brittle trees. Everything seemed sleepier than usual, like the school had gone into hibernation for the winter.

The bus eased into the parking lot, and Millie spotted Zuki from the window. She was standing under the main archway, like she was trapped in a photograph. Normally Zuki was the kind of person who sent color out into the world, but instead it looked like all the gray in her surroundings was swallowing her up. She looked sad. And Zuki was never sad to be at school.

Her expression morphed as soon as Millie stepped onto the sidewalk.

"Hi!" Zuki waved, beaming from ear to ear.

Millie walked toward her. "I haven't heard from you in days. What happened with your parents? Were you in trouble? Did they take away your phone?"

"Oh, that," Zuki said with a shrug. "They were more

embarrassed than anything. I think if I'd just stayed home, nobody would've even cared. But now your parents know, and, well . . ." Her voice trailed off. A moment later, she waved her phone in front of her. "But I got my phone back, so we can text again!"

"Your dad looked really angry when he picked you up," Millie pointed out. She couldn't get the image out of her head—his fingers latched tight around Zuki's arm, and the way he flung her into the car like she wasn't a person at all.

"Come on," Zuki said quickly. "Let's go and find Rainbow and Ashley. I need to hear about their breaks!"

Millie wanted to ask her more, but she followed Zuki anyway.

When Millie walked into the auditorium with Zuki, Ashley, and Rainbow, she was surprised to find Luna waiting for them.

Millie was so happy to see everyone reunited that she felt like a water balloon about to burst. "You're here!" She looked at Luna. "How was Disney World? I didn't think I'd see you today. Since it's the first day back, I thought you'd be with your friends."

Luna gave a harmless shrug. "I *am* with my friends."

Ashley's entire face brightened.

They spent the rest of their lunch hour talking about their

vacations and presents and funny stories. And even though they didn't practice their routine, it didn't matter.

They were together again.

☆ ★ ☆

As the days went on, rehearsals went back to normal. For a while, everything *felt* normal.

But Millie couldn't stop watching Zuki. She watched the way Zuki's demeanor would jump from animated to hyper-elated. The way Zuki's eyes never seemed to quiet, like they were forever watching an alarm clock. The way Zuki was always moving, moving, moving, like she was on a high-speed train that was impossible to catch.

Millie worried that if her friend went any faster, she might never come back.

CHAPTER FORTY

"Try that again—it should be one, two, tri-pa-let, four." Scott clapped his hands and sang the notes.

Millie clenched her teeth so hard they hurt.

"Come on," Scott urged, clapping a beat like a human metronome. "Da, da, da-da-da, da."

Millie played the notes, but halfway through her dad interrupted her.

"No, that's not right. Try it again." He continued clapping, and every time the sound snapped through the room, Millie winced like she was in pain.

"Dad," she begged exasperatedly. "I can do it on my own."

"But you're not." He put his hands down and frowned. "Every time I walk past your room, I can hear you getting it wrong. And as soon as you hit those sixteenth notes, you start rushing."

"Well, maybe you should stop walking past my room," Millie mumbled under her breath before she could help herself.

Scott lowered his chin. Millie's eyes widened.

"I don't like your attitude," he warned.

"I'm sorry. I'm just—" Millie squeezed her flute like she wished it would break in half. "I don't like it when you're always telling me how to practice."

"I'm trying to help, Millie," Scott said.

"But I don't *need* your help!" Millie cried.

Scott looked wounded. Millie felt like someone had sucker punched her in the stomach. She hadn't meant to hurt his feelings, but still, she needed *space*. Was that so much to ask?

"You don't want *anyone's* help. That's part of the problem. You complain about flute lessons, you never want to practice, and you still haven't challenged the second chair for your spot back." Scott let out a heavy sigh. "You're not even trying anymore."

"I don't care about second chair," Millie huffed. "I've told you already, but you never listen to me. I *hate* playing the flute."

"I think the problem is that you don't like to work hard," Scott challenged.

Millie's eyes began to well up. She worked hard at school. She worked hard at J-Club. She even worked hard at being a good friend.

Why didn't any of those things matter?

"Now I want you to start again from the beginning. Watch the tempo, okay?" Scott raised his hands. *Clap, clap, clap.*

Millie shut her eyes, played the notes, and hoped the sooner she got it right, the sooner her dad would leave her alone.

☆ ★ ☆

Millie stepped into the empty quad, thumbs tucked under the straps of her backpack. "Sugar Pop" was stuck in her head, and she started walking in time to the beat without even realizing it.

She mouthed the lyrics to herself before letting her feet fall into a few of the dance steps they'd been practicing during lunch.

"Nice step-ball-change," Luna said.

Millie froze, embarrassed, and looked up to find Luna making her way down the gymnasium stairs. "I didn't know anyone was watching."

Luna grinned. "You never have to apologize to me for dancing!" She stopped in front of Millie. Her curly hair was twisted into two French braids. "Do you have tutoring today?"

"Yeah. I'm headed over to Mrs. Seo's classroom now." Millie paused, noting the lack of a bag hanging from Luna's shoulder. "What are you doing here?"

Luna motioned toward the gym doors. "Helping to set up for tomorrow's assembly. And by 'set up,' I mean I'm listening to the upper-level students fight about whether the banners should be facing the doors or the stands." She turned back to Millie and rolled her eyes. "I can't believe I volunteered for this."

"Do you get anything for it? Like extra credit?" Millie asked.

"No, but I get to skip dance class today, which seemed like a good idea at the time," Luna replied.

"But I thought you loved dance," Millie said, surprised.

Luna widened her eyes. "Oh, I do! It's my favorite thing in the world. But . . ." She looked around the quad like she was worried someone might overhear. "Ruby's mom is a co-owner of the studio, so Ruby thinks that makes her the queen bee. And lately it just feels like more of a clique than a dance school. It's kind of been taking the fun out of it."

Millie could sense her flute nearby like a ghost, haunting her. "I feel that way about music. Not the clique part, but the part about it not being fun anymore. I kind of miss the days when flute was something that was just for *me.*"

"Yeah, I get it." Luna paused, thoughtful. "But do you know what helped me? Finding a way to dance outside of school and classes that was just *fun* again. Like rehearsing with J-Club." Her face soured. "Though now that Zuki is acting so strangely, that's not really the same anymore either."

Millie's chest tightened. "You noticed that, too." It wasn't a question.

"How could anyone not?" Luna pursed her lips. "She argues about everything these days. I have English with her, and she even started talking back to the *teacher.*"

Millie frowned. That didn't sound at all like the Zuki she

knew. "I know she's been acting a little different since we got back from the holiday break . . ."

Luna's eyes softened. "I'm pretty sure whatever is up with Zuki has been going on way before the holidays. I think she's just getting worse at hiding it."

"You think Zuki's hiding something?" Millie felt dizzy. That couldn't be right. Zuki was her best friend. She might not have wanted to talk, but that didn't mean she was *hiding* something.

Was she?

Luna's eyes darted between Millie's, searching for something. And then she sighed. "All I know for sure is that most students don't go to the counselor's office as many times as Zuki does unless they're in trouble or something is going on with them personally."

"I don't know what to do." Millie's worry roiled through her. "Every time I ask if everything's okay, she says she's fine and changes the subject."

"You can't make someone talk who doesn't want to," Luna replied.

"I guess so," Millie said quietly. And then she lifted her shoulders hopefully. "But you still like being in J-Club, right?"

"Of course I do," Luna said seriously. "Hanging out with you all is my favorite part of the week." She looked back over her shoulder and made a face. "I better go. Who knows where they've put those banners at this point." She flashed a warm smile toward Millie and hurried back up the stairs. "See you tomorrow! Good luck with tutoring."

Millie waved and carried on past the quad.

☆ ★ ☆

"This is fantastic, Millie. Well done," Mrs. Seo said after she finished reading Millie's essay. She handed the stapled pages over and folded her arms together, turning to Ashley, who was casually adjusting their tie. "And how's your essay coming along?"

Ashley scratched the back of their neck. "Technically we're still on school hours, and since you aren't my teacher and I'm only here as a volunteer, I don't think I should have to answer that right now."

Mrs. Seo sighed, eyes full of humor. "Mm-hmm. Clever." She turned to Rainbow. "What about you? Or are you only here as a volunteer, too?"

Ashley snorted. "Rainbow's going to be valedictorian one day. She doesn't need tutoring."

Rainbow blushed darkly. "I—I don't mind if you want to read my essay."

Mrs. Seo let out a gentle laugh. "Sounds like you've already got it covered." She leaned against her desk, just as Ashley stood up to grab another cookie from the nearly empty plate. "So how are rehearsals coming along? Ashley tells me you're all very busy preparing for Pop Showcase."

"Yes, very busy," Rainbow squeaked, looking at Millie for an extra word or two.

Millie nodded in agreement. "We've been trying to perfect the choreography. We thought we'd go with the official dance moves, but now . . ." Her voice trailed off as she thought of Zuki's sudden changes. Not only had she convinced the group to change the choreography to one of the live-performance versions, but now she wanted them to change up the song *entirely*.

To say it was causing friction would be an understatement.

Mrs. Seo hummed. "You've all been working so hard. I bet everyone could use a little break. Maybe you could take an afternoon off to do something fun?"

Millie felt an ache spreading through her chest. J-Club *was* supposed to be fun. But it didn't feel the same as it used to.

"Zuki is a tyrant," Ashley mumbled through bites of cookie. "I don't think she knows how to have fun when it doesn't involve bossing everyone around."

"That's not true," Millie said quickly, feeling like she had to defend Zuki.

But Ashley was unfazed. "Yes, it is. She's always liked being in charge, but she's taking it to a new level. The other day she even tried to lecture Luna on her *dancing*."

"She's probably just getting stressed out about the performance. It means a lot to her," Millie tried.

Ashley crossed their arms. "I'm not the only one who thinks Zuki is being too controlling."

Millie paused before turning to Rainbow.

"Um—I don't—I'd rather you left me out of it," Rainbow managed to say through quick, terrified breaths.

"We *all* feel the same way," Ashley pointed out. "Even Luna."

Millie chewed her lip, glancing between them and at Mrs. Seo, who had mostly made herself busy with paperwork to give them the illusion of space. "I'll talk to her. I know Zuki doesn't mean it. She just wants the group to do well."

Millie waited for one of them to agree, but they didn't. Ashley went back to eating their cookie. Rainbow seemed intensely preoccupied with the grooves of the desk.

Eventually they all started talking again. But not about J-Club. And definitely not about Zuki.

Millie hoped it was a phase that would end sooner rather than later.

And maybe talking to Zuki herself was the only way to make things right.

CHAPTER FORTY-ONE

Millie couldn't stop thinking about what her friends had said. The conversation she needed to have with Zuki would be uncomfortable, but it had to be done. And Millie had to be the one to do it.

She just wasn't quite ready yet.

Millie was sitting on her bed, flicking through her Instagram feed and avoiding talking to anyone at all when she spotted the newest post from Chiyo. Generation Love had its own main group page, but all the members had individual social media accounts, too. And Chiyo—even though she was arguably the most popular—only updated her account a few times a month.

The latest photo was of Chiyo holding a violin. The caption was in Japanese, so Millie clicked the button to translate the words into English.

It has been many years since I've picked up my violin. Thank you, old friend, for reminding me that music is and always will be my whole heart.

Millie stared hard at the picture and spotted the sheet music off to the side. Chopin's Nocturne in C-Sharp Minor.

Chiyo liked classical music?

Millie's heart thrummed. She'd had no idea. Chiyo had never mentioned it in an interview before, and she'd certainly never seen any videos of her playing an instrument.

Millie had so many questions she didn't even know where to start. How old was Chiyo when she first started playing the violin? Had she loved it from the very beginning? And what made her stop playing for so many years?

But all Millie's wondering didn't stop her from opening up a new browser window and searching for Chopin's Nocturne in C-Sharp Minor violin solos.

She watched video after video, letting the sad, beautiful melody draw her in, until she felt like she was on a cloud drifting toward another world. When she ran out of videos, she hesitated, thumbs hovering over her screen. And then she typed:

Nocturne in C-Sharp Minor flute solos.

When the sound poured through the speaker, she closed her eyes tight and leaned against her headboard. Normally the sound of the flute made her chest tighten and her throat go dry, like her body was rejecting the noise. But none of that happened this time.

All she heard was something wonderful.

And it was nice to think that in her own small way, she had a connection to Chiyo. They had both grown up playing classical music. Chiyo probably took lessons and studied music in school. Maybe her parents made her practice every day.

Maybe there was even a time when she had hated it, too.

When the song ended, Millie opened her eyes, her gaze drifting over the room until it landed on her flute case.

She wasn't sure exactly what made her set her phone down and reach for her instrument. And she wasn't entirely sure why she had such an itch to dig through her old sheet music in search of any Chopin.

But she found it. A hidden gem in a book of flute arrangements. One she'd heard before, but had never practiced. Never *wanted* to practice.

But this wasn't practice. It was just for fun. For her. Maybe that was what made all the difference.

She set the music on her stand, put her flute to her lips, and played the first note.

☆ ★ ☆

On the bus, Millie squeezed the key chain Zuki had made her between her fingers. It reminded her of the early days, when the thought of J-Club rehearsals filled her with hope rather than dread.

The bus pulled up to the curb, and Millie slid her backpack over her shoulders to follow the trail of students outside.

Zuki was waiting near the main gates like she always was, waving excitedly when she spotted Millie on the sidewalk. At least she *seemed* like she was in a good mood.

Millie's smile felt unnatural. "Hey. I was hoping to see you this morning."

"You see me every morning!" Zuki narrowed her eyes. "Oh, before I forget, we need to have a serious conversation about J-Club."

My thoughts exactly, Millie's mind hissed.

Zuki wagged her finger like she was giving a lecture. "I think it's time we reinstate our meetings after school. We could do three days a week instead of just the one. And maybe Luna can finally ask about using the dance studio. I'm thinking Wednesday, Thursday, and Friday? Obviously we have to talk to the others, but if we're going to do well at Pop Showcase, we *have* to do this."

Millie felt weak. "But I'm grounded, remember? I can't stay after school."

"You stay after for tutoring," Zuki said simply. "Just come to J-Club instead!"

"What? No!" Millie's voice was clipped. "I can't do that. My parents would be furious if I lied again. They still don't even know about our band."

Zuki pushed out her lip. "You won't even try? This is J-Club we're talking about. We promised to make it the best it could possibly be!"

Millie didn't remember promising anything like that. "I'm really sorry, Zuki, but I can't stay after school. Not without asking, and I can't ask without risking even our lunch rehearsals. Besides, Luna can't get us the dance room. Ruby and Annabelle still don't know she's in J-Club."

Zuki let out a noise, frustrated. She tapped her foot against the pavement. "Well, that's not good enough! I'm going to have to call an emergency meeting and set up some new rules."

Millie winced. "Please don't do that. I think—I think everyone is kind of feeling like there are a lot of rules already."

"What's that supposed to mean?" Zuki challenged, and very quickly Millie realized all the joy had fizzled out of her voice. It had been replaced with hurt.

And Millie just didn't have it in her to keep pushing. She missed her friend and she wanted her back. Even if it meant going easy on her.

"Nothing. I only meant we're all practicing so hard, and I'm worried about stressing everyone out even more," Millie said quickly.

Zuki relaxed. "Hmm. Well, if practice goes as badly this week as it did last week, I'll *have* to say something. And as vice president, you're going to have to back me up." She spun quickly and marched through the courtyard.

Millie trailed close behind, watching Zuki's matching key ring swing back and forth like a pendulum. It no longer felt like a sign of their friendship.

It felt like a responsibility that was getting heavier and heavier to hold on to.

CHAPTER FORTY-TWO

Zuki became more like lightning than electricity. Once she snapped at Luna for missing an intro, even though everyone knew it was Zuki who'd messed up. She seemed to talk over everyone, all the time, like she was the only person in the world who existed. And sometimes she'd start shouting about new ideas, and changing songs, and switching the dance choreography, like it was as easy as plucking a card from a deck and placing it somewhere else.

She didn't just make suggestions—she gave orders.

"This isn't working." Zuki marched over to her phone and paused the music. "Ashley, you're way too close to Millie, and Millie, you aren't hitting the pose right." She attempted to demonstrate. "It needs to be bigger! Think about how Chiyo is onstage."

"*Now* we're supposed to be like Chiyo?" Ashley muttered under their breath. "Yesterday you told us we were upstaging you."

If Zuki heard them, she pretended not to. "And Luna, you're a little pitchy. It's making it hard for me to concentrate."

Luna looked genuinely embarrassed.

Zuki turned to Rainbow. "You too, Rainbow. The harmonies need to be perfect, and they're just not there yet."

Rainbow's face turned bright red.

Ashley crossed their arms, defensive on behalf of the group. "Are you kidding me? You think *Rainbow* is pitchy? She's the best singer in the room by a long shot."

Zuki tensed. "I'm the lead singer. Your voices are supposed to be complementing mine."

"Maybe that's the problem," Ashley bit back. "If you let Rainbow sing lead, we might actually have a chance at not embarrassing ourselves onstage."

"This is *my* group," Zuki barked, eyes flashing. "I make the rules."

Ashley narrowed their eyes, and Rainbow shrank even farther into herself. All Millie wanted was for Zuki to go back to normal. The Zuki who yelled at her friends and bossed people around and was taking all the fun out of J-Club was a stranger.

Luna crossed her arms. "Nobody here signed up to follow anyone's 'rules,' Zuki. This is supposed to be fun."

"It *is* fun," Zuki argued. "But none of you are listening to me. We need to be amazing, and what we're doing isn't working."

"It's *you* who isn't working," Ashley said. "You just don't want to see it." Zuki's nostrils flared, but Ashley didn't stop. "Pop Showcase is mostly full of choir and theater majors. We're already the odd group out, and we're going to stand out even more if we don't have a strong lead singer. And I'm not saying you're a terrible singer, but Rainbow is clearly better. Don't we want the best shot at not getting laughed off the stage?"

"I—I never said—" Rainbow sputtered, too frantic to finish her sentence.

Zuki's entire body seemed to shake. "There wouldn't even *be* a band if it wasn't for me! If you don't like it, go start your own!"

Millie's ears burned. "I—I thought we were all in this together."

Zuki looked at Millie like she didn't fully understand what she was talking about. But instead of trying to, she turned on Luna next. "This is *your* fault. You've been hurting the group because you keep missing rehearsals. Because you still won't tell Ruby and Annabelle about J-Club. You're making it impossible for us to improve."

Luna opened her mouth to argue, but Ashley jumped to her defense.

"This isn't Luna's fault. You've been treating us like garbage for weeks, ever since we came back from winter break. And I know you might be going through something, but that doesn't give you the right to be a bad friend."

Luna looked surprised. Ashley was usually the one arguing *with* her, not defending her.

Zuki balled her fists. "You don't even know what you're talking about. I'm trying to fix J-Club. I'm trying to do what's best for all of us."

"No, you're not." Ashley shook their head stubbornly. "All

you care about is controlling everybody. If you really wanted what's best for the band, you'd do the right thing and let Rainbow sing lead."

"But this is *my*—" Zuki sputtered.

"This isn't the Zuki Showcase," Ashley interjected.

Zuki's eyes began to well up, but when Millie reached for her, she pulled away. Her voice was nearly inaudible. *"I need this."*

"What do you mean?" Millie asked, desperate to put her friends back together. Back to how they were.

But Zuki's eyes flashed too suddenly. "If you're going to take my spot, then you can do the whole show without me. I don't care anymore—I quit."

She stormed out of the auditorium without another word.

CHAPTER FORTY-THREE

Millie waited for Zuki after class, but she never showed up. She couldn't find her near the bus stop either, or during lunch the next day. And Zuki wasn't the only one involved in a disappearing act; Rainbow and Luna had been avoiding everyone since the fight, too.

It didn't make sense. Everything was falling apart. And Millie knew why Zuki was mad, but Luna? Rainbow? Millie had seen Ashley at lunch, but they'd hardly said a word to each other.

Had Millie done something wrong? Is that why so many of her friends were avoiding her?

She had to find out. Because the *not* knowing was torture.

Millie took a detour after Math and found Rainbow halfway to her next class. The moment they made eye contact, Rainbow averted her eyes and picked up speed.

"Did I do something to make you mad?" Millie asked abruptly. She could hear the shake in her own voice. The fear that she'd hurt Rainbow without even meaning to.

Rainbow stopped, eyes pinned to the floor, and sighed.

"I—I feel like everyone put me in an uncomfortable situation with Zuki."

Millie's shoulders felt too heavy to hold up. "I know. It's awkward for all of us."

"No," Rainbow said, and stepped closer. "It's awkward for *me.* Because I never said I wanted to sing lead. Ashley just volunteered my name like that without even asking me. It wasn't nice to be cornered like that, and I don't like people using me to win an argument. And it's especially bad because of what Zuki is going through." Rainbow clamped her mouth shut like she'd said too much.

"What do you mean?" Millie's stomach sank. "Do you—do you *know* something?"

Rainbow shook her head. "I've just been noticing things, that's all. Like, this one time in PE, someone slammed their locker too hard, and Zuki practically leaped out of her skin. She was so scared. And—and I don't think it's normal to be that scared, you know?"

Millie felt a lump growing in her throat. "If something's wrong, I want to know. I want to *help.*"

Rainbow pushed her glasses up her nose. "You should talk to her."

"But she won't let me," Millie said. "She's been avoiding me all day."

"Just . . . give her time," Rainbow said quietly.

Millie stared at the floor. She should've said something. She should've talked with Zuki when she first realized something was off, instead of letting it get this far.

"I don't know how to fix this," Millie admitted.

Rainbow looked sullen. "I don't either. But I think it's better if I eat lunch by myself for a while, at least until things blow over. I don't like confrontation."

"I get it," Millie said sadly. "I'll try to talk to Zuki, okay?"

Rainbow nodded once before dropping her eyes and hurrying off to class, leaving Millie alone in the courtyard.

Millie felt like she'd broken up with her friends. Or rather, like *they'd* broken up with *her*.

Luna was back to sitting with Annabelle and Ruby every day at lunch. Rainbow was hiding somewhere on campus, preferring solitude to company. And Zuki was doing such a good job of avoiding everyone that Millie hadn't seen her in days.

Ashley was the only one who still ate lunch with Millie in the courtyard, but they hardly said a word, and Millie got the feeling it was only a matter of time before they left, too.

She couldn't take it. Not speaking to Zuki felt like her stomach was full of fire ants, eating her from the inside out.

Millie made up an excuse to leave class early and headed across campus to the orchestra room. She knew Zuki was in class, and she had to see her. She missed her friend, and she believed in her heart that Zuki missed her, too.

Zuki appeared just after the bell rang, with her orange backpack hanging behind her and a mess of key chains jingling like a chorus with each step she took. The J-Club key chain was still there.

Maybe it was a sign everything was going to be okay.

When she spotted Millie, Zuki's face struggled between a smile and a frown.

"Hey," Millie attempted to break the ice. "I've been looking everywhere for you."

Zuki shrugged. "I've been busy."

"Look, I know you don't want to talk about it, but—"

"I *don't* want to talk about it," Zuki interrupted. "The others can do whatever they want. It's their band now."

"You don't mean that," Millie tried. "Tell me what's wrong. Is something going on at home?"

Zuki's face tensed. "This has nothing to do with me. It's *them*. They wanted J-Club all to themselves and now they can have it."

Millie frowned. "Why are you acting like this?"

"Like what?" Zuki blinked stubbornly.

"Like you don't care. Because I know you do. And you should be trying harder to keep the group together," Millie said.

"It doesn't matter anymore," Zuki said coolly. "I was getting bored anyway. All we do is rehearse, and it's not even fun. Ashley and Luna are always fighting, Rainbow barely says a word, and you just agree with everything I say."

Millie froze, hurt. What was happening? Why was Zuki acting like this? A few days ago, J-Club was the most important thing in the world to her. And all of a sudden she didn't care? It didn't make sense.

Not to mention, Ashley and Luna were in a better place than they'd been in months, Rainbow was finally opening up to the group, and Millie most *definitely* didn't agree with everything Zuki said.

Did she?

"That's—that's not true," Millie argued.

"Yes, it is," Zuki pointed out. "It's like you don't want me to be mad at you. And real friends tell each other the truth."

"What are you even talking about?" Millie growled, heart racing. She didn't know how to react to this. How to *deal* with this.

Were they falling apart, too?

"You're the one who doesn't tell the truth," Millie said suddenly. "You won't tell me what's really happening with your parents, or why you've been seeing the school counselor so much, or why you haven't been the same since Christmas. If friends tell each other the truth, then tell me what's wrong!"

"Who cares?" Zuki barked back. "Telling you about my parents won't change anything. It won't make them care. It won't make my dad less angry at me. It won't make my mom want me to live at her house full-time so I don't have to—" She stopped, tears flowing down her cheeks. "You wouldn't get it, because your parents are perfect."

"My parents aren't perfect," Millie countered.

Zuki shook her head. "Why, because they make you take flute lessons and care about whether you're failing your classes or not? You have no idea. And everyone is trying to take away the only thing in my life that makes me happy."

"That's not what we're doing!" Millie's voice sounded like a plea, but Zuki was already pushing past her. "Zuki, you're my friend. Stop walking away."

"That's what people do when they're not friends anymore," Zuki said coldly before disappearing into the crowd.

Millie stared after her, not sure what to say.

CHAPTER FORTY-FOUR

The kitchen table was covered in pages of notes, most of them finished in Millie's hurried scribbles. She had two kinds of handwriting: her natural one and the one she used when her parents were watching. It had become such a habit for her to switch between the two that if her teachers ever compared her homework to her other notes, they probably wouldn't believe they'd been done by the same person.

Millie set her finished vocabulary assignment to the side and took out a blank sheet of paper to start her English essay.

J-Club wasn't an incentive for good grades anymore, but it didn't matter. Millie liked succeeding in school, and she wasn't about to throw all her hard work out the window by letting her grades drop.

Jane appeared with a mug of coffee, eyeing Millie's essay from over her shoulder.

"It's hard to concentrate when you're watching me like that," Millie mumbled.

"Hmm? Oh, I just wanted to see how you were doing," Jane replied innocently.

"You could always just ask," Millie said.

Jane frowned and sat in one of the empty chairs. She set her mug down and steam snaked its way into the air. "You've been in a funny mood lately. Is everything okay at school?"

Millie rolled her eyes. "School is fine. So is band, since I know you'll ask that next."

Jane didn't look away. She tapped a nail against her ceramic mug. "I noticed your phone isn't ringing as much as it used to."

Millie froze. Had her mom really noticed something that didn't relate to studying? Something that didn't relate to music?

"Is everything okay with Zuki?" Jane pressed.

Millie couldn't help herself—she felt like a flimsy twig, ready to snap.

So she did.

"I don't have time for friends. I'm either practicing or doing homework. And since when did you care about my social life?" She knew she'd gone too far, but she was committed now. She let a frown settle onto her face and glared.

Jane narrowed her eyes. "I don't like this new attitude of yours. Clearly you're picking up bad habits from the other kids at school, which is one of the things your dad and I wanted to avoid."

Millie set her pen down too hard, and Jane raised an eyebrow. Millie was edging very close to being grounded. *Again.*

Not that it mattered. None of her friends were even talking to each other.

"They're not bad habits," Millie said. "I'm allowed to be in a bad mood once in a while. It's not the end of the world. It's *normal*."

"Well, talking to your mom this way isn't normal," Jane said. "Not in our house." She watched Millie carefully. "Did you and Zuki have a fight?"

Millie's eyes began to water and she bit down on the inside of her cheek just so she wouldn't have to answer.

"I see," Jane said quietly. "Friendships can be hard sometimes. It's one of the reasons your dad and I always wanted you to focus on school instead. Because friendships come and go, and they can take over your life when they shouldn't."

"How would you even know?" Millie barked. "You've never cared about friends in your entire life!"

Jane blinked, momentarily stunned. Millie *never* spoke to her parents like that. Not even when part of her wanted to.

Her mom took a deep breath, concentrating on her words. "You're obviously under a lot of stress with school, which deserves a discussion. But right now, I think you need some time to calm down. Because the way you're speaking to me is completely unacceptable."

Millie's gaze practically burned a hole into the table.

Jane sighed. "Just try to remember what's important. You have a family who loves you—more than anything." She tucked a strand of hair over Millie's ear. "Even when you're angry."

When she took her coffee and disappeared into the next room, Millie sank back in her chair and crossed her arms.

Her mom didn't get it. Friendships weren't separate from family. One wasn't more important than the other. Sometimes they *were* family. A different kind than having parents, but still a family.

Millie had two parents who were raising her and who loved her and believed they had her best interests at heart, but they never made her feel like she belonged. But with J-Club, with her friends, she felt like she had a real place in the world.

Wasn't that what family was supposed to make you feel?

Her parents would never understand why she was upset.

Which meant Millie was once again all on her own.

CHAPTER FORTY-FIVE

Millie scrolled through a list of Generation Love interviews. She was sitting on the couch, wrapped in a blanket with a pillow in her lap, for no reason other than because it felt cozy. Comfortable.

Her parents always said she was born ready for cuddling. They said the only way to get her to sleep when she was a baby was by letting her curl up against one of their chests, because if they set her down, she'd immediately start to cry. So they'd sleep in shifts, one of them always holding Millie close against their heart, forever kissing the side of her head.

Sometimes Millie wondered if it hadn't been the cuddling she craved. It was the human contact. And not being in touch with her friends felt like someone had ripped half of her heart away.

She clicked on another video, watching Chiyo's smiling face appear on the screen. She made a heart with her hands, and bounced on her toes. Millie couldn't think of another human being who was as happy and excitable as Chiyo. Except maybe Zuki, before everything changed.

The rest of Generation Love appeared, one by one, each getting a huge reaction from the crowd. Each of them had their own individual fan base outside the group, which Millie always thought was cool. She liked the idea that there was someone out there for everyone. That it didn't matter how different you were—someone out there would appreciate you just for being yourself.

She read the subtitles as Chiyo spoke to the host about the ups and downs of the group's success. Generation Love was known for being incredibly positive but also honest about what being in the spotlight could sometimes feel like. It had always made them relatable. *Human.*

And then Chiyo began to recap a period of time when the group disagreed about where their album was going. There had been rumors Chiyo was planning to go solo, and it had affected how the others felt about any new material. But in the end, Chiyo had showed them that she had no intention of leaving "her family," as she put it. She hadn't signed up to be a solo artist—she'd signed up to be part of a team. A team she grew to love.

The crowd cheered after her answer, just as proudly as Millie remembered. She'd seen most of their interviews at least a couple of times each. But what she'd forgotten were the words.

Family. Team. Love.

Chiyo had fought to keep the band together. They'd all fought for one another, and they didn't give up, even when things got hard.

Millie's heart came to life behind her rib cage.

If J-Club was going to stand a chance, then she had to fight for them, too. She had to find a way back to her friends. To what *mattered*.

She wouldn't give up until they were a family again.

CHAPTER FORTY-SIX

Ashley was in the tech room, dressed in a black shirt and black pants. They were so busy prepping for the band concert that they barely heard Millie when she stepped into the small room.

"I thought you might be up here," Millie said softly. She was dressed in black, too, but she was wearing her old recital dress. It still fit, although the neckline was itchy, and Millie wished the arms weren't so tight.

Ashley pushed their chair away from the equipment. "You performing tonight?"

Millie nodded. There was still nearly an hour before she had to be onstage. "I wanted to talk to you about Zuki. And Rainbow." She felt like there was a rock in her stomach. "Do you think maybe you could apologize about saying Rainbow should sing lead? I think it hurt Zuki's feelings. Rainbow's, too, actually. And I just want things to go back to normal."

Ashley shook their head. "But I'm not sorry. I told Zuki the truth, which is more than anyone else has done."

Millie flinched. "I do tell her the truth."

"No, you don't." Ashley sighed. "Look, I know you two are basically a pair, but Zuki has been acting too controlling for a while. Even before winter break, she was trying to force all of us to have those personas or whatever. She just assigned us a member of the band like she was handing out personalities. It was weird. And she made herself the lead singer without even asking anyone, when she is obviously not the best singer."

"I know, but still, Zuki really needs this group. So do I," Millie said desperately. "School isn't the same without all of you. Besides, you lost a friend a long time ago. Do you really want to do that all over again?"

"Luna was different," Ashley said almost protectively. "We used to be even closer than you and Zuki before she ditched me."

"But you two are friends again now," Millie tried. "You fixed what was broken. Can't we do the same with J-Club?"

"But it's not fixed with Luna," Ashley pointed out. "I don't know if we'll ever be fixed."

Millie frowned. "What happened between you two?"

Ashley's eyes trailed over the tech equipment. "We'd been best friends since we were kids. And at some point, people at school started talking about crushes, and dating, and who they'd imagine getting married to. They had all these ridiculous games, and they always revolved around matching a boy and a girl together. And it always made me uncomfortable for a lot of reasons. But mostly because I never looked at boys the way any of the girls in my classes would, or vice versa." Ashley paused. "I only ever looked at Luna."

Millie was quiet for a moment, letting her understanding sink in. "You like Luna."

"I started getting so nervous around her. I was terrified people would find out and make fun of me. They already gave me a hard time about having short hair," Ashley said. "But mostly I was terrified our friendship would change."

"Did you tell her how you felt?" Millie asked.

"I didn't have to. It was obvious. And I guess Luna was embarrassed of me or something because she stopped talking to me one day and found different friends." Ashley was stoic. "I never cared if she didn't feel the same way about me. It just hurt to be rejected by the one person in the world who was supposed to understand me."

"You should tell her," Millie said. "Maybe that's something good that can come out of J-Club—you two can fix things."

"I know I gave her a hard time about keeping J-Club a secret," Ashley admitted. "Which wasn't cool because I do actually understand why it's hard for her to leave her friends. Telling the world who you really are can be scary." They looked away. "But I guess I hoped she'd changed. That maybe this time, things would be different."

"So that's why you joined J-Club?" Millie asked.

Ashley laughed. "I thought it was a sign that Luna missed our friendship somehow. Because J-Pop was always *our* thing, even when we were little."

Millie stared at the floor. "I know I'm not important to you the way Luna was, but you're still my friend. And I don't want to lose you."

"Look, if you're worried about me leaving you alone at lunch, don't be." Ashley shrugged. "I'm kind of used to eating with people now."

Millie smiled. The conversation hadn't exactly gone the way she'd planned in her head. Part of her still hoped Ashley would agree to apologize to Zuki and everything would be better.

But at least it was something.

CHAPTER FORTY-SEVEN

Outside, it was pouring rain. Millie felt like she was betraying J-Club's courtyard table by eating inside, but she didn't have a choice. Not unless she was okay with a soggy hamburger, which she definitely wasn't.

The cafeteria was quieter than she'd remembered. Even the table Millie and Ashley sat at seemed to stretch on forever. Were there always so many empty chairs?

It felt like a weird memory. Familiar, but still all wrong.

Or maybe it wasn't like a memory at all—maybe it was more like a bad dream.

Millie took a bite of her hamburger. Ashley was eating a bowl of fruit they brought from home. And a few tables away, Luna was sitting with her other friends.

J-Club felt like a lifetime ago. Millie missed everyone so much that it made her bones ache.

Rainbow emerged through the double doors. When she spotted Millie, she hurried toward her with her head down. She quickly planted herself in one of the empty chairs, eyes pinned to the table like she was worried someone might spot her.

"Rainbow!" Millie said, surprised. At first, she was just happy to see her again, but then she noticed the way Rainbow opened her mouth and hesitated, like she had something important to say but didn't know how.

Something was wrong.

Rainbow leaned in. "Have—have you talked to Zuki lately?"

Millie and Ashley exchanged a glance before shaking their heads. Rainbow looked concerned, so Millie added, "She still won't talk to us. She said we weren't friends anymore."

Rainbow peered up carefully. "I don't think she meant it. I think . . . I think she might need her friends now more than ever."

Ashley frowned. "What do you mean? Did you hear something?"

Rainbow looked like her brain was fighting for the words to explain herself. Or maybe it was fighting for courage. "Not exactly. But I'm sure you must've noticed how Zuki never talks about her parents and that she has bruises on her skin underneath all her bracelets." She hesitated. "And in PE today, Zuki refused to change into her gym clothes. She was in the coach's office for a long time. They were talking about something, and Zuki was crying. And then she got sent to the counselor and didn't come back."

Ashley frowned. "You think Zuki's parents . . . ?" They hesitated. "You think they *hurt* her?"

"I don't know," Rainbow said, breathing out slowly. "But I'm worried she needs us, and we haven't been there for her because of this silly fight."

The memory crushed Millie like a wave. "I saw her dad. On Christmas." She met Rainbow's and Ashley's eyes. "He was really mad. He even grabbed her really roughly, right in the driveway. And at the time I wondered why Zuki didn't look scared. Because he was *scary*. But she looked . . . empty, I guess. Like she knew what to expect. Like . . ."

"Like it had happened before," Ashley finished.

The three of them fell silent, all thinking over their words.

Millie spoke first. "If Zuki's in trouble, we should be there for her. All of us."

Ashley nodded. "I agree."

Rainbow looked around nervously. "Okay. Well, I should probably go before . . ." She stood up and turned to leave, but Annabelle's voice stopped her.

"There you are, Rainbow!" Annabelle flashed a smile while Ruby stifled a laugh beside her. Luna froze in her chair. "How's practicing for Pop Showcase going?"

Rainbow seemed to shrink.

Ruby snorted. "Is it even *possible* to practice not vomiting onstage?"

Rainbow looked queasy. "That was a long time ago . . ."

"Oh my God," Annabelle said, pretending to retch. "What if you puke on someone in the front row? What if they have to cancel the show?"

Ruby cackled. "Seriously. You should just drop out. There's

no point in ruining Pop Showcase for everyone. Besides, do you really belong there? Do you even *listen* to pop music?"

"She's probably not even singing. She's probably going to perform a séance or hypnotize the entire school with crystals." Annabelle snorted. "Wait. Are your *parents* going to be there?" She looked at Ruby and they burst out laughing.

Luna tensed beside them.

Rainbow's shoulders shook, but she stood her ground. She didn't run. And even when her voice wobbled, she spoke anyway. "I don't care what you think."

Annabelle and Ruby were too immersed in their laughter to even hear her.

Rainbow only balled her fists tighter. "I feel sorry for you."

Ruby turned, her smile going stiff. "What did you just say?"

But Rainbow wasn't finished. "You pick on people because you're miserable on the inside. You want people to feel sad and small because *you're* sad and small. But I don't care, because someday we'll graduate, and I won't have to look at you ever again. But you'll still be miserable. And there won't be anyone for you to pick on because you'll be in the real world, and your popularity won't matter anymore. You'll be just as sad and small as you've always felt."

Annabelle's face hardened. A few people from nearby tables turned to stare. And Rainbow stood her ground, alone but full of trembling strength. She'd stood up for herself. She'd fought back.

And Millie knew if they were going to be there for Zuki, they needed to be there for Rainbow, too. Because friends showed up for each other.

Millie only had to glance at Ashley before the two of them were out of their chairs. They stood beside Rainbow, making it clear she wasn't alone. Not anymore.

"Seriously? You think your dorky friends are going to suddenly make everything better?" Annabelle scoffed.

"We don't have to make everything better. Rainbow is perfectly capable of doing that herself," Ashley noted with a smirk.

Rainbow's hands shook, and Millie resisted the urge to hold her just to give her strength. Because Rainbow needed this moment. She needed to show Annabelle and Ruby that she could stand up for herself but that she had friends behind her, too.

"You're all losers," Ruby said. "That's why you're all in the loser club. What was it for? Japanese cartoons? It's the perfect place for you, really. It's the club nobody cares about. The club nobody will ever remember."

They started to laugh, and then Luna stood up abruptly.

"It's called *J-Club*," Luna seethed, "and it's a way better place to be than this ridiculous lunch table."

Annabelle and Ruby looked stunned. Even Rainbow seemed taken aback, but her shoulders seemed to tremble less.

Luna grabbed her bag and marched toward Rainbow, looping her arm through Rainbow's. "Come on, Rainbow. These jerks aren't worth anyone's time."

The nearby crowd began to rumble with surprise, awe,

and . . . laughter? When Millie looked around, she realized nobody was laughing at *them*—they were laughing at Annabelle and Ruby.

And as they walked out of the cafeteria, the four of them side by side, Millie was sure she heard some people cheer.

CHAPTER FORTY-EIGHT

After the incident at lunch, Millie sent Zuki a text to say J-Club was having an emergency meeting in the theater. There was a chance she might not turn up and an even bigger chance that she would ignore the text completely.

But Millie didn't care. If Zuki *didn't* turn up, then she'd organize an emergency meeting every single day until she did.

When Zuki appeared at the edge of the stage, face stoic and her arms folded in front of her, Millie let out a sigh of relief.

The brightness that was normally so present in Zuki's eyes had drained. She looked tired. Maybe even a little out of place, which didn't make sense. J-Club used to be her entire world.

But she made her way to the stage and sat down, all five of them in a circle.

It was silent.

Millie cleared her throat. She'd have to do this herself. "I guess I'll start by saying thank you to everyone for coming."

"Why am I here?" Zuki cut in. "I'm not even *in* J-Club anymore."

Millie tried not to let her hurt show. "We miss you," she said simply.

Zuki hesitated, searching the room for a sign of a pending argument. But there wasn't one.

"We want you to come back," Millie said.

Rainbow spoke next. "J-Club isn't J-Club without you."

"Friends fight sometimes, but it doesn't mean we have to stop being friends," Luna pointed out.

Ashley looked at Luna thoughtfully before glancing at Zuki. "I'm sorry I was so blunt. Sometimes I don't think about what I'm saying before I say it, and I end up hurting people's feelings. I need to work on that."

Zuki didn't reply.

"I think maybe what we need is to clear the air," Millie said slowly. "So maybe we could each take turns telling each other how we really feel? Like this is a safe place to be honest with each other—as friends—so that we can move forward?"

Rainbow nodded. "I like that idea."

"Me too," Luna and Ashley said in unison.

Zuki sighed. "Fine. But I'm not going first."

"Okay. Well, I guess I can start." Millie paused. She hadn't really planned anything special to say. But maybe it was easier to be honest when she wasn't trying to plan her words so carefully. "It hurt my feelings when you said I'd do whatever you wanted just because I was desperate to have a friend. And it hurt my feelings when Ashley agreed with you."

Zuki looked up at Ashley and frowned. "You agreed with

me? Because it's not true—I just said that because I was mad. Millie has been an amazing friend, and you shouldn't be telling her stuff like that."

Ashley held up their hands. "Look, I just said I say things without thinking." They turned to Millie. "But I'm sorry. I still think it's a little true, but I shouldn't have said it."

Zuki opened her mouth to argue, but Millie spoke instead. "It's okay. I'm not mad anymore. And you're right. It was maybe a little true. But it's not because I'm desperate for friends. I just care about you all. I've never really *had* friends before. And I guess I didn't want to lose you."

Zuki's shoulders fell. "I'm sorry I said I didn't want to be your friend. It was a horrible thing to say."

Millie was trying not to cry, so she nodded and kept her mouth shut instead.

Rainbow shifted in her seat. "Okay, so it's my turn, I guess. Um, well, I didn't think it was nice that Ashley volunteered me to sing lead. It was never my idea, and it put me in the middle of an argument, which is one of my biggest, most horrible fears." Rainbow sniffed. "It takes a lot for me to be around people. I usually prefer hiding away where nobody will notice me. So that kind of conflict . . . it's too much for me."

Ashley held up a hand. "I apologize again. I say things without—"

"Thinking about them. We know," Luna said with a small smile.

Ashley scratched the back of their neck. "I thought it was really cool that you stood up to your friends."

"They weren't very good friends," Luna admitted.

Ashley tapped a finger against their knee. "Then why did you ditch me for them?"

Luna frowned. "What?"

"We used to be close. And then you stopped talking to me out of nowhere, and I—" Ashley started.

"*You* stopped talking to *me*!" Luna exclaimed. "We used to hang out all the time, and then you acted like you didn't want to be around me anymore. You'd barely talk to me, and you always looked like you couldn't wait to get away from me." She shook her head. "I started hanging out with Annabelle and Ruby because you were the one who didn't want to be *my* friend anymore."

"But—but that's not true," Ashley said firmly. "I *did* want to be your friend! More than anything. I still do."

Luna lifted her shoulders. "Then why did you start acting so weird around me?"

Ashley blinked. "You really don't know?"

Luna shook her head. "I just assumed it was because you didn't like me anymore."

Ashley's cheeks darkened. "Well, it was the opposite."

At first Luna looked confused, and then her face softened. "Oh," was all she said before her cheeks darkened, too.

For a moment it was quiet, and then both Ashley and Luna grinned.

Millie raised her eyebrows, amused, and looked around. "Um. Does anyone else want to share how they feel?"

"You know what I'm feeling?" Zuki broke in suddenly. "I'm feeling betrayed. I feel like you all forced me out of J-Club for no reason. I feel underappreciated. And I feel like—" She paused, and tears welled up in her eyes before slipping down her cheeks. "I feel like I lost all my friends. I feel alone. I feel like everything is changing."

Millie reached out to hold her hand. "You aren't alone. I promise. And you definitely didn't lose us."

Zuki sniffed, wiping her nose with her sleeve. "I just really needed this."

Millie frowned. There were those words again. "What does that mean, Zuki?"

"It's silly," Zuki replied, and she tried to laugh even though it came out deflated and heavy. "I thought that if I was singing a solo in Pop Showcase, my parents might actually show up. That they might actually be interested." She shook her head. "But they won't care if I'm just a backup singer. It won't be enough." The tears fell faster. "Nothing I do ever feels like enough."

Millie wrapped an arm around Zuki's shoulders, and the others shuffled closer until there was hardly any empty space in their circle at all.

"What's going on with your parents?" Millie asked quietly.

Zuki shook her head, almost desperately. "I think—I think I'm just hoping for something that's never going to happen.

Only now I finally know it." She smiled weakly. "Kind of like the singing, I guess."

"You're a good singer," Ashley insisted. "You wouldn't have made it through the auditions if you weren't. Just forget I ever said anything, okay?"

Zuki shook her head. "But I can't. Because even if you think I'm good, the truth is Rainbow is a lot better." She turned to Rainbow and smiled. "I think you should sing lead. It's what's best for J-Club."

Rainbow looked frantic. "What?—no—I can't! I've never sung a solo before. And being onstage, with everyone staring at me . . ."

"We'll be there with you," Zuki said. "I want us to be amazing. And with you singing Chiyo's part, I know we will be."

"I can help you with the stage fright," Luna offered gently. "I know some tricks."

"And with the lights, you can barely even see the audience," Ashley added. "Just pretend it's another rehearsal."

"But it's still your choice," Millie pointed out seriously. "You don't have to do anything you don't want to do."

Everyone voiced their agreement, while Rainbow stared at the floor deep in thought.

"You really won't be mad at me if I sing lead?" Rainbow asked quietly.

"You said that it used to be your dream." Zuki smiled. "And I'd be mad at myself if I didn't make the right choice for J-Club. It's all I have."

"You have us," Millie said, squeezing her shoulder. "And we're your friends, regardless of who sings lead."

Zuki looked at Rainbow. "So you'll do it?"

Rainbow smiled, the light finding her eyes. "Okay. I'll do it."

And just like that, J-Club was whole again.

CHAPTER FORTY-NINE

"Choir rehearsals? All week?" Zuki looked like someone had given her the worst news of her life. After everything that had happened over the past several weeks, J-Club was behind. Their dancing was rusty, their singing was off, and they needed every spare second possible to get their routine back on track.

Ashley wasn't as visibly disappointed as Zuki, but their voice still faltered. "They like to use the theater for the acoustics, I guess. But it's during lunch."

"Which means we can't rehearse," Luna finished. "What about after school? Could we use the orchestra room again?"

"Normally, yeah, but the orchestra room is being repainted. They had us in the old band room yesterday," Zuki said with a sigh. "Plus, Millie has tutoring after school."

Millie nodded. She might have gotten her grades up, but her parents still didn't know anything about J-Club.

"I could try to ask the dance teacher about a space," Luna started. "Everyone knows I'm in J-Club anyway. But they have rehearsals right now, too, with the big recital coming up. So I can't promise anything."

"We could rehearse at my house," Rainbow offered. "I know my parents wouldn't mind. And they, um, sort of have a dance studio."

"What?" everyone asked in surprise.

Rainbow lifted her shoulders timidly. "My mom teaches kids on the weekends."

"You've had a dance studio at your house this whole time and you never told us?" Zuki asked.

"I—I don't usually invite people over," Rainbow admitted. "It didn't go so well last time . . ."

Millie offered a smile, but Zuki was still shaking her head like their problems hadn't quite been solved yet.

"But what about the tutoring?" Zuki looked serious. "Would your parents let you skip a day?"

Millie knew the answer, but she didn't want to let J-Club down. Not when they'd worked so hard to get back to how things were.

She'd skip tutoring for one afternoon—but it would have to be a secret from her parents.

"I'm sure one day won't matter," Millie decided. "But I'll have to be back at school in time to make the late bus."

"I live really close," Rainbow said. "We could walk there after school today, if you want."

"Close" was almost an exaggeration. Rainbow lived just opposite the park. She practically lived *next door* to the school.

"Why didn't you just come home for lunch every day?" Ashley wondered out loud as they stepped through the front door. "Instead of eating in the theater?"

Rainbow sighed. "The school has rules about that. But also, I'd rather my parents didn't know I was getting picked on. They'd make it a 'thing.'"

Millie had opened her mouth to ask what she meant when Rainbow's mother appeared in the living room. She was wearing a tunic painted every color of the rainbow, and her straw-colored hair was braided into a crown.

"You brought your friends over!" she exclaimed, pressing her hands together like she was thanking the stars. "It's so lovely to meet you. You can call me Ella— Is anyone hungry? I made apple and kale chips!" Ella wrapped her arms around Rainbow and pressed a cheek to her hair.

Rainbow made a face that was half embarrassment, half appreciation. "We're kind of short on time, Mom. Millie has to take the bus home."

Ella looked up thoughtfully. "Oh, I can drive you home if you like! Do you all want to stay for dinner?"

"No," Rainbow said a little too quickly, her face turning pinker by the second. "We're good." It was obvious she was sensitive about the food. And Millie didn't blame her, after what happened the time she had a birthday party with kids from school.

Luna flashed a warm smile. "It smells delicious in here, though. Maybe we'd have time for a little snack?"

Millie and Zuki both nodded encouragingly.

Ashley shrugged. "I like kale chips."

Rainbow's entire body relaxed, and Ella beamed. "Sure thing! I'll make a plate, and you can take it to the studio with you. Would anyone like water? Tea?"

Rainbow's dad appeared from around the corner. He was wearing coveralls that were spattered in dried clay, and his hair pointed in every direction, almost as if he'd been electrocuted.

"Ah! We're outnumbered!" he shouted, hazel eyes full of laughter.

Ella smiled. "These are Rainbow's friends from school. Come and give me a hand with the drinks, will you, Gary?"

The pair vanished into the kitchen and reemerged a few minutes later with a plate of chips and a jug of water. Rainbow led everyone to the living room, which was full of indoor plants and ceramic ornaments. Above the fireplace was a row of geodes and crystals, all lined up by color to make a rainbow.

"Did you make these?" Luna asked, staring at all the sculptures.

Gary grinned. His beard was sprinkled with bright white hair, and he had happy eyes that turned into crescent moons when he smiled, just like Millie's dad. "Most of them. Rainbow made a couple of them, too, didn't you?" He nudged his daughter, who smiled sheepishly.

"I didn't know you were into art," Millie said.

"Multitalented," Zuki added.

"You're like a professional," Luna gushed.

"You could've easily been an art major," Ashley noted.

"Okay!" Rainbow practically barked. "I know you're all trying to be nice, but this is too much attention. Can we talk about someone else? Something else? *Anything* else?"

Everyone looked at one another for five whole seconds before they burst out laughing. Even Rainbow, who covered her eyes to shield her embarrassment.

"All right." Gary tapped Ella's knee. "We better leave the kids be. Last time we must've really messed things up because it's been years since Rainbow's invited anyone back. We should get out while we're ahead!"

Ella laughed. "Let us know if you need anything, okay? And again, Millie, we'd be happy to give you a ride home if you need it."

"Thanks, but I'm okay," Millie said.

When Rainbow's parents disappeared into the next room, Zuki raised her brows. "Your parents are so nice!"

"And these apple and kale chips are delicious," Ashley said between bites.

"You're lucky. Your mom and dad seem so chilled out," Millie said.

Rainbow smiled, still fighting the embarrassment.

"Millie has cool parents, too," Zuki pointed out. "They let me sleep over on Christmas Eve."

"But Rainbow's seem so happy to let her be who she is." Millie looked at Rainbow. "They seem like they give you space."

"Yeah, I guess they do. Honestly, I thought they were perfect until everyone at school said they were weird," Rainbow admitted.

"They *are* perfect," Ashley argued. "They're perfect for *you*, and that's what matters most."

"Thanks," Rainbow said, her eyes starting to water.

"You're lucky," Zuki said in a faraway voice. "Your parents picked you because they really wanted you. They didn't just get stuck with you. So you'll never have to wonder whether they really love you or not."

Everyone else exchanged knowing looks. Zuki might've been president of J-Club again, but she was *far* from herself. Her light had dimmed, and Millie was pretty sure it was because of her parents.

But Zuki didn't want to talk about it. How could Millie help someone who didn't want to talk?

They spent the next thirty minutes rehearsing in the dance studio, singing as loud as they wanted and laughing in between sections. It was nice having mirrors; it almost felt more official, seeing everyone together. It felt like they were a real group again.

When Millie picked up her phone to check the time, her heart plummeted into her stomach.

Twenty-seven missed calls, all from her mom.

"Oh no," Millie said out loud, glancing through her texts.

Zuki looked up. "What is it?"

Millie read through her messages quickly, her mind moving

too fast to comprehend that her friends were circling around her, concerned.

Her parents had gone to Brightside Academy to pick her up after school because her flute teacher had rescheduled her lesson. They'd been to see Mrs. Seo, who'd told them Millie hadn't shown up for tutoring.

And now they knew she wasn't at the school.

"My mom has been trying to call me," Millie said, her voice barely a sound at all. "I'm in so much trouble."

She dialed the number, pressed the phone to her ear, and waited for the inevitable fallout.

CHAPTER FIFTY

"Millie? Where are you? Are you okay?" Jane sounded panicked.

"Yeah," Millie said. Her hands were starting to shake. "I'm at a friend's house."

And that's when it happened. Jane began talking very quickly about being terrified something had happened and disappointed that Millie would do something like this without asking. She talked about being angry, about trust being broken, and about consequences for being disobedient.

At some point Scott took the phone to yell about how scared they were and how embarrassing it was to show up to Millie's school and find out they had no idea where their daughter was. He reminded her that she was only eleven, that she was a child, and that she didn't get to make her own decisions when she showed no responsibility whatsoever.

When Millie's parents picked her up from Rainbow's house, they had a quick, polite conversation with Ella and Gary. Millie listened as Rainbow's parents told them all about J-Club, and the rehearsal for Pop Showcase, and how hard they'd been practicing. Maybe Ella and Gary thought they were helping—that they were making a good case for Millie—but it only made everything worse.

Because Millie's parents finally knew how far back the lies went.

When they ushered Millie into the car, the lecture didn't stop.

"J-Club? What were you thinking, Millie?" Scott demanded from the driver's seat.

"You told us you were joining Advanced Studies. And what about the tutoring? Was that even real?" Jane asked.

Millie bit the edge of her lip, wiping tears away with her fingers.

"This is unbelievable. I don't even know who you are right now," Scott said, shaking his head.

"That's the problem," Millie muttered under her breath.

His eyes flashed in the rearview mirror. "What, now you're talking back to your parents, too?"

Millie couldn't help the angry tears from spilling over. "You didn't know me before either. You never bother to learn anything about me."

"What are you talking about?" Jane turned to look at Millie. "This is not our fault. We didn't force you to lie to us, or to make up a fake club, or to sneak around with your friends while you were failing your classes. You made those choices."

"Because I can't breathe!" Millie exploded.

"Don't talk to your mother like that!" Scott yelled.

"You never listen to me! All you care about is flute, and grades, and your rules. You don't let me take a single step without telling me I'm doing it wrong." Millie started to sob, taking in big, heavy gulps of air.

"We're your parents! We know what's best," Scott said firmly. "You don't have to like it, but you don't get to just change the rules whenever you feel like it."

"And you *certainly* don't get to lie to us," Jane said.

"I wouldn't have had to lie if you'd just listened to me," Millie argued. "The only part of my life that I don't hate is J-Club and being with my friends."

"Well, that makes me sad," Jane said. "But that still isn't an excuse."

"Every kid goes through stages. But I honestly thought we could trust you more than this," Scott said.

They still weren't listening. They still didn't understand what it felt like.

"You're done with J-Club," Scott said sternly. "In case that wasn't obvious."

Jane sighed and pinched the bridge of her nose. "Obviously you're not doing this Pop Showcase or whatever it is either. And I'm not sure I'm comfortable with you hanging out with these friends of yours. They're clearly a bad influence, and I'm not happy about it."

Millie's face turned hot. "If you make me quit J-Club, then I'm quitting flute."

"You don't get to make that choice, Millie," Scott warned.

"Yes, I do!" Millie cried. "If you take away J-Club, I will never play the flute again!"

There was more shouting, more lecturing, and more of Millie's parents refusing to see Millie's side.

But one thing was final: she was grounded.

CHAPTER FIFTY-ONE

During lunch the next day, Millie told her friends that she wouldn't be able to perform in Pop Showcase. She expected them to be upset or disappointed or even a little angry.

But they weren't. All they cared about was Millie.

"I'm really sorry you're grounded, but don't worry," Zuki said. "As long as we get to hang out, that's what's important."

Millie's worries turned to fear.

How could she tell them her parents didn't want her hanging out with them? And did she really have to obey?

It wasn't even an option. They were her friends no matter what, and being grounded wasn't going to get in the way of that.

But if her parents pulled her out of Brightside . . .

Millie tried to shake the thought away. She didn't want it in her mind, where it was making things warped and dark and ugly. All she had was *now*, and she needed to make it count.

Rainbow smiled encouragingly. "Yeah, you have us no matter what."

"You aren't mad at me for ruining our group?" Millie asked quietly.

Even though everyone shook their heads immediately, it was Zuki she turned to first. Because Zuki had been there from the start. J-Club was how they'd become friends.

"I didn't start J-Club to perform in Pop Showcase," Zuki admitted. "I did it to make friends—and I did. Maybe we're nerds or dorks or whatever, and the rest of the school may not even know we exist, but we found each other. So who cares about a concert?"

Millie looked around the table. "Sometimes I feel like I've known you all for years. Isn't it strange that it's only been since September?"

Everyone nodded in agreement, but it did nothing to lift the mood.

"How long do you think you'll be grounded?" Luna asked.

Millie sighed. "For the rest of my existence, probably."

"Well, at least we have school," Rainbow offered.

Millie tried to force a smile. Zuki seemed to be doing the same, though Millie wasn't sure why.

It wasn't like Zuki's parents were pulling *her* out of school. She'd still be here next year. She might even get another chance to audition for Pop Showcase.

But what did Millie have to look forward to? She was afraid to guess.

"Maybe your parents will be less mad by the time summer

break comes along," Ashley said. "We could hang out—make an unofficial J-Club that doesn't have anything to do with school."

"A loophole," Luna noted. "I like it."

Ashley grinned.

"You two have changed so much this year." Zuki snorted. "Remember when you couldn't even look at each other?"

They both rolled their eyes but laughed anyway.

"Because of a misunderstanding," Luna pointed out.

"It's not just us—we've *all* changed," Ashley said. "I guess I've learned that I don't always have to push people away. And that needing friends doesn't have to be as scary as it sounds."

Luna looked around. "I finally feel like I can be myself. Like I don't have to hide."

Rainbow gave a timid smile. "I feel safe at school for the first time in . . . well, ever, really."

Zuki pressed her lips together, trying to hold back tears. "I guess—I guess I don't feel alone anymore." She looked around and her eyes glistened. "I feel like I finally have a family."

They turned to Millie and waited for her answer. And she didn't know if it was silly or poetic or profound in any way, but she knew what she wanted to say. She could feel it in her heart.

"My whole life, I've felt like I was half asleep. Like I didn't know where I was supposed to be or how I was supposed to fit in the world." Millie shrugged. "But now I feel awake. I feel like I belong."

The mood at school had already been sad enough. But at home? It was like standing in the middle of the Arctic tundra. It felt like the ice had shattered beneath Millie's feet, and she was falling down, down, down into a black hole.

She was waiting for a decision from her parents. Waiting for them to take Brightside away from her forever. Knowing their verdict was coming only made the days feel colder because every day with her friends felt like the lead-up to a goodbye.

So she drifted through the week like she really was lost in the snow, without anyone to pull her back to safety.

But at least there were no more lies.

CHAPTER FIFTY-TWO

"Millie, can you sit down with us in the kitchen for a minute?" Jane called.

Millie hesitated by the doorway. She was already wearing her pajamas. They were covered in little Gudetama drawings and were maybe a size too big, but very comfortable.

She'd been doing a pretty good job of avoiding her parents, and they hadn't exactly been putting up a fight about it. They hadn't even brought up the afternoon in the car when everything exploded and they'd found out the truth about J-Club.

It was weird. Millie expected the hovering to get worse and for the rules to become even stricter. But instead, everything felt like it was on pause. Like the aftermath still hadn't been decided. Millie hadn't practiced her flute in days, and her parents hadn't said a word about it.

But maybe all that was about to end.

Maybe *now* was the aftermath.

Millie swallowed her nerves and took a seat at the table.

Scott and Jane watched her, their faces devoid of any expression at all. Millie tried to appear neutral, but it was too hard. She carried her emotions with her everywhere, on display for the world to see.

"Millie," Jane started, "we want to talk to you about school."

Millie's eyes welled up then, like a flash flood without warning. This was it—they were pulling her out of Brightside Academy. She was never going to see her friends again.

They were going to take away the one thing that made her heart feel full.

"We're really sorry we've been so hard on you," Scott said, his voice echoing like they'd all been transported into an empty auditorium.

Millie blinked. Had she heard him correctly?

Jane's eyes softened. "We heard what you said—about feeling like you couldn't breathe—and maybe we're to blame for some of that."

"Not all of it," Scott interjected. "You did lie to us, which is never, ever okay."

Jane lowered her chin. "But maybe we've been pushing you in a direction you're not comfortable with. And even though we've been here, we haven't been here for you in the way you needed. And that's our fault."

Millie's brain tumbled and tumbled. She couldn't make sense of anything they were saying.

They were *agreeing* with her.

"We asked to sit down with all of your teachers," Jane admitted. "We were concerned about how you'd been doing in school after we found out you'd been secretly going to J-Club. We wanted to know the truth about your grades."

"And your behavior," Scott added. "Because in my experience, when someone gets caught skipping class, it's usually not the first time."

Millie frowned, defensive. "But it *was* the first time. And it was just tutoring, I—"

Jane held up a hand to stop her. "We know, honey. We spoke with Mrs. Seo and everyone else. And it turns out your teachers think you're an incredible student."

Millie froze.

Scott gave a small smile. "They said you're always on time and that you try really hard in class. They said they've never had a student show as much improvement as you did—especially after your first-quarter grades. They said they can tell you really put the work in and that you take school very seriously."

"They—they really said all that?" Millie asked.

Her parents nodded, and Millie struggled to maintain her composure. Because she *did* try her best, but she didn't think anyone else had noticed. Or that anyone else cared.

She'd started school doing everything so wrong; she had never imagined things could turn around so much.

"Mrs. Seo in particular, said she was very impressed by how disciplined you were with tutoring. She said you never missed a session before that day and that your friends would stay after school to help you with your homework." Jane smiled. "She also said she heard you kids talking about J-Club, and how you'd moved rehearsals to lunch so you wouldn't fall behind on school."

"That was a very responsible decision to make," Scott said. "And we're really proud of how far you've come."

They were proud of her. And it had nothing to do with music.

Millie's tears spilled over.

Jane moved to the chair beside her and wrapped her arms around Millie's shoulders, squeezing gently. "We love you. So much. And we're going to try to be a lot better about listening to you from now on, okay?"

"But you have to promise that the lying will stop. The secrets, too." Scott lifted his shoulders. "We want to trust you, and we want you to trust us back. Maybe we can all work a little harder at it."

Millie nodded, sniffling into her mom's sleeve. "Okay. I promise." She paused. "So . . . does this mean I get to stay at Brightside Academy?"

Jane pulled away and ran her fingers through Millie's hair. "As long as you keep your grades up the way you have been, then yes." She looked over at Scott. "We think maybe this was a good move for you after all."

"Maybe for us, too," Scott admitted with a gentle laugh.

Millie gave both of her parents a hug.

"One more thing before you run up to bed," Jane said. "Could you maybe explain to us what Pop Showcase is, and where we can buy tickets?"

CHAPTER FIFTY-THREE

Millie: My parents said I can be in J-Club again! And they want to come to Pop Showcase!

Rainbow: YAYY!!!

Ashley: That's awesome.

Luna: omgggg this is the best news!

It took Zuki a few extra minutes to respond.

Zuki: AHH YESSSS! Okay we need to talk about costumes. Are we imitating the outfits in the music video? And what about colors? Are we matching? How does everyone feel about pinks and lilacs?

Ashley: No.

Zuki: To which part?

Ashley: All of it.

Luna: never mind the costumes, I want to know what Millie's parents said! What made them change their minds?

Rainbow: yeah, me too! Does this mean you aren't grounded anymore?

Millie: Nope not grounded. They said they were sorry for making me feel bad. I guess they talked to my teachers and found out I was doing well in school. Oh, shout out to Ashley's mom for saying good things!

Ashley: 👍

Luna: That's amazing!

Rainbow: i'm so glad your parents understood!

Millie: I'm just happy I don't have to lie anymore and that they want to come to Pop Showcase. I never thought they'd be interested in something that wasn't flute. It feels really nice.

Zuki started to type something but deleted it. She started typing again but deleted that, too.

Ashley: My mom said I could invite you all over for pizza after school this week, if you want. No pressure though, I don't care either way.

Luna: you sound positively thrilled about it 😃

Rainbow: 😃😃

Ashley: Whatever, the offer is on the table.

Millie: I'll ask my parents and let you know tomorrow!

Rainbow: same!

Luna: ditto!

The three dots appeared to show Zuki was typing. When her reply appeared five minutes later, it was barely a reply at all.

Zuki: Okay.

Millie could sense something was wrong, so she left the group chat and sent a text just to Zuki.

Millie: Are you okay?

It took her another fifteen minutes to reply, even though Millie could see that she'd read it.

Zuki: You and I both used to have parents that weren't interested in J-Club, but now we don't. I'm happy for you but it also reminds me that I'll never have that.

Zuki: But I'm glad you're back in J-Club.

Zuki: AND that you can do Pop Showcase. Really.

Millie: I'm sorry. Do you want to talk about it?

Zuki: No.

Millie: I think of you as family.

Zuki: You do?

Millie: Yeah! And maybe family is about more than just sharing DNA.

Millie: Maybe some families are chosen.

Zuki: I'd rather talk about costumes, to be honest.

Zuki: But thanks.

Zuki: Thanks for being my friend.

Millie: Thanks for being mine.

CHAPTER FIFTY-FOUR

Ashley's living room was decorated in red party streamers and paper lanterns covered in yellow stars. An archway of colorful balloons separated the living room from the kitchen, and there was music playing from a nearby speaker. A stack of pizza boxes was sitting on the counter, along with several bottles of soda and a birthday cake shaped like a giant bumblebee.

"It's your birthday?" Millie's mouth hung open, and she looked around at the others, desperately hoping she wasn't the only one who didn't know to bring a gift.

Zuki squealed, staring at the decorations with delight. Rainbow looked like she wasn't entirely sure if she was in the right house.

Ashley rubbed the back of their neck uncomfortably. "It's whatever. My mom is into parties."

Luna smiled. "I remember you always hated when people knew when your birthday was. You used to get so annoyed, like it was supposed to be some huge secret."

"Yeah." Ashley sighed. "I didn't want to tell any of you either, but I guess the balloons kind of give it away. My mom doesn't do anything in moderation."

Mrs. Seo entered the room. "Welcome, welcome! Help yourselves to pizza. Rainbow, there's a vegan option just on the table."

"The cake is vegan, too," Ashley added. "And there's no meaning to the bumblebee. It was just the only design that wasn't covered in flowers or sports equipment, neither of which I like."

After pizza, everyone sang "Happy Birthday" to Ashley while they blew out their candles. Mrs. Seo served cake and sorbet, and she took about three hundred photos over the course of the dinner. When they were finished eating, Mrs. Seo ushered everyone into the living room to relax.

Ashley slumped into one of the couches. "Does anyone want to watch a movie?" There was a collective sound of approval, and Ashley reached for the remote.

"I can't believe you didn't tell us it was your birthday," Rainbow said. "I would've brought you something."

"I don't like presents," Ashley grumbled, flicking through the video library.

Luna looked down at her hands awkwardly. She'd removed something from her bag—something small and wrapped in tissue paper. Now it looked like she was wondering if she'd made a mistake.

Ashley noticed, and their whole body went still. Whatever expression Luna was wearing, Ashley was wearing it, too.

With a sigh, Luna passed the item to Ashley. "I didn't want to show up empty-handed when I knew it was your birthday. But it's nothing big, so don't worry. It's barely a present."

"You remembered?" Ashley asked quietly.

Luna looked up. "Of course. It's the same day as my brother's. Don't you remember? That's how we met—you both had your birthdays at that beach. The one with the pier and the funnel cake."

Ashley couldn't hide their smile. They carefully unwrapped the gift to reveal a small jar filled with tiny colorful stones.

"Sea glass." Ashley's voice was almost inaudible.

They looked at each other like they were sharing a secret. Or maybe it was a memory.

After a moment, Ashley cleared their throat and motioned to the TV. "Does anyone have a preference?"

Zuki lunged for the remote and began scrolling through choice after choice, while Rainbow offered commentary on all the films she'd already seen. Luna and Ashley avoided each other's eyes but couldn't stop smiling.

They decided to watch the first episode of a dorama none of them had seen before, and halfway through Millie got up to get a drink of water. She found Mrs. Seo in the kitchen, putting away the last of the pizza in the fridge.

"Did you need something?" Mrs. Seo looked over her shoulder and smiled.

"Just some water, if that's okay," Millie said. "I didn't want to bug Ashley, so I thought I'd just get it myself."

Mrs. Seo reached into the cabinet for a clean glass and filled it at the sink. "Are you excited for Pop Showcase? It's soon, isn't it?"

Millie took the glass and cupped her hands around it firmly. "I'm nervous. But excited, too." She'd been onstage plenty of times before, at flute recitals and solo performances. But this felt different. She *wanted* to be there, for one. Before, being onstage made her feel jittery and breakable, like one wrong step would shatter her into a million pieces.

These nerves were different. They felt like magic swirling around Millie's fingertips.

She felt like magic.

"That's good," Mrs. Seo said. "I'm so glad Ashley gets to do this with all of you. I've never seen them look forward to something so much before."

Millie and her friends found one another when they really needed it. She imagined them all lost at sea, searching for an escape from a storm. And J-Club was their lighthouse; the constant that brought them all together. The thing that made them feel safe.

She would never stop being grateful to Zuki for putting up those flyers and for being her friend when nobody else would.

She wished there was a way to repay her for giving her a family through J-Club. And she knew what Zuki wanted the most, but it was impossible for Millie to give it to her.

Because she couldn't force Zuki's parents to love their daughter more. She couldn't make them stop hurting her.

She felt powerless.

Millie frowned. "Can I ask you something?"

Mrs. Seo looked surprised. "Of course."

"What are teachers supposed to do if they suspect someone doesn't have the best parents?" Millie asked carefully.

Mrs. Seo's expression stilled into something more thoughtful. "There are a lot of rules in place for things like that. And if there was ever a time where a student seemed to be in danger, then the teacher would have an obligation to report it. Because a student's safety is very important. It can also be very complicated."

Millie's mind flashed to Zuki. She wanted her to be safe more than anything. And even if she didn't have proof, she could feel something was wrong. It was in Zuki's eyes. Something she wasn't telling anyone about.

"How do you help someone if they won't tell you what's wrong?" Millie asked.

"That's a very big question indeed," Mrs. Seo began. "I think all we can do is try our best and be present in their lives as much as they'll allow us. And it can be hard when we feel like something is out of our control. But being there for your friends? That's something we *can* control. And it's very important."

"But if I saw something . . . And if I told someone . . . Would a teacher even be able to fix it?" Millie asked.

Mrs. Seo was quiet for a moment. "Is this about Zuki?"

Millie's eyes widened. "I didn't—I don't—" She felt panicked.

"It's okay," Mrs. Seo said gently. "Ashley already told me." She sighed. "It's not my place to talk about this with you, but I don't want you to worry, okay? There are other people looking out for Zuki, just like you are."

Millie relaxed a little. "I just want her to be safe."

Mrs. Seo nodded. "Just be there for her, like you're doing. A good friend is really important. No matter what age you are."

Millie returned to her friends, watching them quietly as they laughed at all the funny parts in the show. She wanted to believe Mrs. Seo was right—that there were people who would make everything with Zuki okay again. She needed to believe it because the alternative was terrifying.

Zuki deserved better than the parents she had.

And Millie wished being eleven didn't stop her from fixing a problem so *big*.

CHAPTER FIFTY-FIVE

Millie pulled the red curtain back and peered into the crowd. The sound in the audience was like static on a radio, but soft around the edges. Everyone was still finding their seats and making idle conversation with the people around them. There were a lot of parents and siblings and grandparents, but most of the room consisted of fellow students.

That made Millie especially nervous.

But at least she looked the part. Even though Zuki had wanted costumes for the group, they'd each decided to wear whatever felt right for their personality. For Millie, that meant a Bulbasaur T-shirt, jeans covered in holes, and her red Converse.

Zuki was beside her, looking like she'd just stepped off the set of a Generation Love music video. Her pink-streaked hair was tied up in twin buns, and she was wearing a pink sweater over a pair of white shorts and knee-high socks. She didn't look nervous; she looked distracted. Her eyes were busy searching for someone in the crowd. Judging by the way her shoulders fell, she couldn't find them.

"They aren't here?" It was a question Millie already knew the answer to.

Zuki turned around and smiled—a broken, tired smile. "I just wanted to get a look at the crowd. There are so many people! I'm so nervous. Are you nervous? I bet Sierra Cooper is out there somewhere—she's in my Math class and she said J-Club would *never* make it to Pop Showcase because nobody cared about Japanese music. I'm so ready to show her how wrong she was!"

Millie knew she was lying about not looking for her parents, but she smiled anyway. "Come on. We're supposed to meet the others backstage. Luna said something about fake eyelashes."

Zuki nodded, casting one last glance at the crowd before letting the curtain fall.

They wove through the small gathering of performers, making their way down a hall and up a set of stairs to one of the dressing rooms. Rainbow was perched on a chair in front of a huge mirror, wearing a loose-fitting black dress, a bomber jacket with Generation Love's symbol, and her signature argyle socks. A small heart was painted below the corner of her eye—something Chiyo often did at concerts.

Luna was hovering in front of her, sprinkling glitter onto Rainbow's hair like it was pixie dust. She was dressed in a striped jumpsuit that hung off one shoulder, and it wasn't just her hair that sparkled: Luna shimmered from head to toe. She leaned back, surveying her work, and exchanged the glitter for a tube of bright red lipstick.

"Is this really necessary?" Rainbow squeaked. She was wearing contacts especially for the performance, and her glasses were nowhere to be found. "I don't really wear makeup."

"Come on, you're a theater major—you know the stage lights wash you out," Luna tutted, carefully painting Rainbow's lips. "There. Perfect." She stood back and looked around. "Who's next?"

Ashley glowered, adjusting the collared shirt beneath their vest-and-trouser set. It almost looked like they were going to a wedding, except on their feet were a pair of crisp white sneakers. "I already let you put blush on me, but I draw the line at lipstick."

Luna rolled her eyes. "You'll thank me when the photos come out and you don't look like a corpse."

"I know how lighting works," Ashley mumbled. "But I also know there's a difference between 'a little bit of color' and full-on face painting."

Zuki threw herself into an empty chair and straightened her spine. "Millie said you have fake eyelashes? Are they big ones? I definitely want red lips—and can you put glitter in my hair, too?"

Luna clapped. "Yes! Okay, you do the lipstick, and I'll get the eyelash glue."

When they were all polished up and ready for the stage, the five of them stood in front of the mirror, staring at one another like they could barely recognize themselves.

"Wow," Zuki gushed. "We look so . . . professional."

Millie laughed. "I didn't know my eyes could look this huge!"

Rainbow flattened her hands over her clothes self-consciously. "It feels weird not being in a uniform at school."

Even though they didn't exactly match, they still looked like they belonged together.

A band of misfits.

Millie took a deep breath. "Is everyone ready?"

The energy in the room crackled.

Zuki clasped her hands together. "Let's do this."

Millie's heart pounded a million miles a minute. Her ears began to ring. She could feel a rush of adrenaline racing through her, like a fire willing itself free.

The theater was blanketed in darkness, but she could still see a slight shift in the crowd. Her parents were there, somewhere. And it occurred to her that they were finally about to see her— *really* see her.

Were they excited? Were they nervous? Did they think she could do this?

Could she do this?

Millie closed her eyes and let out a slow breath.

In the darkness, she felt someone's hand close over hers. A reminder that she wasn't alone.

She squeezed their hand back so they would know they weren't alone either.

The music started, the lights turned on, and Millie began to sing in perfect harmony with her best friends.

The beat took over, and Millie step-ball-changed and shimmied across the stage, and suddenly the group was hitting pose after pose while the spotlights danced above them. Right on cue, Rainbow took her place front and center and sang a riff straight into the melody.

Millie and her friends spun in time to the music, their voices soaring into the room so easily that she felt like she was in a dream. Luna moved like her soul was connected to the sound waves. Ashley, with their fluid but precise movements, was the epitome of cool. Zuki's enthusiasm was infectious. And Rainbow was *alive*. It was like a shooting star had taken control of her body, and she was dancing across the stage, throwing a hand out to the crowd with the attitude of someone who'd performed a million times before.

And Millie had never been prouder to call them her friends.

When the dance sequence started, the lights flashed before sending the stage into different colors of the rainbow. All five of them danced with everything they had, nailing every step of the choreography the way Luna always told them they would. Millie became so lost in the performance that she forgot there was a crowd at all. All she knew was that she was a part of something special. Something unforgettable.

They hit another pose, and then another, and sang the final verse of the song with their whole entire hearts. And then they all came together, hit their last pose, and felt the spotlights illuminate the stage.

When it was all over, Millie remained frozen, feeling her breath caught in her throat.

Her heart thumped. And thumped. And thumped.

And then the audience got on their feet and erupted in cheers.

CHAPTER FIFTY-SIX

"A standing ovation!" Zuki cried, shoveling another scoop of frozen yogurt into her mouth. "I'm still in shock."

Millie giggled euphorically as she took another bite—hers was coconut flavored and covered in pieces of mochi. "Me too. Didn't it seem like they were clapping for forever?"

"I'm not surprised at all," Luna said. "You were all amazing."

"We did have the best choreographer in the school," Ashley said smugly, and Luna grinned beside them.

Rainbow hadn't stopped smiling since she walked offstage. She looked dizzy with joy. "I'm just so glad I didn't throw up."

"You were *incredible*," Millie gushed. "Did you hear how many people were complimenting you when we got backstage?"

"I had no idea you were a secret diva," Zuki added.

"You had *so* much attitude," Luna agreed. "I loved every second of it."

Rainbow moaned and covered her face with her hands.

Laughter flooded the small outdoor seating area. There was a pink parasol attached to the glass table, which was pointless since it was neither sunny nor raining. It was ideal—a little warm, no breeze at all, and every star visible in the velvety night sky.

It was the perfect end to a perfect day.

Millie could still feel her parents' arms around her, hugging her tightly and telling her how proud they were. She hadn't known that love could feel like that—like it went in two directions instead of just one.

Maybe she hadn't given her parents enough credit for trying their best, but maybe being right in one moment didn't mean you were right all the time. Maybe parents have room to compromise, too.

And Millie would never stop being grateful she had parents who weren't too stubborn to admit they had changed their minds.

"Thank you," Zuki said suddenly. "All of you. For doing this with me."

"Thank you for being the best J-Club president anyone could've asked for," Millie said.

"Next year we should pick a song where everyone gets a solo," Rainbow added. "Do you remember when Generation Love did that at a concert? It was amazing!"

"Yes!" Luna and Ashley agreed in unison.

Something shifted in the air, like there'd been a power cut. It was eerily silent. The kind of silent that could only precede bad news.

Zuki's eyes began to water. "I, um, I have something to tell you, actually." She swallowed. "I'm not going to be in J-Club next year. I'm . . . not coming back to Brightside Academy at all."

Millie's chest felt hollow. "What do you mean?"

Zuki tried to smile. "I'm going to live with my grandma in New Mexico."

"But that's—" Millie started, shaking her head like she couldn't comprehend the distance. It was so far. So *final*.

"I know," Zuki said.

Rainbow looked down at her half-eaten dessert. Ashley leaned back in their chair.

"Is this because of your parents?" Luna asked quietly.

"The school counselor has been talking to me a lot this year. They've been talking to my parents, too. And after Christmas . . ." Zuki blinked like she was hoping to get rid of the memory. "My grandma thinks it's better if I live with her."

"Is it temporary?" Millie asked softly.

Zuki shook her head. "I don't think so."

For a long time, everyone was quiet.

It was Ashley who spoke first. "Good." Their voice was firm. "I'm not happy you're leaving, but I'm happy you'll be away from your parents."

"Yeah, me too," Luna said.

Rainbow nodded in agreement, but Millie couldn't bring herself to move. She knew this was a good thing—the right thing—but she was going to lose her best friend.

She wasn't prepared for that.

"How long have you known?" Millie asked. Her stomach felt

like quicksand, and all her other organs were sinking into it. She couldn't feel anything. She could hardly breathe.

Zuki's shoulders sank. "I found out around the time I said I quit J-Club. I just wasn't ready to talk about it. And then when I was, we were so close to performing. I didn't want to make everyone sad. I didn't want the show to feel like a goodbye."

Ashley might've been right about the move being a good thing for Zuki, but it didn't feel good. It felt like the earth was splitting beneath Millie's feet, and everything she loved was falling straight through it, into the darkness where she'd never see it again.

She wasn't ready to say goodbye to Zuki.

"We'll still keep in touch," Zuki said. "I mean, it took me years to find anyone who loved Generation Love as much as I do. Our friendship was fate."

"Fate has a weird sense of humor," Ashley said sadly. "But I think you're right. I mean, how else would the five of us end up together? Look at us. We're like weird poster children for our majors."

Millie couldn't help but laugh. "Am I the awkward band geek?"

Ashley shrugged. "I'm the unsociable theater tech."

Luna scrunched her nose. "I guess that makes me the popular dance major. Except I am *not* ditsy, so don't even suggest it."

Ashley held up a hand. "I wouldn't dare."

Rainbow lifted her brows. "Mine doesn't make sense. I'm shy and a theater major. They don't really go together."

"Yeah, but you come to life onstage," Luna defended. "In any audition show, that's always everyone's favorite."

Zuki frowned. "What does that make me?"

Everyone looked at each other.

"A melodramatic orchestra major?" Ashley offered, and everyone laughed. Even Zuki.

"Okay, maybe *yours* is the one that doesn't make sense," Rainbow said with a shrug.

Zuki lifted her hands. "I don't mind being an enigma. As long as I get to be strawberry-mousse pink."

"Oh, we're still doing the color thing? I thought we'd canceled that," Ashley said dryly.

Zuki stuck out her tongue, and Luna giggled.

"I know what you are—you're a leader," Millie said, and her voice started to shake. "You brought us all together. We would never have found each other without J-Club."

"A few state borders won't change that," Zuki said.

A tear fell down Millie's cheek. "You promise?"

"I promise," Zuki said.

And Millie wanted to believe it. Because she couldn't imagine a world without Zuki in it.

CHAPTER FIFTY-SEVEN

There was a knock at Millie's bedroom door. She looked up from her bed, the framed photo of her friends wedged between her hands. Some of the glitter had fallen off and gotten stuck to her skin, but she didn't mind. It reminded her of being onstage. It reminded her of the lights and the magic and the crowd. It reminded her of Zuki.

And she wanted to remember it forever.

"You can come in," Millie called toward the door.

Her mom appeared. She was still wearing the dress she had worn to Pop Showcase, and she smelled of vanilla perfume. "Are you all ready for bed?"

Millie moved the frame back to her bedside table. She tucked her legs under her quilt and watched her mom sit down beside her.

"You were wonderful tonight," Jane said. "I know we keep saying it, but it's true."

Millie tugged at the stray threads of her blanket. "I know I hadn't told you about J-Club before, but I'm glad you were there. It wouldn't have felt right if you weren't."

"Your dad and I," Jane started, "we've been talking. And we

think maybe it's time to let you make up your own mind about what you're passionate about."

Millie looked up and frowned. "What do you mean?"

She looked serious. Gentle, but serious. "If you really hate playing the flute this much, then you don't have to do it anymore. It's your choice."

Millie's eyes widened. "Really? You mean it?"

Jane nodded. "I think it's time we let you grow up. Even if that means growing out of the dreams we had for you."

Millie thought for a moment. "What about Brightside Academy?" She was a band major. If she quit flute, she'd have to quit the school.

"You don't have to go if you don't want to," Jane said simply. "We'll support you no matter what you choose."

But Millie wasn't sure about the alternative. If she didn't go to Brightside, what was going to happen?

Her life had changed so much since the beginning of the school year. She had *friends* now. She didn't want to go back to being lonely.

"I don't want to be homeschooled again. I know it works for a lot of people and a lot of families, but it didn't work for me." Millie wanted to believe that was okay.

"I know," Jane said. "We thought maybe you could go to the local public school, if that's something you'd like."

"You wouldn't be mad?" Millie asked.

Jane shook her head. "No. It will be an adjustment, but we'll be okay with it if it means you won't feel so pressured."

"Can I have some time to think about it?" Millie asked. It was a big decision. All she'd wanted for the past few years was to finally be able to quit flute. To chase a different dream.

And now that she had the option . . .

She just wanted to make sure it was the right one.

Jane kissed Millie's forehead. "Of course. Let us know what you decide. But for now, get some rest."

Millie curled up beneath the blanket and watched her mom pause near the door to flick the light switch. She blew a kiss, pulled the door shut, and left Millie in the darkness.

Millie listened to the sounds of faraway footsteps and cars passing in the street. She could see the light from a neighbor's house. And she could still smell her mother's perfume, like she'd left a ghost behind to help Millie sleep.

But she couldn't sleep. She was wide awake, with too many thoughts tumbling through her mind like a parade of acrobats in a mystical circus.

But even while she lay awake in bed, she dreamed.

CHAPTER FIFTY-EIGHT

Returning to school after J-Club's big performance was surreal. It felt like the world had shifted a little bit. Like someone had put a different lens on a camera, and everything was a different shade than it was before.

Millie sat in the courtyard with all four of her friends, eating lunch and laughing about how they were still finding glitter all over their rooms.

"This is why glitter should be banned," Ashley grumbled. "Permanently."

"No way." Luna pouted jokingly. "The world is so much prettier when it's sparkling."

"You don't need glitter to look pretty," Ashley said, and then stiffened like they hadn't quite meant to say that out loud.

Luna's eyes widened, and then a smile stretched across her entire face. The others burst into waves of giggles.

A few students walked past their table, eyes lingering on the group. One of them raised their hand in a wave, smiling, before carrying on past the quad.

Zuki blinked. "Did . . . did someone just acknowledge us?"

"I didn't think anyone else in this school even knew who we were." Millie looked around at the rest of the outdoor tables, all full of students. She spotted a girl with strawberry-blond hair she recognized from her Math class. When she met Millie's gaze, she smiled.

So Millie smiled back.

"I preferred being invisible," Ashley muttered under their breath. Judging by their flushed cheeks, they hadn't entirely recovered from earlier.

"I'm still trying to decide how I feel about it," Rainbow admitted. She lifted a brow, voice lowered. "Everyone keeps telling me they liked our performance, and I keep waiting for the comments about me puking onstage or eating weird food. But they never come."

"That's because nobody cares about what happened in first grade," Luna said earnestly. "Ruby and Annabelle are just immature and mean because deep down they hate themselves. Speaking of . . ." Her eyes trailed across the courtyard, where her former dance-major friends were just leaving the cafeteria.

They hesitated as they approached Millie's table, eyes clearly falling toward Rainbow, and then—they kept walking without saying a single word.

"Okay," Rainbow said, breathing out a sigh of relief. "I definitely prefer this alternate reality."

They all laughed until their cheeks hurt. And every time

Millie's mind drifted toward the thought of Zuki moving, she pushed it away. Their goodbye would come eventually, but for now?

She wanted to enjoy the little time they had left, making the happiest memories they possibly could.

☆ ★ ☆

Millie sat down next to her parents on the couch. They were halfway through a movie about a woman who was trying to find her lost son. It wasn't anything Millie was interested in, but she had to admit the soundtrack was incredible.

Jane passed the popcorn (covered in M&M's, of course) and whispered under her breath, "That was a pretty song you were playing upstairs. When did you learn that?"

Scott growled a warning. "Hey—you know the rules. No bugging Millie about flute."

Jane pouted innocently. "I'm sorry."

Millie relaxed into a grin. "It's okay. I don't mind you asking sometimes." Her eyes watched the screen, even though her thoughts were everywhere else. It was weird to *want* to play the flute. And it was even more weird to not feel any pressure from her parents about it. "It's a song Chiyo was playing on the violin. She's a singer from Generation Love."

"I know who Chiyo is," Jane said. "I *have* been paying attention, you know."

Scott frowned. "Is that the one with purple hair?"

"*Pink*," Millie and Jane said in unison, in the same tone of mock irritation.

Scott made a face and snatched the popcorn bowl. "Fine. If you want to be like that, you can all go make your own snacks."

Millie and her mom looked at each other.

"Want an Oreo milkshake?" Jane asked.

Millie grinned. "Yes, please."

The two of them jumped up from the couch and headed into the kitchen, just as Scott threw up a hand and said, "So I guess I'll just find out if she reunites with her son all on my own?"

Millie grabbed the ice cream out of the freezer while Jane plugged the blender in, and a few minutes later they were sitting at the kitchen table with their milkshakes. Millie used her spoon to fish out the big chunks of Oreo, just the way she liked it. When she looked up, her mom was watching her with a sad smile on her face.

"What?" Millie asked, wiping her face self-consciously.

Jane shook her head. "Just thinking about how fast you're growing up, that's all." She tapped a fingernail against her glass. "I know you think I didn't notice, but I *always* notice. Maybe . . . maybe that's why your dad and I pushed a little too hard. We know we won't have this time with you forever." Her eyes glistened. "We wanted to make sure we didn't waste it."

Millie shifted in her seat, thinking. "I know friends and J-Pop won't get me into college, but they make me happy. I—I don't feel like that's a waste. And I don't want you to feel like that either."

Jane let out a slow breath and smiled. "If you're happy, I'm happy."

Millie smiled back. "Thanks, Mom."

"So"—Jane placed her hand flat against the table—"do you want to talk about your friend moving away? How are you feeling?"

Millie's throat tightened, and she leaned back against her chair. "I feel terrible. I feel like I only just found her and now she's being taken away from me. I feel like it's not fair. But also, I feel guilty—because I know moving is what's best for Zuki."

"You'll still be friends, no matter where she is in the world," Jane said. "But I'm sorry you're sad. I know how much you care about her."

Millie stared at her milkshake. "Maybe she could come over one of these weekends? Before school ends?"

"I think that's a great idea. You should make the most of the time you have left." Jane lifted an eyebrow. "As long as those grades stay up, right?"

Millie grinned. "Yeah. My grades are good."

Jane took a sip of her own milkshake.

"Um, Mom?"

"What is it?"

"Since we're being honest and stuff, I also want to tell you that I don't like chicken legs. They're greasy, and the bone kind of grosses me out."

For a moment Jane said nothing, and then—she burst into laughter.

And Millie couldn't help but laugh, too.

They stayed in the kitchen for a long time, talking about food and boba tea and Japanese dramas, and even Scott gave up on the movie and decided to join them. Millie felt like they were all different notes that had finally found the right harmony. They were a chord. A unit. A *family*.

For the first time in a very long time, Millie felt like everything was going to be okay.

CHAPTER FIFTY-NINE

The energy was different on the last day of school. It felt lighter, like you could do anything and not get in trouble for it.

Not that Millie ever wanted to get in trouble again. She was happy to stick by the rules from now on.

After class, she hurried to the theater, snaking her way through a crowd that was determined to get home as fast as possible. But Millie had made a promise, and she didn't intend to break it.

She opened one of the side doors to the auditorium, watching as the light spilled across the empty chairs. She saw them right away—her friends, waiting for her up on the stage. Climbing the steps shakily, she saw Zuki in the middle, her orange backpack tight over her shoulders. She didn't look empty or full, bright or dark. She looked calm.

And even though Millie's heart felt broken in a thousand places, she knew calm was good.

Zuki needed to breathe, the same way Millie once did. Maybe now she finally could.

"I guess we're all here," Zuki said, smiling softly.

Ashley made a face. "I really wish we'd done this over text. I hate goodbyes."

Luna nudged Ashley's shoulder. "Be nice," she whispered playfully.

Rainbow frowned. "It's bad enough that we're having to say goodbye to Zuki, but to Millie, too? Who's going to run J-Club next year?"

A smile crept over Millie's face. "About that." She raised her shoulders. "I decided I'm going to stay at Brightside Academy."

"Really?" Rainbow beamed.

Luna clapped her hands. "Oh, that makes me so happy!"

Even Ashley grinned. "You don't mind having to play the flute for another year?"

"I don't mind if it means I get to spend more time with my friends. My parents said they'd ease off the practicing," Millie explained. "Who knows, maybe I might even start to like it again."

"I'm seriously jealous," Zuki said. "I so wish I had more time with you all." She looked around the auditorium longingly. "I'm going to really miss this place."

Millie took her hand. "We'll stay in touch." She looked around. "All of us."

Zuki nodded sadly, and Rainbow reached for her hand. Luna clasped her fingers through Rainbow's and held her other hand out to Ashley. For a moment Ashley and Luna stared at each other, a look of peaceful recognition passing over their faces.

And then Ashley took Luna's hand and held firm.

The five of them stood, hands joined together like a row of paper dolls.

No, Millie thought. Not paper dolls. Paper dolls could be severed or torn or ripped into pieces.

Their friendship was stronger than that. *Bigger* than that.

"So this is really it." Millie's voice danced across the stage.

"Yeah," Zuki said. "This is goodbye."

They stood in silence for a long time, holding hands like they didn't want the moment to get away from them.

Maybe in life, some things had to come to an end, even when you didn't want them to. Maybe part of growing up was learning to say goodbye.

But maybe some goodbyes didn't have to be forever.

And Millie could feel it in the deepest part of her heart: someday they'd all find each other again.

They looked out into the imaginary audience and took a bow.

Acknowledgments

I owe the most enormous thank-you in the world to my brilliant editor, Trisha de Guzman. Getting to work on this story with you was truly an honor. Our little book has grown so much since that first phone call, and I'm beyond grateful Millie and company had your editorial magic to help bring them to life. Thank you for handling this book with so much love and care!

I am also eternally grateful to my super-agent, Penny Moore. Five acknowledgments later, and I still can't believe this is real life. Thank you for always believing in my words and for being the best teammate to have fighting in my corner. You're the best.

Thank you to the truly fantastic team at Macmillan and FSG for turning this story into a real book and for all your help and thoughtfulness behind the scenes. Special shout-out to Taylor Pitts, Cassie Gonzales, and Celeste Cass—I'm so grateful for all that you do!

And a very special thank-you to the mega-talented Jen Bartel, whose artwork has been hanging on my office walls long before

I ever knew who was doing the cover art for this book. You brought Millie and her friends to life so perfectly. Total dream come true.

Thank you to the team at Aevitas Creative Management for being so supportive of my books and career, and to all the incredible booksellers, librarians, book bloggers, and reviewers who help get stories like Millie's into the hands of the readers who need them most. You're all superstars.

To all the readers, new and old—thank you for reading. If it weren't for all of you, I wouldn't be able to keep doing this job that I love. I know some of you write to tell me that my books have made your worlds a little brighter and a little less lonely, and I want you to know that every time you pick up a book of mine, it does the same thing for me. I'm beyond grateful to each and every one of you.

To the friends I've had over the years: thank you for sitting next to me so I wouldn't be alone. Thank you for the hundreds of notes and texts and phone calls. Thank you for being the people I looked forward to seeing every day. But most of all, thank you for the memories.

And to my family and friends today, who listen to my worries and encourage me even when I'm plagued with self-doubt—thank you. This job would be a million times harder without you.

Ross, Shaine, and Oliver—you three are my everything. Thank you for being patient when I'm working long hours and juggling deadlines. Thank you for bringing me cups of chai, sharing your snacks, and looking after my Animal Crossing island. And thank you for letting me be your family. Writing is my favorite job, but hanging out with you three is my favorite kind of existence. I love you all times infinity.